THE
ENGLISH
Short Story

1945 - 1980

A CRITICAL HISTORY

TWAYNE'S CRITICAL HISTORY
OF THE SHORT STORY

William Peden, General Editor
University of Missouri-Columbia

The American Short Story before 1850
Eugene Current-García, Auburn University

The American Short Story, 1850–1900
Donald Crowley, University of Missouri-Columbia

The American Short Story, 1900–1945
Philip Stevick, Temple University

The American Short Story, 1945–1980
Gordon Weaver, Oklahoma State University

The English Short Story, 1880–1945
Joseph M. Flora, University of North Carolina-Chapel Hill

The Irish Short Story
James F. Kilroy, Vanderbilt University

The Latin American Short Story
Margaret Sayers Peden, University of Missouri-Columbia

The Russian Short Story
Charles Moser, George Washington University

—THE—
ENGLISH
Short Story

1945 - 1980

A CRITICAL HISTORY

Dennis Vannatta
University of Arkansas at Little Rock

Twayne Publishers

The English Short Story
1945–1980
A Critical History

Copyright © 1985 by G. K. Hall & Company

All Rights Reserved

Published in 1985 by Twayne Publishers
A Division of G. K. Hall & Company
70 Lincoln Street, Boston, Massachusetts 02111

Printed on permanent/durable
acid-free paper and bound in
the United States of America

First Printing

Book production by Marne Sultz

Book design by Barbara Anderson

Typeset in 11 pt. Garamond
with Perpetua display type
by Compset, Inc. of Beverly, MA

Library of Congress Cataloging in Publication Data

Main entry under title:

The English short story, 1945-1980

(Twayne's critical history of the short story)
Bibliography: p. 175
Includes index.
Contents: Chronology — Introduction — The English short story, 1945-1950 / John J.
Stinson — [etc.]
1. Short stories, English—History and criticism. 2. English fiction—20th century—
History and criticism. I. Vannatta, Dennis P. II. Series.
PR829.E533   1985   823'.01'09   85-8574
ISBN 0-8057-9358-5

Contents

Chronology

1945   Clement Attlee elected prime minister. Death of Caradoc Evans. Anna Kavan, *I Am Lazarus.*

1946   National Health Service Act passed. Death of H. G. Wells.

1947   Dominions of India and Pakistan established. Graham Greene, *Nineteen Stories. No Scottish Twilight: New Scottish Short Stories,* edited by Maurice Lindsay and Fred Urquhart.

1948   William Sansom, *Something Terrible, Something Lovely.*

1949   *West Country Short Stories,* edited by Lewis Wilshire.

1950   Angus Wilson, *Such Darling Dodos and Other Stories.*

1951   Sir Winston Churchill reelected prime minister.

1952   Death of George VI. Elizabeth II accedes to the throne.

1953   Death of Dylan Thomas.

1955   Sir Anthony Eden elected prime minister.

1956   Death of Walter de la Mare. V. S. Pritchett, *Collected Stories.*

1957   Harold Macmillan elected prime minister. Death of A. E. Coppard.

1958   Muriel Spark, *The Go-Away Bird and Other Stories.*

1959   Alan Sillitoe, *The Loneliness of the Long-Distance Runner.*

1960   *Introduction: Stories by New Writers* first published.

1961   *Arena* begins publication. *London Magazine* begins publication.

1962   Death of Karen Blixen (Isak Dineson).

1963   Sir Alec Douglas-Home elected prime minister. Death of Aldous Huxley.

1964   Harold Wilson elected prime minister. Robert Graves, *Collected Stories.*

1965   Death of W. Somerset Maugham. Doris Lessing, *African Stories.*

1966   Death of Evelyn Waugh. *Alta* begins publication.

1968   Death of Anna Kavan. Muriel Spark, *Collected Stories.* James Stern, *The Stories of James Stern.*

1969   British troops rushed to Ulster. Death of Osbert Sitwell. Edward Upward, *The Railway Accident and Other Stories.*

1970   Edward Heath elected prime minister. Death of E. M. Forster. Roald Dahl, *Selected Stories.*

1971   Gabriel Fielding, *Collected Short Stories.* Glyn Jones, *Selected Short Stories.*

1973   Graham Greene, *The Collected Stories of Graham Greene.* Doris Lessing, *Collected African Stories.*

1974   Harold Wilson reelected prime minister. Death of H. E. Bates. Gwyn Jones, *Selected Short Stories.*

1975   *Beyond the Words: Eleven Writers in Search of a New Fiction,* edited by Giles Gordon.

1976   James Callaghan elected prime minister.

1978   Roald Dahl, *The Best of Roald Dahl.* Doris Lessing, *Collected Stories* (vol. 1, *To Room Nineteen;* vol. 2, *The Temptation of Jack Orkney).* *Modern Scottish Short Stories,* edited by Fred Urquhart and Giles Gordon. V. S. Pritchett, *Selected Stories.*

1979   Margaret Thatcher elected prime minister.

1980   Kingsley Amis, *Collected Short Stories.*

Introduction

The Short Story in Postwar British Culture

To understand fully any specific body of literature or any specific genre, we must, of course, understand something about the society from which it springs. It is no revelation to observe that the years immediately following World War II were for all nations involved at the best a period of transition and at the worst a time of near chaos. The contemporary British short story is the product of a society in often painful flux.

If the problems facing postwar British society were less dramatic than those facing Germany, Poland, Italy, Japan, or China, they were nevertheless severe, rooted both in the immediate effects of the war and, more fundamental, in old sores that had been festering since the turn of the century and before. That Britain's problems were long-standing is best dramatized by Lord Churchill's defeat in the 1945 and 1950 elections—a stunning and perplexing circumstance to casual observers, considering Churchill's almost mythic status as World War II savior. Yet the people were not rejecting Churchill so much as the Conservative party, whose policies had, in the eyes of many, both led to and failed to lead Britain out of the economic slump of the 1930s. Britain did not face the depression alone, of course; it plagued most of the industrial world and was actually less severe in Britain than in, for instance, the United States. Many of Britain's problems in the post–World War II period had their roots, in fact, in issues dating from before World War I. Only the most jingoistic Britisher could deny that the empire was slowly fading in scope and vitality throughout the twentieth century. The beginning of the end had been signaled sym-

bolically by the death of Queen Victoria in 1901. Of much more practical note, however, had been the devastating effects of the Boer War
in the 1890s—a grueling, seemingly endless struggle that had caused
Britishers to question not only their empire's military strength but,
more important, its moral and ethical strength. Clement Attlee and
his Labour party's victory over Churchill, then, indicated that the British were looking for new leaders with innovative ideas for dealing with
problems old and new.

Britain emerged from World War II—perhaps its proudest moment
as a military power since the defeat of the Spanish Armada—with the
look of a conquered nation. Many of its cities were in ruins; its factories
and railroads were worn out in the effort to supply the war machine;
worse, a huge war debt compounded the problems, requiring a nation
whose balance of payment deficits were centuries old to attempt to
export products in greater quantities. Producing for export requires
money; there was little. It requires efficient factories; the factories were
worn out. Britain found itself in the economically untenable position
of needing to borrow huge sums of money in order to reach the potential of paying off old debts. One of the results was that with exports
going to pay off debts rather than to bring in capital or material goods,
consumer goods were scarce, and the government enacted strong rationing measures—frequently more stringent than rationing imposed
during World War II.

Large loans from the United States and, especially, the Marshall Plan
helped Britain regain a measure of economic vitality. Economic problems, however, have continued to plague Britain since the war. Moreover, many of the measures taken by the Labour party and subsequent
governments to combat the economic woes have had as great an impact
on the British character and way of life as inflation, unemployment,
and declining production. One of the more radical measures was the
nationalization of certain industries and utilities such as coal, gas, elec-
tricity, and various transport industries. Nationalization met with approval in some sectors, bitter invective in others; it was not a
resounding success, and some nationalization acts were rescinded. Of
even more pervasive impact on British society has been the growth of
the welfare state, especially in health and housing. The welfare state
has also had mixed results but seems, nevertheless, a permanent feature
of British life. The emergent European Economic Community seemed
one possible broad solution to the economic problems, but Britain was
reluctant to join for practical and for symbolic reasons: her ancient

island status might be compromised, spiritually if not geographically, by such a union with the Continent. Join she did eventually, but the Common Market has not been the godsend some envisioned.

Other problems or issues important in postwar Britain are less specifically economic in nature but frequently result in part from economic issues or in turn cause economic problems. If the decline of the empire could be said to begin with the death of Victoria in 1901, the end itself could clearly be seen by 1947 with the loss of the "Crown Jewel," India. Over the next few years, other countries in Asia and Africa gained their independence, and Britain's stature as leader of the Commonwealth began to erode to something closer to *member* of the Commonwealth. A related problem, growing more severe over the years, is that of race. The influx of large numbers of Asians and Africans has exacerbated housing and unemployment problems, led to ideological and even physical confrontations, and fed the fires of a sad, desperate bigotry. Even worse is the "Irish question," the bloody legacy of centuries of British exploitation, racism, and brutality—a question with only one answer, obvious to all but more difficult to embrace with each new act of terrorism and retaliation.

The list of Britain's problems in the post–World War II years is lengthy: youth disaffection and violence, government corruption and scandal, increasing agitation for Welsh independence, the "brain drain," and so on. And though Britain managed to avoid the bloody conflict in Vietnam, victory in World War II did not usher in an age of blissful peace. The Jewish-Palestinean question lay largely in Britain's unwilling hands until 1948; the Persian nationalization of British oil interests in 1951 brought the nation to the brink of war once more; the festering Israeli-Egyptian problem culminated in the Suez crisis of 1956, almost plunging Britain into war again and straining, briefly, relations with the United States. Lurking behind and in the midst of all this was the cold war and the numbing possibility of nuclear warfare.

It is, perhaps, not simply engaging in facile stereotype to observe that the stiff upper lip in face of trouble is part of the British character. There seems to remain something endearingly "British" about the British even in the worst of times, times of radical and fundamental change. Still, the Britain of post–World War II is not the Britain of 1939 and certainly not of 1899. What this means for the British short story since the war remains to be seen.

• • •

Worldwide, the years immediately following World War II marked a period of transiton in literature as well as in social and economic areas. The imposing shadow of modernism still lay over the literary world; yet it seemed a shadow cast by some glorious giant receding into the sunset. Kafka, Joyce, Proust, Conrad, Lawrence, Woolf, and Fitzgerald were dead; the best work of Faulkner, Hemingway, Dos Passos, Mann, and Malraux lay behind them by 1945. Who could replace them, what general aesthetic would replace modernism, was not clear.

In retrospect, we might observe that for a number of years *no* one replaced the deceased or aging giants of modernism. In Germany, the voices of Böll and Grass would not be heard for a number of years. Russian and Eastern European writers were for the most part decades away from the time—only very recently—when their works could be published in the West (or anywhere else). Camus and Sartre were of course active in French letters, but both seem more properly associated with the war than with the period after. The one movement to gain international recognition in French fiction, the New Novel, would not begin to make its presence felt until more than a decade after the war. In the United States, the years immediately following the war are notable for the appearance of a number of writers—Salinger, Ralph Ellison, Mailer—who offered great promise but who for one reason or another failed to fulfill it.

One might argue, indeed, that contemporary Western fiction still is rolling in the wake of modernism, especially if by Western fiction one means that of Europe and the United States. For the fiction of Europe and the United States pales, in general, when compared to the work of such Latin American and Third World figures as Jorge Luis Borges, Gabriel García Márquez, Jorge Amado, Mario Vargas Llosa, Carlos Fuentes, Manuel Puig, G. Cabrera Infante, V. S. Naipaul, and Salman Rushdie.

Still, when people adversely contrast post–World War II fiction to modernism, usually they are referring in general to the novel. A different picture emerges if we look at the short story. Modernism has its great figures in this genre, to be sure: Joyce, Mansfield, Kafka, Anderson, Lawrence, Hemingway, Faulkner, to name a few. In retrospect, however, it is clear that most—excepting Kafka and Faulkner—were working within the fairly limited range of what is often referred to as the "epiphanic" short story. With its one or two major characters in everyday situations moving toward a climax of psychological revelation with no subplots, no overt drama, often little or no physical action, the epiphanic story became such a dominant mode that it threatened to suffocate the genre. The postwar years, in contrast, saw the revival of the short story, especially in the United States, Ireland, and Latin America. The United States is experiencing what might be called its golden age in the genre, with Eudora Welty, Flannery O'Connor, Carson McCullers, Grace Paley, John Updike, J. F. Powers, Donald Barthelme, and others withstanding comparison to the best of the modernists, and younger writers such as Raymond Carver, Ann Beattie, Jayne Anne Phillips, Bobbie Anne Mason, Max Apple, and many others continually reinvigorating the form.

·   ·   ·

British fiction, like the nation, was in a state of transition in the years immediately following World War II. Of the leading figures before the war, Conrad, Woolf, and Lawrence were dead by 1945, and so too was Ford Madox Ford; of the transitional figures, Huxley's best fiction was behind him and all of Forster's. Graham Greene, Evelyn Waugh, and George Orwell continued to write interesting fiction after the war; but, although Waugh is undergoing something of a rediscovery, thanks largely to a television production of *Brideshead Revisited,* only for Greene could we make a strong claim for truly major international status.

Just as the painful uncertainties besetting British society in general had their roots in the end of the Victorian Age, the malaise of post– World War II British literature was not entirely new. Although modernist works are richly interesting, the crowning achievement of British fiction was the nineteenth-century novel. Austen, the Brontës, George Eliot, Dickens, Thackeray, Hardy, and others composed a group rivaled only by the great French and Russian masters. If we turn to poetry and drama during the modernist period, the picture becomes gloomier. Save Auden, no British poet of the period can be considered more than a minor voice.

The post–World War II years by and large continue the decline in British poetry and drama. In poetry, Dylan Thomas stands a giant among a field of competent but unexciting figures. In drama, Harold Pinter is one of the major figures of our age, but he seems to have blossomed from an otherwise fallow field.

The contemporary British novel deserves some consideration, however. Although it may not be quite so exciting as the modernist British novel, and the modernist novel not quite so grand as the nineteenth-century novel, several interesting figures emerged in the post–World War II years. Whether Graham Greene and William Golding deserve inclusion among the seminal figures in contemporary fiction is questionable, but at least we can with justice ask the question. They cannot, at any rate, be ignored. Other British writers of the period whose fiction has received occasional high praise include Laurence Durrell, Anthony Powell, Joyce Cary, Evelyn Waugh, Anthony Burgess, John Fowles, and the resurrected Barbara Pym. Of late, younger writers such as Margaret Drabble and D. M. Thomas have been praised. One might, to be sure, point out that few of these writers are boldly innovative—as, for instance, Beckett, Barth, Borges, García Márquez, and Robbe-Grillet often are. Durrell's *Alexandria Quartet* follows a modernist impulse, as does Golding's powerful *Darkness Visible*; and his *Lord of the Flies* and Burgess's *A Clockwork Orange* join the rich British tradition of dystopian fiction. Fowles's *The French Lieutenant's Woman* and Thomas's *The White Hotel* come closer to cutting new paths; as entertaining as they are, however, future critics might well judge them to have been overpraised.

Ironically, Britain's major contribution to postwar culture has not come in the high culture areas of art, classical music, serious literature, and so on (although certainly we should not overlook British scientists' contributions to computer and genetic engineering, nor the philosophical circles hovering about Wittgenstein at Oxford) but in varieties of popular culture. BBC radio has been a trendsetter for decades (and has also provided one outlet for short stories); and British television at its best, and possibly at its average, surpasses its American counterpart, as Americans are coming to realize. Since the Beatles' invasion of the early sixties, British rock 'n' roll groups have garnered fame and fortune. And in literature, if we grope to determine the true value of "serious" contemporary British fiction, we have no trouble with such popular fiction forms as science fiction, the detective novel, and fantasy where Arthur Clarke, Agatha Christie, J. R. R. Tolkien, E. R. Eddison, C. S. Lewis, Mervyn Peake, and many more reign.

• • •

We come then to the British short story in the post–World War II years. (For the purposes of this survey, "British" signifies writers from England, Scotland, and Wales, although upon occasion a writer from outside the boundaries of Britain but spending a significant portion of his or her life there—Doris Lessing, for instance—will be discussed.) Who are the major figures in the contemporary British short story? In what ways does it reflect the tensions and conflicts in British society as a whole? How does it fit in the development of the British short story in general? What is its place in world fiction today and particularly in the context of the rejuvenated short story?

One of the most notable, and surprising, features of the contemporary British short story is its variety—surprising because hackneyed and ill-considered estimations of what is "typically British" in art and life would have us believe that the entire culture is of a kind. The Welsh short story writers who made their presence felt in the middle decades of this century—Caradoc Evans, Gwyn Jones, Glyn Jones, Margiad Evans, Gwyn Thomas, Rhys Davies, Alun Lewis, Kate Roberts, and, of course, Dylan Thomas and Roald Dahl—would object strongly to having their identities blurred in some stale cliché about what is "British." As early as 1941, in *The Modern Short Story: A Critical Survey,* H. E. Bates drew our attention to the virtues of the Welsh short story where, in the words of John Stinson, "the grotesque and the eccentric, the lyrical and the pastoral, often exist side by side." The strength of the Welsh short story began to wane somewhat in the fifties, but as late as 1971 an interesting anthology, *Twenty-Five Welsh Short Stories,* was published.

The Scottish short story has never achieved the status of the Welsh and English story; yet *No Scottish Twilight: New Scottish Short Stories* (1947), edited by Maurice Lindsay and Fred Urquhart, served notice that Scottish short fiction was not to be overlooked. Especially during the fifties, Urquhart, Neil Gunn, Eric Linklater, Ian Finlay, Muriel Spark, Naomi Mitchison, and others published excellent short stories, not provincial but colored by the Celtic language and heritage. If the Scottish short story has never taken quite so strong a hold on our imaginations as others, perhaps it is because the Scots have not of late been quite so loudly and militantly jealous of their ethnic identities as the Welsh and Irish.

Variety in the contemporary British short story is manifested in ways other than national origin. British writers most frequently set their stories in England, Scotland, and Wales, to be sure, but other locales are represented: the Continent, Africa, India and Southeast Asia, and elsewhere. The characters are most often British; but they converse with, and confront, Americans, Germans, Japanese, and, more important, the Arabs, Indians, and Africans who immigrated to the London area and these same peoples in their own lands in the far reaches of the Commonwealth. Concomitant with variety in settings and characters is variety in theme, tone, conflict, and technique: from the witty, urbane, often satirical studies of English middle-class life (Angus Wilson and V. S. Pritchett among many others) to darker studies of the frayed edges of the empire (Lessing's African stories, the Indian stories of Ruth Prawer Jhabvala, and so on); from the social realism of Nell Dunn to the ghost stories of L. P. Hartley; from the war stories of Roald Dahl to the feminist fiction of Penelope Gilliatt.

Not only is the contemporary British short story more varied in subject matter and style than we might expect, but we also might be surprised—considering the relative paucity of critical attention they have received—at the number of fine writers of short fiction produced by Britain in the four decades since World War II. Some of the names—Graham Greene, W. Somerset Maugham, Muriel Spark, Dylan Thomas—would be familiar to American readers, but largely because of their accomplishments in other genres (Greene, Spark, Thomas) or because their reputations were well established before World War II (Maugham, for instance). Ironically, most of the best contemporary British short story writers are little known beyond Britain's shores.

If frequency of mention in the four essays that constitute this survey is an indication of the most important writers, then V. S. Pritchett, H. E. Bates, William Sansom, Sylvia Townsend Warner, Doris Lessing, and Elizabeth Taylor are notable. Bates and Warner wrote finely crafted short fiction over decades-long careers. Taylor is perhaps the least well known of the group, but, in the words of Dean Baldwin, she "is a master of creating scenes and conversations that on the outside betray nothing of significance but that resonate with emotional power." William Sansom is one of the few British short story writers, at least until the seventies, whose work is notable for technical experimentation. Lessing is internationally known, of course, but perhaps more so for the novel than for the short story. Yet she is also a superlative writer of short fiction in which she dramatizes many of the seminal issues of our age, including the race question, feminist concerns, and leftist political movements.

The situation of V. S. Pritchett is curious. John Stinson speaks of Pritchett's "mastery of the [short story] form." Dean Baldwin calls Pritchett a "formidable talent." Walter Evans praises Pritchett's "wisdom, breadth of vision, irony" in his "vigorous, witty" short fiction.

Despite this and similar high praise, Eudora Welty's contention that Pritchett is the best short story writer in the language is probably better known, to American audiences at least, than are his short stories themselves. There are some signs that this is changing; still, Pritchett must rank as a major figure in the short story who is one of the most neglected by critics and readers alike.

Should, then, the contemporary British short story be considered an unfairly neglected body of work that, if scholars and readers would only give it its due, would be found to make a considerable contribution to the genre as a whole? Time, as ever, will be the final judge. It is interesting to note that, although they find much to praise in certain works, three of the four scholars contributing to this survey—John Stinson, Dean Baldwin, and Jean Pickering—express serious reservations about the state of the contemporary British short story. It may be significant that only Walter Evans, writing about the seventies, is generally more positive than his colleagues, for he has chosen to weight his discussion toward new, younger writers.

If it is true that the contemporary British short story is, with important exceptions, not the vital form that it was only a few decades ago, what has happened? In what terms, and why, does it fail to reflect, interpret, and engage the contemporary world that produced it?

One factor that may be interpreted as either a cause or a result of the malaise is the uncertain market for the short story in postwar Britain. Stinson, Baldwin, and Pickering all comment on the shrinking number of publishing outlets, and Evans does, too, by implication, pointing out that many stories first appeared in American publications. Even if we conclude, however, that the market for short stories in postwar Britain was dismal—and none of our contributors goes quite that far—such a circumstance still would not account for the falling off in vigor and quality during the period. Short story publication in America, after all, has not been a lucrative concern for decades; publishers bring out collections more from a sense of moral obligation than with any faith in the prospects of profit, and there are no American journals publishing short fiction with the visibility and economic viability of, say, the *Saturday Evening Post* before the war. Yet the short story in America not only is aesthetically healthy but may be experiencing a golden age.

We must look, then, beyond the mere economic circumstance of a declining market to more fundamental issues. *What* do postwar British writers write about and *how* do they write about it?

What is surprising about the content of the postwar British sto-ries—given the weakened economy, the class conflicts, the race and Irish questions, the decline of empire, the cold war, and all the other problems that plagued a society in transition—is how infrequently these major questions are at issue in the stories. Earlier it was noted that no one can hope to understand fully any body of literature without understanding the culture that produces it, but to a perplexing degree this observation does not apply to our subject. Stinson notes Angus Wilson's satires in the late forties on the middle class and its inability to change, but few of the other writers whom he discusses reflect their age so directly. Stinson speculates that the British short story declined in popularity after the war because readers had their minds on "larger issues" and were drawn more to nonfiction; yet perhaps if the short story writers had engaged more of these larger issues they might have reclaimed their audience. Baldwin notes that social and political con-cerns are reflected in the short fiction of the fifties—a decade that witnessed the rise of the "angry young men"—but that for the most part the decade produced a short story more "of grumbling than of revolution." Pickering points out how surprising it is that the short story should fail to engage social problems during the sixties, given the social nature of traditional British short fiction. And although Ev-ans devotes a section of his essay to short stories embracing a "social vision," he concludes that "for the most part the writers in our study seem relatively untroubled by the present menu of horrors facing the human race."

To be fair, writers have always leaned more toward the novel to project social concerns and perhaps toward drama to explore philo-sophical ideas. The short story, like lyric poetry, has always seemed more suited to the dramatization of individual emotional and psycho-logical concerns. (And perhaps few of us would really want to read stories dramatizing the problems of, say, socialized medicine.) Still, short story writers of other nations have more successfully reflected social concerns and have done so in ways that invigorated their fiction. Irish short-story writers have always found it impossible, even if they had wanted, to escape their troubled culture. American writers, black and white, whose short fiction touches on the race question in the United States are too numerous to mention. A virtual industry grew up in America around feminist fiction, long and short. And short sto-ries set against the backdrop of the Vietnam War and the drug culture of the sixties were so common a few years ago that the subjects strike many readers (and most editors) today as hackneyed. More historically important, perhaps, are the short story writers who have begun to appear from behind the Iron Curtain—most notably those in Penguin's Writers from the Other Europe series—such as Danilo Kĭs, Tadeusz Boroski, and Milan Kundera, all of whom write stories searing in their social awareness. British short story writers cannot be absolved, then, for their failure to reflect the age in which they live.

But perhaps we are in point of fact wrong. Perhaps British writers really do incorporate important contemporary issues into their short fiction, but those issues fail to engage us, to make a lasting impression on us, because the vehicles in which they appear, the stories themselves, are not sufficiently engaging. A genre remains vital through change; it grows as writers find new ways to dramatize themes old and new. If no new ways are found, regardless of what issues may or may not be dramatized in the action, the genre stagnates and eventually dies. If the short story in Britain has stagnated, it may be that the problem is rooted in a failure of growth, a failure of innovation.

John Stinson correctly observes that, after the cataclysm of World War II had plunged the world into an era of accelerated change and uncertainty, the "neat and tidy" short story with a clearly defined introduction, complication, climax, and logical resolution seemed dated; moreover, the delicate atmospheric short story of Chekhov seemed too frail to reflect an increasingly grim reality. Innovative forms were required to reflect this new world, but of all the writers whom Stinson discusses, only William Sansom comes close to the experimental. To be sure, the late forties witnessed little innovation in the American short story either, but American writers soon began to seek out new forms. Baldwin finds little experimentation to comment on in the British short fiction of the fifties. The sixties were a period of great experimentation in America, the Continent, and Latin America; but Pickering observes that most stories of the same decade in Britain had an old-fashioned air in subject and technique. Evans's essay offers some hope. He discusses a number of writers in the seventies who experiment to varying degrees in their short fiction—not all successfully but some encouragingly so. Yet despite Evans's decision to seek out innovative writers, he concludes that "the bulk of writers . . . favor more traditional modes."

Much the same could be said for the literature of any period, no doubt; traditional or conventional stories always outnumber the innovative. And innovation is not necessarily a virtue. A good deal of experimental literature—perhaps most of it—is crushingly uninteresting. We can with confidence predict, however, that it is not among the traditional writers but among the writers who shock us, puzzle us, anger us that future generations will find the seminal writers of our age. Few of them, it now appears, will come from Britain.

Perhaps the central problem is something undefinable in the British aesthetic character. Except for a brief, and we might say uncharacteristic, flowering in the early decades of this century, the British simply cannot boast of a rich short story heritage. It is strange that cultures can be rich in one genre, poverty-stricken in another. The Irish have produced great short story writers, poets, and dramatists but relatively few major novelists (with one extraordinary exception, of course). The French have contributed outstanding prose writers of all varieties to the world's culture, but their poets do not in general compare to the great English lyric poets. The Russians have excelled in the novel and short story, but aside from Chekhov, they have produced little outstanding drama. American drama, too, is a relatively infertile field. Perhaps it is simply the fate of the British to excel in poetry and the novel but not in the short story. There are worse fates.

We could all be wrong, of course. The worst place to see the game, after all, is down on the field of play. Distance affords objectivity, and objectivity in turn, at least one kind of wisdom. Perhaps the future will cast a kinder light on the post–World War II British short story than we now surmise. At the least we should remind ourselves that not only the greatest writers deserve our consideration. The following essays contain discussions of many writers who likely are unfamiliar to most readers, especially in America, but who are nevertheless capable of producing interesting and occasionally exhilarating short fiction.

• • •

A *note on the apparatus of this volume:* All short fiction collections and writers discussed are listed in the primary bibliography following the essays; quotations from the collections are not footnoted. A selected, annotated bibliography of important secondary sources is also included.

Finally, I would like to thank William Peden for his advice and encouragement on this project from conception to completion.

Dennis Vannatta

University of Arkansas at Little Rock

THE ENGLISH SHORT STORY, 1945–1950

The English short story, always something of a stepsister in the house of fiction, went, nonetheless, into World War II in a state of reasonably good health. During the war years themselves it fared as well as could be expected, perhaps slightly better. Past history, most notably World War I, provided a reasonable expectation that the aftermath of war would produce changes in the social and artistic climate that might be either salubrious or injurious for the short story. As it turned out, the short story suffered no sudden chill or serious illness, but it did seem older, cautious, withdrawn. Although the short story did not become an invalid, neither was it, by the end of the forties, a robust presence whose engagingly vigorous health commanded attention.

As the forties came to an end, the outlets for short fiction in newspapers and periodicals noticeably narrowed (a phenomenon discussed more fully later in this chapter). Publishers, always wary of bringing out a collection of short stories by a single author, became more reluctant still. In his introduction to the *Little Reviews Anthology: 1949,* the editor, Denys Val Baker, notes that "publishers are now a good deal less willing to consider a book of short stories than they were two or three years ago."[1] Still, the picture was not unrelievedly gloomy. A number of writers who had brought the British short story between the wars to a state of noteworthy artistic accomplishment and prominence were still alive and active. These were, most notably, W. Somerset Maugham, A. E. Coppard, H. E. Bates, V. S. Pritchett, and Graham Greene. Each produced at least one volume of short stories between 1945 and 1950, but only Pritchett continued to produce a large number of consistently good short stories.

Although, in retrospect, there are some obvious reasons for the relative decline of the short story form in Britain; other reasons are not so easily discernible. To start with the obvious: British life was thoroughly disrupted by the all-consuming effort of total war. Although the end of the war did indeed produce some of the exhilaration that

1

might have been expected, it also saw a depletion of the nervous energy that had kept the nation going. Britons drew on their remaining psychological resources to get their lives back in order while still having to cope with wartime rigors and constraints—rationing, shortages, a quotidian drabness that led to a languor of spirit that some social historians feel has been chronic with Britons even to the present day.

Books about the war (histories, personal accounts, thinly disguised fictions, biographies, and documents) crested to near flood stage in the period from 1945 to 1950. Understandably, books in the social sciences enjoyed a boom: studies of the origins of totalitarianism, the history of Nazi Germany, the Anglo-American-Soviet alliance, the morality of nuclear weaponry, the postwar economy of a devastated Europe, the cold war, the possibilities of a third world war. One is perhaps surprised only by the rapidity with which books on the Nazi death camps and morality in the age of the Bomb appeared.

It has become commonplace to say that far fewer great works of fiction came out of World War II than might have been expected. The usual explanation for this is that reality had become a beast of monstrous proportions—one that simply could not be contained between the covers of a book; reality had beggared fiction. As a result it is possible that many readers were in the process of making some indictment, if only subliminal, about the "failure" of fiction. If the novel could not cope with the nature of reality, the short story seemed even less well qualified for the task. Well-crafted, tidy stories with strong plot lines and definite endings were already out of fashion; now they seemed hopelessly passé. So too did the Chekhovian story of atmosphere and character.

Whether a significant drop-off occurred in the reading of fiction in Britain after the war cannot be determined definitively. Sales figures alone are no accurate indicator; Britons, particularly in a straitened economy, make far heavier use of circulating libraries than do Americans. It is fair to say, however, that in the immediate postwar period, fiction produced no great stir. The world being in the pass it was, many readers seem to have felt a kind of moral obligation, or at least a social compunction, to read the important books of political theory, psychology, history, statesmanship, and foreign policy and to have begun to think of fiction as something like a fondly remembered toy, something not quite serious, not quite adult. When fiction was read, it was frequently for escapist purposes, as is evidenced by the great popularity of historical romances in the period.[2]

Not surprisingly, the subject of much of the war and immediate postwar fiction was the war itself. Readers had a voracious appetite for stories about the war, and they were fed a heavy diet of quickly concocted fictions. Many mediocre stories were written to tried-and-true formulas; many more were journalistic stories full of reportage about military life and training, the feel of combat, and technical details of weaponry and maneuvers, as well as descriptions of various kinds of war service on the home front.

Short Fiction of the War

Isolating the best British short stories of the war is no easy task; no one has performed for Britain the valuable service that Charles A. Fenton did for the United States with his judicious anthology of 1957, *The Best Short Stories of World War II: An American Anthology.* The best writer of stories about the war was unquestionably H. E. Bates (1905–74). His collections *The Greatest People in the World* (1942), *How Sleep the Brave* (1943), and *The Stories of Flying Officer X* (1952), which added three new stories to the first two volumes, were popular successes and helped give the short story of war a good name.

Bates's "The Cruise of the *Breadwinner*" (1947), a war story of about twenty-five thousand words, is typical in the easy assurance of its construction, the strong, sometimes lyrical simplicity of its prose, and its exact observation of detail. The story is one of initiation, of a sixteen-year-old boy, a crew member on a lugsail fishing boat on government patrol in the channel, coming of age. The one day on which the narrative takes place sees the *Breadwinner* much more heavily engaged in activity than it had ever been before; the crew picks up both an R.A.F. and a Luftwaffe pilot and is shortly thereafter strafed by a German fighter. The story is believable in its realistic details and effective symbolism.

Nicholas Monsarrat (1910–79) achieved great popular success in Britain and America with *The Cruel Sea* (1951), one of the better World War II novels in English. *Depends What You Mean by Love* (1947) contains three long short stories of a little over twenty thousand words each. These are finally crafted stories of war that blend selective realism with romanticism; stock qualities and sentimentality, the obvious dangers with Monsarrat's type of story, are here largely, but not entirely, avoided.

In "Heavy Rescue," Bill Godden, a working-class man of fifty, has lost much of his purpose and feeling of self-worth in the depression. His once loving and beloved wife has long been a shrew, and his fifteen-year-old daughter is now tartlike and smart-mouthed. Godden joins a London air-raid rescue squad mostly out of patriotism and human decency but also simply because he needs a job. Soon he rediscovers the camaraderie he knew in World War I; war relieves his psychological depression even more than his economic problems. Much of the story takes place during the period of the "phony war" when Godden, promoted to squad leader, and his colleagues wait expectantly and train for the time when Hitler's bombs will finally fall. By the time they do, Godden is almost a fully resurrected man who, ironically, dies a hero's death: after a successful rescue, he is buried under tons of debris as a bombed-out house collapses on him. The story, though, does ring true; the time and events were extraordinary—the mundane and the heroic frequently blended in the proportions Monsarrat serves up here.

Godden's love of his fellow man is not too very different from that which prompts the captain of a severely damaged warship to bring her in against very long odds in " 'H.M.S. Marlborough Will Enter Harbour.' " More discernible in Monsarrat are the limitations that some critics descry in Bates's fiction of this period—a treatment and style somewhat too facile and a tendency to romanticize situations.

Another popular writer who deserves brief mention because of his prolific production and the wide range of his audience in both Britain and America is Gerald Kersh (1909–68). Between 1941 and 1946, Kersh turned out the astonishing total of thirteen books (and this while he was in the army); his output remained high in the postwar period, no fewer than thirteen of his stories appearing in Esquire in the years 1945–50. Clean, Bright, and Slightly Oiled (1946), although classified and reviewed as fiction, is much more a series of near-autobiographical sketches about army life than a collection of stories. In "How Not to Become an Officer," for example, "Kersh" is much nearer to being the author himself than to being a persona. Kersh's fiction is generally journalistic and his writing sometimes flat. Frequently, but not always, he is content to evoke from his readers the expected sentimental responses he calculatedly thinks they want. Kersh, an effective self-advertiser, sometimes gives way to posturing. Whether he is quite at his best or not, his strong qualities—authenticity, pith, immediacy, verve, readability—frequently do manage to break through.

Much more consistent artistry characterizes the first collection of adult stories by Roald Dahl (1916–). *Over to You: Ten Stories of Flyers and Flying* (1946) reflects Dahl's experience as an R.A.F. fighter pilot and wing commander. He presents not only vivid scenes of aerial combat but also poignant portraits of airmen on base and on leave. Dahl writes a graceful, lucid, unpretentious but carefully crafted prose. What he achieves in this collection is one of the objectives of any accomplished short story writer: the sharp, credible individuation of character and scene that manages, almost paradoxically, richly to suggest the truth of universal experience. Young airmen in war, we are convinced, would behave exactly as they do, but we come to understand something not just about R.A.F. men at war but about youth, anxiety, valor, stress, foolishness, and death. Dahl's work is of qualified excellence, his craft at a few points seeming, especially in its ironies, to become almost too assured; a slightly facile quality begins to emerge. A well-assimilated Hemingway influence, however, seems at times detectable, as in the powerful story "A Piece of Cake."

Three Masters of the Form: Maugham, Coppard, and Greene

The short story in Britain did not set forth clearly on any new path during the war period to 1950. Indeed, comments about the state of the short story at the time were mostly complaints that the British short story lacked form and direction. Although it seems remarkable for its querulousness and, more particularly, its naïveté, this comment of an anonymous reviewer in a 1945 *Times Literary Supplement* is typical: "The new type of short story that has come into fashion in the course of the last few years has broken with the old tradition inasmuch as it tends to discard any necessity for plot and construction and regards the happy ending with supercilious disgust. Taking Mr. Wyatt's present selection [*English Story*, fifth series] as a test, one of the chief aims of the modern short-story writer is, it would seem, to harry rather than entertain the reader."[3]

Such dissatisfaction among critics with the British short story of the time was widespread although not universal. The absence of an underlying, agreed-upon aesthetic of the short story was frequently noted. It was neither one thing nor the other, said several critics. One lamented the "bewildering number of different styles." No one remarked happily on the protean possibilities of the form nor on artistic diversity being, if only potentially, a sign of health. More particularly, there were animadversions on the baleful influence of Chekhov (and, less frequently, Mansfield) upon British writers of the forties. A number of these critics found that altogether too many of the stories they read had neither character nor plot, but only quivering sensibilities.

W. Somerset Maugham (1874–1965) exerted a beneficent influence on the short story in Britain in that the popularity of his stories kept people reading at least his own efforts in the form. An early admirer of Chekhov, he came to feel that his own reputation was diminished because critics seemed capable of measuring the excellences only of the Chekhovian story—a story far different from Maugham's. In an urbane address on the short story, delivered to the Royal Society of Literature (published in slightly altered form in *Points of View*), he quotes Chekhov's observation that "people don't go to the North Pole to fall off icebergs. They go to offices, quarrel with their wives, and eat cabbage soup." But Maugham protests that "people *do* go to the North Pole, and if they don't fall off icebergs they undergo adventures as perilous and there is no reason in the world why an author shouldn't write very good stories about them."[4] And, indeed, a great many of Maugham's stories are very good; he usually had the honesty and grace, however, to admit that they were kept from excellence by certain limitations.

Creatures of Circumstance (1947) was the last volume of Maugham's to contain stories previously unpublished in book form. He was more or less back in favor with the critics by this time, his age and the enormous bulk of his production earning him genuine respect if not unqualified admiration. Some British reviewers now seemed ready to side with Maugham in his battle with the exponents of the Chekhovian short story.

Creatures of Circumstance consists of fifteen stories, all written since 1934 and previously published in magazines. The familiar Maugham virtues are on display: lucidity, ease, clarity, congenial and engaging narration, polish, a definite plot line. Maugham is successful in his effort to give the reader the feeling that he is at his ease, perhaps in his armchair at his club, with after-dinner brandy and cigar, being told a story in a straightforward and relaxed way by an urbane man of the world. Despite their detractors, many of Maugham's stories possess a degree of genuine artistic accomplishment, although it is a rather small one; Maugham seldom attempts incisiveness, depth, or poetic quality, even as the man in the armchair telling us his polished anecdotes would not be at all likely to attempt those effects.

Although some of the stories in *Creatures of Circumstance* are slightly weak, there are three or four noteworthy successes.

"Winter Cruise" deserves to be far better known, its adroit styling enhancing its comedic effects. The story proves that Maugham can go beyond his colder, more ironically detached observations of character to the richer, warmer treatment of pure comedy. The comedy arises in "Winter Cruise" from the near-perfect union of character and situation. Miss Reid, an English spinster, has always fancied herself a jolly soul and a catalyst for good conversation. In fact, though, she is a crashing bore. The crew of the German freighter on which she is the sole passenger, being driven to distraction by her relentless cheeriness and conversation, decides to administer the prescription of the ship's doctor, who ascribes her condition to a dammed-up libido. The cure involves a late-night visit to Miss Reid's cabin by an embarrassed twenty-one-year-old radio operator. The comic treatment before and after the visit is assured and adept; there is also a slightly serious side to the relationship, and this is handled sensitively and with some poignance.

"The Colonel's Lady" and "Sanatorium" are engaging and fairly well-known stories, thoroughly accomplished within Maugham's usual limitations. The former is essentially a well-told anecdote, but "Sanatorium," in which Maugham's familiar Ashenden appears as the focal character, is a story of love, death, and intertwining human relationships. The story is more than sufficiently involving, but it is marred by clichéd characterizations and a whiff of sentimentality.

"The Unconquered," is a story in which Maugham's narrative ironies are muted. Annette, a young French schoolteacher, is brutally raped by a drunken Nazi soldier during the first week of the invasion. Later, feeling lonely, the soldier returns to the farm where Annette lives with her parents; shortly thereafter she discloses that she is pregnant. The story economically delineates the changing relationships and subtly changing emotions among Annette, her parents, and the German soldier. It is Annette, though, who never wanders too far from her initial emotional reaction; underlying all else is her perception that the German is the hated enemy—uncultured, obtuse, and arrogant beneath his sentimentality and common humanity. At the end of the story Annette, with cool rancor, announces to the soldier and her parents (now urging Annette to accede to the soldier's proposal of marriage) that she has just drowned the healthy newborn, the father's proud image of himself. The young Nazi gives "the cry of an animal wounded to death." This story rises above the level of the anecdote, because some

relatively complex internal fiber of emotion is bared through dramatization; the tinge of melodrama is mitigated by the sad fact that even
stranger dramas were enacted on the stage of World War II.

• • •

Like Maugham, A. E. Coppard (1878–1957) favored the simple and
the straightforward, achieving a naturalness and an ease in his narrative
style. Whether it be an omniscient author or a storyteller introduced
within a frame, the narrative voice is always natural and compelling,
sometimes leisurely ingratiating. Coppard's stories, however, convey
the impression that their wellspring is the folktale; with Maugham it
seems to be the dinner-table anecdote. In Coppard there are poetry,
resonance, and depth; in Maugham, except when he is at his absolute
best, there are only matter-of-factness and well-bred common sense.
Along with Hardy, one of the influences upon Coppard was clearly
Chekhov.

Coppard's *The Dark-Eyed Lady: Fourteen Tales* (1947) is perhaps his
weakest volume, and none of the pieces is included in *The Collected
Tales* (1948). In *Dark-Eyed Lady* the light, playful touch sometimes
found in his stories seems here slightly wrong when employed in con-
junction with serious, sometimes tragic themes. One is surprised to
find two stories ("Hail Columbia" and "The Gold Watch") that deal
with Jewish life, replete with dialect; these are not quite embarrassing,
but they are not Coppard at his best by any means. "Apes Don't Shave"
and "The Sullens Sisters" (where a light touch for a serious theme does
seem to work) are stronger, more characteristic efforts from this
volume.

• • •

A major short story writer, although not very active in the form
between 1940 and 1950, Graham Greene (1904–) produced some
good, if not his best, stories during this decade. In the preface to
Nineteen Stories (1947) Greene called them "scraps," "merely the by-
products of a novelist's career." Many reviewers having taken their cue
from Greene's own modest dismissal of his efforts, it is not surprising
that Greene thought to take back his earlier statement in his introduction to the *Collected Stories* (1973): "I realize that since the beginning I
have really all the time been a writer of short stories—they are not the

'scraps' I thought them." An unbiased judgment would place the truth somewhere between the two positions. A few of Greene's stories are incontrovertible masterpieces, and many others approach excellence; but to claim, indiscriminately, that Greene has assured himself a place as one of the great short story writers of our time is surely a mistake. A few of the stories are frankly paltry and many others merely competent.

Nineteen Stories reprints the stories of *The Basement Room and Other Stories* of 1935; to them are added "The Innocent," "A Drive in the Country," "Across the Bridge," "The Second Death," "A Little Place Off the Edgeware Road," "The Case for the Defence," "When Greek Meets Greek," "Men at Work," and "Alas Poor Maling." *Twenty-One Stories* (1954) contains the same stories as *Nineteen Stories* but deletes "The Lottery Ticket" and "The Other Side of the Boarder" and adds "The Hint of an Explanation," "The Blue Film," "Special Duties," and "The Destructors." Readers familiar with these stories will probably agree that, on average, the stories included for the first time in *Nineteen Stories* are slightly weaker than both those of *The Basement Room* and the new ones in *Twenty-One Stories*.

In general, the best stories are lean and rock-hard; the lucid plot lines move with quickness and ease while allowing for an almost magical conjuring up of character and mood. Greene has distilled the essence of the thriller but turned it to his own religious/metaphysical ends. Events in many of his stories carry an uncanny weight since a dread significance—salvation/damnation—underlies the actions of his characters. Many of the stories float on a heavy current of atmosphere, here largely associated with a gray, somewhat foreboding London, reminding us of one of Greene's masters, Conrad.

None of the new stories of *Nineteen Stories* is a masterpiece like "The Basement Room" (1935) or "The Destructors" (1954), and two or three are very small efforts. "Alas, Poor Maling" is a slight, whimsical sketch of an unfortunate fellow plagued by loud, involuntary stomach rumblings that imitate "the opening bars of a Brahms concerto" and an air-raid siren. "The Case for the Defence" is the sort of product that used to be found among short stories in newspapers, except that even here Greene's touch has an absolute assurance. A defendant in a murder case is acquitted despite what would have been the positive identification of several eyewitnesses; they are confounded when the defense dramatically produces an identical twin of the defendant. In a final ironic twist, as the twins leave the courtroom together, one—no one knows which one—is pushed to his death under a bus by the swell of the crowd behind him.

"Men at Work" (which originally appeared in the *New Yorker*) is more significant. Here is an ironic portrait of bored paper shufflers at a wartime ministry trying hard to get through a make-work day in a building where inconsequence proliferates and partitioned little offices out in the corridor have a way of spawning subsections of their own. The last sentence, strategically placed for full ironic effect, provides a view of other men at work—R.A.F. pilots high in the skies over London.

"When Greek Meets Greek" (which originally appeared in *Esquire*) is an extremely droll story whose comic plot centers on the unwitting encounter between a con man and his niece on one side of the game, and a con man and his son on the other. In the final comic turn, son and niece fall in love and carefully position themselves to con father and uncle.

Stories of Wit and Irony:
Pritchett, Warner, Wilson, and Sitwell

The only major already-established writer not yet discussed is V. S. Pritchett, unless it be suggested, not implausibly, that Sylvia Townsend Warner belongs in that group. These two, along with the most accomplished newcomer on the scene, Angus Wilson, write witty, ironically detached comedies of character. All three have a penchant for dealing with the eccentric, the bizarre, the quaint, or the garish, frequently for the purpose of social satire. Eccentricity is also, as shall be seen, no small component of the short stories of writers such as Henry Treece, Osbert Sitwell, or most of the Welsh writers.

H. E. Bates in *The Modern Short Story* (1941) writes that "what contemporary British writers of the short story are doing is excellent, but it is comparatively easy."[5] His point seems to be that comic portraiture and caricature are comparatively easy when contrasted to the illuminations of truth in the lives of "ordinary" people that masters of the short story form in the tradition of Turgenev and Chekhov had captured so expertly. Pritchett and Wilson, and, to a lesser degree, Warner, are more in a line of English comedy descending mostly from Dickens and, less obviously, Thackeray.

The movement toward rich comedy and away from delicacy, evanescence, poetic realism, or symbolic naturalism is characteristic of

Pritchett and Warner. Whether the appearance of the eccentric in these writers portended anything at all, except a happy discovery that rich comic/satiric veins in the short story were yet to be mined, is difficult to say. (Some contemporary readers might still hold to Flaubert's dictum that "art is not made to paint exceptions," but many more, decidedly, would not.) It is true that in British writers of the period the grotesque does appear occasionally, and when it does, it is usually as a radical critique of rationalism. Greene's "The Destructors" provides one example, and the title story of Osbert Sitwell's *Death of a God* another. Rather than employing the bizarre and the grotesque to dramatize metaphysical or spiritual truths, as do many American writers, and even occasionally Dickens, contemporary British short story writers tend to use it more for the exploration of some truths about man in relation to the society in which he lives.

V. S. Pritchett (1900–) writes a type of short story that changed relatively little from *The Spanish Virgin and Other Stories* of 1930 to *On the Edge of the Cliff,* published in 1979. There is no good reason that it should have. Pritchett has achieved his own mastery of the form and is obviously comfortable in the broad but familiar terrain he has made his home, the comedic/satiric short story of character; in general his satire is more compassionate than caustic.

It May Never Happen and Other Stories (1945) is typical. Pritchett's prose—wry, descriptive, and evocative when it needs to be—amusingly and pointedly discloses various kinds of eccentricities, usually in lower-middle-class life. "The Saint," a deliciously funny story that originally appeared in *Horizon,* illustrates well some of the ways in which Pritchett manages his material to excellent advantage. The story is broadly humorous, but it also possesses pith, wit, and character while achieving, quite remarkably, sharp thematic implication and a fine economy, suggested in the strong, angular beginning: "When I was seventeen years old I lost my religious faith."

The narrator and his family have recently been converted to the "sect called the Church of the Last Purification, of Toronto, Canada." The sect's chief article of belief is that evil is but an illusion; "error" is belief in evil. The church's adherents deny the reality of such phenomena as influenza, cancer, consumption, unemployment, and insanity, maintaining "that since God could not have made them they therefore did not exist." The young narrator comes to have powerful doubts and is thus the recipient of a heart-to-heart talk from an avuncular leader of the sect. The talk proceeds as the two punt on a river, but reality intrudes. The church leader proves inept at punting, and soon, in navy blue suit and waistcoat, he finds himself a victim of total immersion. Drenched, with blue suit covered with yellow pollen, he pretends that nothing untoward has occurred, but the narrator finds the experience instructive.

"It May Never Happen" has for its protagonist another teenage boy, this one recently entered into the damp, somewhat misshapen world of the small but earnest mercantile enterprise so redolent of Dickens. There is also a Dickensian eccentricity of character wryly and expertly detailed, although Pritchett's style is compressed rather than expansive.

· · ·

Sylvia Townsend Warner (1893–1978) should best be remembered as a short story writer, although she was a prolific writer who produced, in addition to twelve volumes of short stories, novels, poetry, biographies, and authoritative studies of Tudor church music. Warner was already fairly well known to some American readers when *The Museum of Cheats* appeared in 1947. Eight of the stories in this volume had, in fact, appeared previously in the pages of the *New Yorker,* another reminder of that magazine's contribution as an international outlet for superior short fiction.

The Museum of Cheats contains twenty-two stories of several types, the longest being the thirty-seven-page title story. Many of them achieve rather subtle effects through graceful stylistic turns. Warner reveals herself to be a skilled fantasist in some of the stories, and in all, she achieves verisimilitude and compression through her exact rendering of the minutiae of her characters' daily existence. Having created full-dimensional worlds and situations alive with nuance and possibility, Warner is content to let her readers do a great deal of the work; much may be discerned only by the intelligent reader, and many of her endings are ambiguous.

Warner, for example, skillfully employs the open ending in "Poor Mary," where some truths, both poignant and droll, about human nature are ironically but convincingly presented. Time and circumstance have weighed heavily on the husband and wife of this tale. He has been a conscientious objector assigned to agricultural labor during World War II, and thus has led a lonely existence. She, as a member of the military, has been near the center of wartime activity. Weary and dispirited, she has become sloppy in mind and body, but he is self-contained, domestic, deeply contented. Poor Mary, who admits to having had an affair, now supposes that she is ready to have her husband back, and he is willing to take her back, too. At the end of the story he thinks of the pleasures of bed with her, but she seems to come second to the joys of rusticity: "They would lie in the Wordsworthian bed, their smells of dung and of metal would mingle, her shoulder would feel like greengages. . . . And probably his last waking thought would be of the alarm clock, poised to wake him at five-thirty, and of the limpid innocent morning in which he would go out to his work." His serenity is apparently more than a willed narcosis, a withdrawal from the insanely destructive outside world. But we cannot be sure. And can she accept the same balm for the psychic wounds she suffered out there in that real world and live with him in his romantic idyll? Probably not, but the weight of ultimate interpretation falls upon the reader; Warner deliberately withholds enough relevant evidence so that readers are compelled to enter fully into the situation and draw their own conclusions.

Noting the frequent appearance of Warner's stories in the *New Yorker,* some readers might feel that she deliberately trades on Americans' notions that delightful quaintness and idiosyncrasy are inherently English. The title story, "The Museum of Cheats," is likely to arouse this suspicion, but it is not altogether well founded. In this ironical history of an endowed museum that specializes in objects of superstition, Warner implicitly says something significant about human vanity and self-interest, not just English eccentricity. The narrative tone is deliciously dry as it details an often ignoble and debased kind of eccentricity in several characters, but Warner's view is not misanthropic; it is compassionate and amused even while it is critical.

Other stories are about relatively ordinary civilian life during the war; "A Speaker from London" is a two-sided view of the ongoing class struggle at home even as England fights an external enemy for survival.

· · ·

Angus Wilson's *The Wrong Set* (1949), a collection of thirteen stories only three of which had previously been published in magazines, signaled the arrival of a major new talent. Wilson's forte, an abbreviated comedy of manners, is ultimately predicated on the social upheavals that occurred in Britain after World War II. Wilson (1913–) presents us with an array of vulgar or eccentric people, all of them, however, totally believable; the tone is generally one of slightly amused detachment not unlike Warner's, but readers will, to varying degrees, discern some acidulous commentary beneath the flat, precise tones. Certainly Wilson is not on the side of vulgarity, sham, pretension, decadence, and hypocrisy; but the question remains open whether the moral bias is sufficiently present so that Wilson should be classified a satirist. Whether he is writing satire or social comedy, however, the accuracy of his work, combined with a ruthless irony, results in some of the most consistently witty stories of the period.

That irony, resulting in this case from the manipulation of point of view, produces some delightful but slightly disturbing wry humor in the title story, "The Wrong Set." Here the narration is confined to the point of view of the chief character, Vi, but the reader will realize before he has finished the story that he ought not to accept things at Vi's valuation. The reader might initially feel, too, that Vi is an implausible bundle of contradictions, but as the story progresses he will come to see that Wilson's depiction is droll but accurate: Vi *would* be exactly like that. Vi values respectability but lives with a man without benefit of marriage; she values social status but is one of two pianists at a slightly raffish nightclub; from a lower-middle-class background, she is a Conservative and a person alive to the Red Menace. The story is an ironically oblique character study, and its rich characterization makes possible superbly comic ironies. That these can be achieved in such a small space indicates that Wilson was, from the very first, a master of the short story craft.

Wilson has a penchant for skillfully exposing the grotesqueries of his characters, particularly upper-middle-class ones; frequently, this exposure is witty and subtle, but the conclusion of another story, "Raspberry Jam," provides a jolt the reader does not anticipate. The story deals with a young boy's friendship with two elderly, decayed gentlewomen. We will probably—and this is how Wilson plays his trick—see these two as familiar literary types: charming eccentrics, noble relics from a richer past now shamefully devalued by the vulgar, tasteless world of the present. The ending of the story, however, in which the two old sisters excitedly and viciously torture to death a captured bird in the presence of the horrified boy reveals how deeply the two have descended into madness.

"Crazy Crowd" is a portrait of a different type of eccentricity. Here "craziness" is the kind a family carefully cultivates and nurtures because it gives a titillating boost to their collective egos. They are filled with self-congratulation and hug themselves daily with the delight of it all; a young male visitor finds their behavior diverting at first, but then is soon driven to anger and near-distraction.

Other Wilson characters are either beset by, or are the victims of, a dangerously naive romanticism. An earnest female student in "Fresh-Air Fiend" thinks to let a little fresh air into the relationship between her university professor and his alcoholic wife. This, she is certain, will give him a psychological boost, which she feels he badly needs. What it produces instead is a nervous breakdown of the professor.

Throughout all the stories of *The Wrong Set* Wilson presents us with people who cannot, or will not, fairly assess themselves, people who cannot come to honest terms with themselves or the reality of their social situation. Within this context Wilson paints his exquisite miniature portraits, full of psychological and social nuance captured through skillfully ironic shadings. One should note the fact, too—for whatever it is worth—that Wilson's subtlety and wit were not lost upon the reading public; *The Wrong Set* was a definite success as indicated by sales figures of the time.

• • •

Osbert Sitwell (1892–1969), who with his sister Edith and his brother Sacheverell formed a famous, self-advertising, and eccentric literary trio, wrote the kind of English comedy that was frequently Dickensian yet designed, in his own words, to allow effective "hand-to-hand battles against the Philistine."[6] *Death of a God and Other Stories* (1949) contains only one story, "Staggered Holiday," that had not appeared in previous collections. The effects of the blitz upon some elderly invalids taken for daily outings to Kensington Gardens is its subject. What is noteworthy about the story is the first impression that some easy and rather tasteless fun is being had at the expense of the pitifully infirm. Actually, however, the story compounds irony and compassion in an effectively strange and provocative way.

War appears also in "Death of a God"; here World War I lies at the center of a fable about the destruction of the illusion of Order in the world; forces deeper, darker, and more powerful than the rational emerge and prevail.

Varieties of the Eccentric:
Treece, Sansom, and Kavan

Henry Treece (1912–66) is sometimes misidentified as a Welsh writer, probably because he has written fairly extensively about Wales and perhaps because he is known in America for his *Dylan Thomas: Dog among the Fairies* (1949). Treece, a poet, published his first and only volume of short stories, *I Cannot Go Hunting Tomorrow*, in 1946. (Four of the stories had previously appeared in *English Story*.) The dust jacket refers to "the author's native Wales"; actually he was born in Staffordshire and grew up in the Midlands, although he did have Welsh ancestry on his mother's side and Wales is the setting for a few of the stories.

"I Cannot Go Hunting Tomorrow" is a highly polished story about Roman Britain and the difference in culture and modes of thought between the occupying Romans and the native Britons. A long-standing friendship between a sober, logical, young Roman captain, Caius, and an Otter chieftain, Gwyndoc, suffers an inevitable rupture when the Briton, closer both to primal nature and to his own people, cannot dismiss as finally as the Roman would like the old ways of his people that include Druidical worship and practice. The story is handled sensitively, and as an artistic representation of the cultural clashes brought by changing history it deserves its place in high school anthologies.

Treece divides his book into three sections: Children, Fantasy, and Situations (the title story belonging to the last class). The stories in the Children section seem at first glance to be stories of initiation, but they lack the psychological acuity and the depth of the universal to fulfill the genre well. The stories mix the macabre and the whimsical, not always to good effect, as young children encounter at close quarters people with severe psychological disturbances. Although Treece skillfully manages the bizarre, he attempts no real penetration into any kind of significant human truth.

• • •

Eccentricity of a different, more artistically significant kind, appears in the work of William Sansom (1912–76), the most important new short story writer of the forties in Britain with the exception of Angus Wilson. Sansom was primarily a stylist who employed odd, angular approaches to his subject and unique, even eccentric (as has often been said) points of view.

Sansom's career began in 1941 with the publication of several stories in periodicals (including two in *Horizon*); *Fireman Flower,* his first collection, appeared in 1944. *Three,* consisting of three stories, including the novella "The Cleaner's Story," appeared in 1945; in 1948 another novella, *The Equilibriad,* was published along with two collections, *Something Terrible, Something Lovely* and *South.*

What Sansom valued most highly was style, mood, and intensity. His stories, when not clearly allegory, incline toward it; he pushes the description of minute, sensuous detail so far that readers' ontological perceptions might even be said to be altered. The early influence of Kafka (most of whose work began to appear in English translation only in the 1940s) upon Sansom has been much commented upon by critics and reviewers, and Lila Chaplin, in her book on Sansom, makes a plausible case for the influence of Poe. Sansom sufficiently assimilated these influences, however, so that a style emerged that was distinctly his own.

Sansom's thematic and emotional range is impressive, as is the technical sweep in *Something Terrible, Something Lovely.* The title story provides a wry and ironic but also sensitive and perspicacious look at two little girls as they encounter an event, small to adult eyes but large to their own, that marks a stage of their passage toward adolescence. "Building Alive," very much like the Fireman Flower stories and, like them, based on Sansom's own wartime experience, is an economical, suspenseful, minutely descriptive narrative of a fireman in London during the V-1 attacks. "From the Water Junction," reminiscent of Kafka's "A Hunger Artist," is a surrealistic story about three boys who have always lived in a water main and will never be content anywhere else. "How Claeys Died," set in a postwar occupation zone of Germany, is a tale that underscores the failure of rationalism and the lack of communication in the world. Many of the stories (such as "The Vertical Ladder") present characters in situations that demand almost feverishly intense concentration, for peril and dread are often near at hand.

Kafka's influence is more recognizable in the novelette *The Equilibriad.* A forty-year-old bachelor awakes one morning to discover that he has been suddenly visited with myasthenia, loss of equilibrium. This, however, he finds no real affliction; it precipitates instead a curious excitement since it changes his angle of vision and seems about to bring him to a cosmic awareness of sorts. He has been having an "affaire" with a female cousin, and as he meets her this day, he discovers things in her that he has not seen before. Something in their relationship is translated as is his basic understanding about the differences between the two sexes and the bonds that can exist between men and women. The story is handled imaginatively and poetically, although, to some tastes, it might seem somewhat portentous.

In 1947 the British critic Ronald Mason wrote (in *Modern British Writing*) that "it may be that writers of imaginative fiction are not common enough in this country nowadays, death and the contemplative life having knocked the bottom out of most progressive work in that field for the last twenty years."[7] Mason went on to make the point that Sansom then richly deserved attention for the imaginative quality of his fiction. "In an age rich in imaginative fiction," however, he thought it possible that Sansom would not be so praiseworthy. Mason's words have proven prophetic; American fiction of the last thirty years has been richly imaginative, and Sansom's fiction, at least in America, has ceased to be well known.

• • •

Another writer of the period whose work was frequently compared with that of Kafka was Anna Kavan, pseudonym of Helen Ferguson Woods Edmonds (1904–68). Kavan first came to attention with the publication of *Asylum Piece,* a novel, in 1940; her novels and stories from that point onward mostly deal with anguish, dementia, psychosis, drug addiction, and dread, the long dark corridors of the psyche being portrayed in relatively unadorned but finely chiseled language. Certain affinities with Anais Nin and D. H. Lawrence have, sensibly, been noted by some, but it seems fair to say that it was the sensationally tortured quality of her personal life that made Kavan something of a cult figure shortly before and, more particularly, in the period after her death. (Much has been written, for example, about her thirty years' addiction to heroin.)

I Am Lazarus (1945) presents fifteen unrelievedly grim studies of mental illness in a style that is sometimes heavily ironic, sometimes coolly anguished. None has a strong plot; all are stark sketches whose controlled ironies are intended to provide heavy indictments of the powers-that-be in mental institutions. In some of the studies we are inside the tortured minds of victims of psychosis or severe psychoneurosis, in others with some observer from the outside; in either case, the author emphasizes the crudely inadequate treatment administered by the psychiatric establishment and its bureaucracy. The attending physicians are usually bluff, hardy types who insist on more walks, less alcohol, the taking up of golf, and good-natured metaphorical kicks in the pants for seriously disturbed patients. That Kavan attempts no balance or even real distancing from the biased view gives intensity and a kind of pathos; but the lack of artistic balance severely limits both the range and depth of her work.

The title story, a poignant sketch of a young Englishman at a Continental sanatorium for the mentally ill, is typical. He has been given insulin-shock therapy and—it is claimed by the authorities—brought back, like Lazarus, from the dead. Getting inside the head of young Mr. Bow, however, one can see that beneath his attempt to conform to expectations there is only emptiness, confusion, and powerful, free-floating anxiety. The indictment of his treatment is not really earned, however; either we accept the author's bias because of some predisposition of our own, or else we do not. Virginia Woolf and Doris Lessing arrive at similar indictments of mental health care professionals, but they do so through more balanced treatment than Kavan. The stark power of her performance is, however, undeniable.

The Welsh Short Story Writers

In the Anglo-Welsh short story of the postwar years, the grotesque and the eccentric, the lyrical and the pastoral, often exist side by side, as they seem to do in so much regional writing.

Caradoc Evans (1883–1945), generally considered the seminal figure in the Anglo-Welsh group, operated from the premise that "cant and humbug and hypocrisy and chapel belong to Wales, and no one writing about Wales can dodge them."[8] His first collection of stories, *My People* (1915), predictably enough, created a furor in Wales. Although Anglo-Welsh writers younger than Evans seldom are led to the indignation that characterized most of his writing, they frequently select the same subjects for some heavily satiric portraiture: the Nonconformist chapel, self-righteous congregations, immoral and hypocritical deacons, secret lusts, and supposedly pious men who covertly worship their real god, money.

The Welsh regional writers are not, however, merely satirizing their fellow countrymen. Taking some lessons from the Irish (and, perhaps, as H. E. Bates suggests in *The Modern Short Story,* one or two from Sherwood Anderson),[9] they know that the universal is discoverable only in the particular, and their works contain more than a sufficient number of poetic truths about the ache of spiritual loneliness, passion, bereavement, and death. The term *Welsh regional writers* must be defined somewhat arbitrarily, but it should include Caradoc Evans, Gwyn Jones, Glyn Jones, Margiad Evans, Gwyn Thomas, Rhys Davies, Alun Lewis, Kate Roberts, and D. J. Williams (the latter two of whom write in Welsh). The work of other Welsh writers such as Dylan Thomas, Richard Hughes, and Roald Dahl has been assimilated into the English mainstream. It was in the short story that the regional writers excelled, and certainly their stories all bear a family resemblance, being, in the words of Gwyn Jones, "lyrical, humorous, sardonic, genial, sensual, tragical-comical-industrial-pastoral."[10] E. Glyn Lewis is correct when he writes that

> until the present time the conditions necessary for the formation of a tradition of drama, or the novel, have not obtained in Wales. These conditions are a fairly high degree of social self-consciousness, where the ultimate problem of the novel, as of all literature—the destiny of man—can be worked out in terms of an intricate pattern of social reactions. In the short story the degree of explicitness and of social self-consciousness need not be so high, so that Welsh writers of fiction in devoting themselves to this medium have revealed a degree of critical acumen in addition to their creative genius; with the result that in the realm of the short story, the Anglo-Welsh are surpassed by very few.[11]

· · ·

The contribution of Gwyn Jones (1907–) to Anglo-Welsh literature, and particularly the short story, is doubly significant. Jones, a scholar, translator, and biographer, founded, with Creighton Griffiths in 1939 the monthly *Welsh Review*. Jones proclaimed in the first issue the presence in Wales of a number of writers of artistic talent and prophesied that they soon would be seen as "the most valuable leaven in English literature since the Irishmen opened insular eyes at the beginning of the century."[12] Only a short time later this prediction had proven to be more accurate than wild-eyed. (The *Welsh Review* had to cease publication until 1945 because of wartime paper rationing, but by the late forties several Welsh short story writers, principally Rhys Davies and Jones himself, were adequately proving Jones's point.) Jones was also a chief force in the establishment and operation of the Penmark Press, issuing books by Alun Lewis, Kate Roberts, and others besides his own.

Two distinct Wales appear in Jones's work. The first is that of the mining valleys, evoked as "river, railway, road on their thin ledges, snaky chains of houses, the dramatic alternation of pit and ferny hillside."[13] This is the pastoral-industrial world of his youth. The second Wales, where he has spent most of his adult years, is the pastoral-paradisal region of West Wales: "the narrow roadway, gorsebloom headland, drift of sheep on the hillside inland, soft blue slumber of the summer sea, noontide swoon of islands."[14]

In *The Buttercup Field and Other Stories* (1945) we find compression, precise forceful language, and an assured use of nonobtrusive symbolism to illuminate the darkness that lies behind such elemental human emotions as passion and revenge. Both the title story and "The Pit" deal with cruel acts of vengeance that arise from passion and sexual jealousy.

"The Buttercup Field" is a story about a jilted lover who exacts a terrible vengeance upon the breathtakingly beautiful girl who left him. On her wedding night he burns down the house she occupies with her new husband, after making sure he has secured them in it. The lyrical qualities of the story, combined with the direct simplicity of its narration (within a frame), give it something of the quality of a Welsh folktale. The burning heat of the summer's day on which the story is told symbolizes the consuming fires of passion and jealousy of long ago. At story's end, the old man who is the teller of the tale reveals, dramatically but plausibly, that it was he who was the jilted lover and murderer of a time that, though long past, he still inhabits.

"The Pit" is a tour de force of suspense. A man with sexual designs on another man's wife finds himself trapped in an abandoned mine. His struggles to find his way out of the mine (where, presumably, the husband has arranged for his entrapment) are engrossing. He does finally escape the pit, but the ending is open: it becomes less certain that it was the husband's hand that arranged his mischance.

The theme of revenge surfaces again in a comic-serious way in "The Green Island," the longest (novella length) and probably the best story of the collection *The Still Waters and Other Stories* (1948). Here an Englishman lusts after a Welshman's wife; she seems to signal that she will not be unyielding, and the Englishman finds an excuse to get her alone on a small island in a bay. He allows their boat to drift away, planning to satiate his sexual appetite with a rich feast that is to be enhanced by the romance of the situation. The Welsh husband knows full well where they are, but he decides on an appropriate and effective vengeance: he tells no one where they are and for a full eight days leaves them stranded there. The couple, meanwhile, is tortured by physical discomfort, the silliness of the situation, guilt, and, for each, the tormenting presence of the other. But this is no simply plotted ironic story with a moral purpose; its lyricism and powerful symbolism invest it with a richness and truth that allow it easily to transcend a merely cautionary tale.

• • •

Rhys Davies (1903–78), son of a grocer in a mining village of South Wales, had been a skilled practitioner of the comic-satiric short story since the publication of his first volume (*The Song of Songs and Other Stories*) in 1927. Davies is somewhat better known to Americans than the other Welsh regional writers, several of his stories appearing, relatively late in his career, in the *New Yorker* and *Esquire*.

Davies's best stories are comic studies of character, where he casts a sly, satiric eye at the foibles of the Welsh and some peculiar twists in their collective personalities. Davies's view is generally detached and droll; there is no real acid in his pen as there is with Joyce and Caradoc Evans. It is with amusement, not contempt, that he allows his characters to pillory themselves or become embroiled in comic situations. Davies generally checks a slight tendency toward sentimentality; he checks somewhat less often slickness and predictability. He might also leave some readers with the feeling that his mining of Welsh materials is somewhat too self-conscious and single-minded in its purpose and perhaps a bit facile.

Davies published two volumes of short stories during the 1945–50 period, *The Trip to London* in 1946 and *Boy with a Trumpet* in 1949. *The Trip to London,* while containing among its eleven stories a few that are simply skilled and polished, offers more that are adroitly compressed, yet very rich in comic character. Relatively flat and unwinking in style, they are all the more deliciously droll and satiric. One such is "The Benefit Concert." Both the subject matter and the drolleries of the flat style and detached, economic narrative are reminiscent of "A Mother" in *Dubliners*. His fellow miners arrange a benefit concert for Jenkin, a disabled collier who is in need of an artificial leg. All seems to begin well enough, but Jenkin, crusty when he is not sniveling, soon comes into heated conflict with the dour deacons of Horeb chapel. Jenkin pumps himself up to righteous indignation when he learns that he is not to receive the evening's full proceeds. The deacons plan to keep for the chapel all proceeds above the cost of the artificial leg; they consider this justified since they have lured the legendary singer Madame Watkins out of fifteen years' retirement for the evening's performance. The comedy reaches its well-controlled high point when Jenkin, in a mixture of guile, greed, and ire, addresses the assemblage at the concert. The story is an excellent one because it presents us with a situation that has a naturalistic verisimilitude, yet is comic to the core and alive with nuances gained by acute knowledge and observation of the people of the Welsh mining town.

Some of the other stories in the volume, including the title story, have a skillful yet undistinctive, even prefabricated quality; they are the kind of product that used to be referred to, fairly or not, as a "magazine" story.

Boy with a Trumpet presents, in its twenty stories, a variety of themes and treatments, the best of them being vivid and in their own way convincing studies of the eccentricity in everyday life that occasionally leads to brutality; an undercurrent of terror is consequently present in some of these stories. Davies's selective realism is used to excellent advantage in those stories where people cross moral boundaries or the borders of normal social behavior; these include "The Fashion Plate," "Tomorrow," "One of Norah's Early Days," and the title story.

An author much admired by other Welsh writers is Kate Roberts (1891–), a writer of delicate short stories whose published work, in Welsh, goes back to the 1920s. In 1946 the Penmark Press of Cardiff published *A Summer Day and Other Stories,* English translations by three different hands of twelve of her stories. Roberts operates within a small thematic range, but her touch, so certain that it gives the appearance of artlessness, is likely to be thoroughly compelling to most readers. Her tone is spare but infused with intimacy and veracity; a reader may wonder only after putting the volume down what depths of sophistication lie beneath the simplicity. The stories are set in two remote valleys of North Wales where the life of the people is hard and constrained. A melancholic note prevails, but it is suffused with a sad beauty. Storm Jameson in her foreword to the volume describes Roberts's world accurately and well: "A narrow world, of peasants, quarrymen, small farmers, shopkeepers, narrowed further by poverty and a severe religion. Yet in most of the stories there is a sense of wide space, like that the immensity of the Welsh sky gives the smallest of these valleys, and of the passage of time—the life in them, often the life of one man or woman, seized and laid bare with subtle precision, is the latest moment in an unbroken line of similar lives."

The Scottish Short Story Writers

In contrast to the high regard in which the recent Welsh and Irish short story is held, the position of the recent Scottish short story is less certain by far. Two Scotsmen, Maurice Lindsay and Fred Urquhart, in a 1947 anthology titled *No Scottish Twilight: New Scottish Short Stories,* aver that "the Scottish short story is by no means enshrouded in any romantic twilight" despite the fact that "in recent years so much attention has been directed to the short stories of Welsh and Irish writers that the reader of short stories may have felt that the medium as a literary form was unknown in Scotland." The anthology offers stories by fourteen mostly younger writers, few of them well known outside Scotland: Margaret Hamilton, William Montgomerie, Maurice Lindsay, Thomas Henderson, Alexander Reid, Dorothy K. Haynes, Naomi Mitchison, Morley Jamieson, J. F. Hendry, Fred Urquhart, Peter Jamieson, Edward Gattens, Robert McLellan, and Coleman Milton. Their stories are almost uniformly well crafted, several are quite entertaining, and a few artistically accomplished. None of these writers, however, with the partial exception of Urquhart, seems to have produced any major volume of published work in the forties.

Fred Urquhart (1912–) in *The Year of the Short Corn* (1949) provides twenty amusing sketches of the inhabitants of the Scottish Lowlands. Since they are character sketches, the plots are extremely slight, and when, as sometimes happens, the character delineation fails to be sufficiently arresting, the story is wafted away like a bit of smoke in a breeze.

• • •

Far better known to British audiences is Eric Linklater (1899–1974), a novelist, biographer, and journalist who endeavored to write richly in several styles and métiers. His unusual collection of stories, *Sealskin Trousers,* appeared in 1947. This slender volume (127 pages) contains five stories that may best be described as adult fairy tales. In his preface to his 1968 collection *The Stories of Eric Linklater,* he candidly remarks that he "read fairly widely, but quite unmethodically, in that vast compendium *The Ocean of Story* (C. H. Tawney's translation of Somadeva's *Katha Sarit Sagara*) and I was, I suppose, impressed by the diffusion of fairy-tale and folk-tale."

Through the universality of fairy tale, Linklater attempts to tap into the collective unconscious; his style, basically simple and deliberately naive, is intended to lull the reader into a frame of mind where he will marvel, yet almost believe. Linklater walks a fine line between silliness and charm, and it must be said that two or three times in this collection he teeters precariously if he does not fall. When they are at their unstudied best, though, the stories are clearly reminiscent of Hans Christian Andersen.

"Sealskin Trousers," a fantasy set in some northern islands that are presumably the Orkneys, concerns a young woman encountering on a rocky seacoast a fellow graduate of Edinburgh University. He is hairy and wears sealskin trousers; he talks somewhat mysteriously with her and then suddenly dives "like nothing human" into the sea to catch a lobster. It is now that he tells the young woman outright that he is, in fact, a seal. He twitches off her glasses and tells her that she can be seal-like too. At the end they swim away together as the narrator, the woman's fiancé, arrives in time to see the last of them. Some talk of "psychobiology" in the story weakens rather than strengthens it; the ingenuous charm is dissipated by explanation.

"The Goose Girl" is a strange mixture of social realism and a folk-lorish sort of fantasy. A young schoolteacher, Robert Tyndall, courts and eventually marries a crofter's beautiful daughter whom he has often seen, before their marrige, leading a mischievous gander out of the house in the middle of the night. The story proceeds in a leisurely, even slightly digressive way that gives a sense of the ordinary and imparts more impact to an ending that the reader should discover, only in retrospect, to be not a total surprise; the beautiful but slightly unusual child of Tyndall and his wife turns out to be not his daughter at all but the gander's.

Adult Stories of Childhood:
Barker, Lehmann, and Manning

Linklater's fairy tales for adults demonstrate that some excellent adult fiction of the period was centered on childhood and adolescence. Three volumes, however—all by women writers and all concerned almost entirely with youth or the world as seen through the eyes of young people—deserve special mention. These are A[udrey] L[ilian]

Barker's *Innocents: Variations on a Theme* (1947), Rosamond Lehmann's *The Gipsy's Baby and Other Stories* (1946), and Olivia Manning's *Growing Up* (1948).

A. L. Barker (1918–) displays in *Innocents,* her first published volume, a gift for conveying delicate and sometimes complex emotions in an effectively dry, understated way. The main theme of the collection involves the tremors of innocence as it is exposed to the frightening or bewildering intrusions of experience. Barker mostly avoids, though, the too-familiar quiverings of youthful sensibilities, managing instead to discover some relatively fresh paths into the minds and feelings of the young.

The long short story "The Iconoclasts" is memorable for its success in heightening a powerful incident by making its perceiver a five-year-old boy who understands little of the significance of events in the story. The five-year-old, Marcus, accompanies a ten-year-old, Neil, on an expedition to an old windmill. The war is on and the older boy wants desperately to be a fighter pilot some day. An inner imperative demands that Neil test himself to see whether he has the requisite courage to be a hero of the skies. He climbs out onto one of the sails of the windmill some ninety feet above ground, hoping by his weight to bring it down so he can safely jump to earth at the bottom of its descent. The axle, though, proves rusted and sticks fast. After dogged but vain attempts to bring the sail down, he becomes exhausted, loses his grip, and falls to earth. He is not yet dead, but the terror of death comes upon him; the five-year-old, with a naive and distorted view, can only look on uncomprehendingly. Neil is, in a sense, a victim of both the war and of savage reality, and young Marcus's inexorable movement toward experience is accelerated by the events of the day. The story, arresting on the surface and structured for deeper meaning, is convincing in its language and its depiction of the psychology of children.

• • •

Four of the five stories in *The Gipsy's Baby and Other Stories* by Rosamond Lehmann (1901–) had previously been published in *Penguin New Writing,* edited by John Lehmann, the author's brother. Lehmann is a delicate writer, sometimes a poetic one, whose subject frequently is sensibility, usually female sensibility. In this collection she sensitively and skillfully captures the delicate flow of gradually increasing awareness among her young people, particularly as they are exposed to class distinctions and other facts of life in the adult world. Lehmann is obviously interested in creating in her readers a strong imaginative response to her characters and situations. The first part of one of the stories, "The Red-Haired Miss Daintreys," is a brief disquisition on fiction in which we are asked to notice that characters cannot really live and breathe in stories with tidy plots. This is not to suggest, however, that Lehmann's stories lack unity; in "The Gipsy's Baby," for example, there is a natural and subtle use of parallel situations that acts as a cohesive element.

The narrator of "The Gipsy's Baby" and "The Red-Haired Miss Daintreys" is the same woman, one who looks back at formative youthful experiences as one of the daughters in a country family regarded as local gentry. "The Gipsy's Baby" is in a darker, more serious vein than the other story, the themes of deprivation, death, grief, and mental disturbance being central. These two stories are probably the strongest, although vivid characterization, humor, and emotional range and depth are present in the other stories as well. The smug or casual dismissals implied in the tag "woman's writer" (sometimes attached to Lehmann) are uncalled for if used in connection with *The Gipsy's Baby*.

• • •

Olivia Manning (1915–80) published her first volume of short stories, *Growing Up*, in 1948. The stories are in a sense chapters delineating the development of girls becoming women. Manning's psychological analyses are penetrating and convincing, although she seems sometimes primarily interested in vivid scene painting and the creation of a sense of place. London, Paris, Ireland, and Transylvania are among the locales that her characters observe minutely and often respond to intensely; thus the reader gets both keen-eyed reportage and a record of vivid impressions. The writing is always lucid, but the plots are thin and sometimes predictable.

The title story, containing much convincing, but in this case not particularly penetrating, observation of character, is a novella about a young woman writer and her relationship with a married London editor. "A Visit" is an effective sketch dramatizing the responses of a sensitive girl as she is deliberately tantalized with thoughts of a jewel box as a possible gift from a wealthy elderly woman. Two stories set in Eastern Europe, "The Journey" and "In a Winter Landscape," are effective for their atmospheric detail.

Minor Figures

No survey of even so short a span as five years can pretend to completeness. Some volumes were not discussed because, subjectively, they were deemed not very significant. Brief comment on several of these might also serve to recapitulate a few tendencies of the period.

A[lan] A[lexander] Milne (1882–1956) published, in 1948, a volume of stories titled *Birthday Party and Other Stories*. Although from the same pen that gave us Winnie-the-Pooh, these stories deal mostly with adults and are intended for an adult readership. In stories that range from satire, fantasy, and murder suspense to slightly whimsical or sentimental realism, Milne displays virtues similar to Maugham's: lightness, ease, and straightforward narration. Milne never strains or tries too hard, and his effects are achieved in a pleasantly relaxed way. "Anne Marie" is an anecdotal story with both cleverness and an easy charm. By rare theatrical skills and a carefully arranged set-up, a magician convinces a small party that he feels his career was ruined by a former female assistant who turned herself into a rabbit to bedevil him. The appearance of the rabbit, exactly as described, produces a sensational effect upon the audience; it is only in the last paragraph that all becomes plausible for the reader as he learns from the narrator, the host of the party, that everything was arranged by him with the magician for twice his usual fee.

Christopher Sykes (1907–) in *Character and Situation* (1949) writes six stories in the mode of Maugham. An air of cosmopolitanism is pervasive, and the narrative style conveys the feeling that these are the stories that one club man recounts to another. Sykes's writing is similar also to that of a fellow Catholic, Evelyn Waugh, who provides an introduction characteristically amusing for its impudence and superciliousness.

Two volumes by Welsh writers of the period to some extent illustrate two of the main impulses of the Welsh short story—the lyrical and the grotesque. Glyn Jones's *The Water Music* (1945) is mostly lyrical and pastoral, although it also has touches of humor; Nigel Heseltine's *Tales of the Squirearchy* (1946) extends the eccentric into the grotesque as extreme oddities sometimes escalate into out-and-out madness in the squires of Wales.

T[heodore] F[rancis] Powys (1875–1953) was a highly individual, even idiosyncratic, writer incapable of easy classification: he wrote country parables and sometimes grotesque allegories; he was influenced

by the Bible, Bunyan, and Langland; and he was a Dorsetshire region-
alist. His *Bottle's Path and Other Stories* (1946) is unlike anything within
the main currents of twentieth-century literature, although some parallels can be found in the works of Dylan Thomas and Sylvia Townsend
Warner. Powys was an acquaintance of Warner, for one of whose books
he contributed the only preface he ever wrote.

William Plomer (1903–73) was born of English parents in Northern
Transvaal, Africa. Since his books (poetry, biographies, short stories,
and novels) have been published in England since the thirties, he probably should be considered British (as he considered himself). *Four Countries* (1949) is a collection of stories that are, for the most part, dramatic
and carefully formed; Plomer suggests in his introduction an indebt-
edness to Maupassant. For this reason (and perhaps others) the book
was sometimes considered an admirable throwback, a happy contrast
to the allegedly more typical product of the times in Britain—formless
stories full of mood and little else but muzziness.

The "four countries" are Africa, Japan, Greece, and England, in each
of which Plomer lived at one time. He provides vivid descriptions of
landscapes and sharp individuating touches often rendered poetically.
The best story is one of the "Stories of Africa," the forty-three-page
"The Child of Queen Victoria"; this sensitive novella, dealing with
conflict between black and white, deserves to be remembered. The
book is moral but never didactic and reflects Plomer's humane values
and sense of decency.

Short Stories in Magazines,
Anthologies, and Annual Collections

So far this chapter has dealt with volumes of short stories by individual authors. It has not yet considered stories appearing in magazines, anthologies, reviews, or annual collections. These were once the
major outlets for short stories, a situation that changed in the postwar
period. Although prior to this time, the public was presumably reading stories in magazines, paradoxically, volumes by single authors did
not (with notable exceptions) sell very well. Thus the magazine, periodical, and anthology market was thought to be vital to the continuing
viability of the form. But its importance was apparently overestimated.
The market did change, but its effect on the short story was not so
great as feared. In fact, the pulse of the magazine market continued to
be a valuable indicator of the healthiness of the form.

During the period 1945–50, the number of markets for short fiction significantly diminished. These years saw the demise of *Writing Today, Selected Writing, English Story,* and *Little Reviews Anthology* as well as *Horizon* (1940–50), a magazine that published occasional short stories and reached a much larger audience than any of the other publications. For short story writers the problems created by the narrowing market were exacerbated when publishers, always wary of collections by individual authors, became even more cautious. The picture, however, was not totally bleak.

Penguin New Writing (1940–50), edited by John Lehmann, published, in addition to poetry and critical surveys of all the arts, short stories by well-known writers and those just beginning to make a reputation, including William Sansom, Rosamond Lehmann, William Plomer, Nigel Heseltine, Anna Kavan, and L. A. G. Strong. In addition to this quarterly (reissued in 1970 by Kraus Reprint and thus available in larger libraries), there were the Penguin sister publications *New Writing and Daylight, Folios of New Writing,* and *Penguin Parade: New Stories by Contemporary Writers,* new series (1947 and 1948).

English Story (1941–50), edited by Woodrow Wyatt, was an irregular book-format collection that appeared on the average of once a year during this period. Its contribution to the form was important, for it was devoted exclusively to short stories and accepted only those not previously published. *English Story* thus encouraged new writers, although familiar names appeared in its pages, too. The general quality was high: it published stories by William Sansom, Angus Wilson, Anna Kavan, Sylvia Townsend Warner, Rhys Davies, Fred Urquhart, Henry Treece, and A. L. Barker.

Modern Reading, edited by Reginald Moore, published twenty-two issues in a relatively inexpensive format between 1941 and 1952. Although some critical essays were included, the collections consisted mainly of short stories of varying styles.

Moore, with Edward Lane, also edited *Windmill,* an occasional publication that appeared twelve times between 1944 and 1948. Each number contained short stories and poetry as well as criticism and articles on the arts. George Orwell, Joyce Cary, Stevie Smith, and C. P. Snow appeared in its pages along with lesser known writers.

New Short Stories, edited by John Singer and published in Glasgow, appeared for only two years, 1944 and 1945–46. It had promised to make a significant contribution, its policy being "to publish the work of those young writers who merit attention because of their actual and potential skill as story-tellers rather than as spokesmen for literary camps."

Two of a number of regional publications deserve mention. The more important was the *Welsh Review* (1939–48), edited by Gwyn Jones, where the Welsh short story, already in full bloom, continued to flower. The review offered encouragement to new writers while also printing the work of such well-known authors as Caradoc Evans, Kate Roberts, Gwilym Davies, and Jones himself. The *West Country Magazine,* edited by Malcolm Elwin and J. C. Trewin, was a quarterly whose existence spanned the years 1946–52; it published stories, articles, and reviews by writers in any way associated with the West Country.

Little Reviews Anthology, edited by Denys Val Baker, first appeared in 1943 and was then issued annually from 1945 to 1949; it reprinted stories (as well as poems, essays, and criticism) from such sources as *Penguin New Writing, Horizon, Windmill, Modern Reading,* and the *Welsh Review.* The 1949 edition contains a valuable annotated bibliography that provides "brief details about contemporary British and Irish little reviews and literary collections."

It should be noted, too, that the United States provided two important outlets for the British short story, one very large (as outlets for artistic short stories go), the other small, but scarcely less important. The *New Yorker* introduced a number of English and Irish short story writers to American audiences. The stories of Sylvia Townsend Warner appeared frequently in its pages, as did those of V. S. Pritchett. Anna Kavan, Elizabeth Taylor, Roald Dahl, and Somerset Maugham were less frequent contributors.

Story, which ceased publication as a quarterly in 1948 but resumed in 1960, had a busy decade; it discovered Norman Mailer, Truman Capote, Tennessee Williams, and J. D. Salinger. In addition to these formidable American talents, it published such British writers as Denys Val Baker, H. E. Bates, Fred Urquhart, and Henry Treece, along with the Irishmen Liam O'Flaherty and Jim Phelan.

The English Short Story, 1945 to 1950, in Retrospect

One who employs a severe set of criteria might find that, at best, the British short story in the period 1945 to 1950 possessed, for the most part, only negative virtues: it was not willfully obscure, overintellectual, or given to overreaching itself for the sake of innovation.

Behind such negative virtues, of course, some will see timidity, where-as others will see good sense. Whatever the reason, British fiction writers of the period were not pushing against the boundaries of their respective forms in an attempt to expand them. But while saying that British short stories of the period were not technically innovative, one should be careful about maintaining that writers operated only in very narrow, traditional, thematic channels. Actually, as much thematic diversity seems to exist in this period as exists in British literature generally. What one might mean by the charge of thematic narrowness is that often there is little direct indication of the social, historical, and psychological forces pressing heavily on Britain and the world at the time, and that themes of war were represented only inadequately. The monumentality of the horror is seldom suggested, it might be argued. A defense against this argument would surely point to ironies, subtleties, shadings: the artistic truth that "less may be more"; and that sharply honed and understated stories can effectively suggest the great weight of large-scale human experience.

These observations about British stories of the forties could be applied nearly as well to those of the fifties and sixties. What separates the fiction of the forties from that of the next decade is the handling of the theme of class distinction. The war did indeed produce the kind of social leveling that might have been anticipated, but clear, unambiguous reflections of this social change were not found in any significant way in British fiction until the fifties. There were, though, some clear intimations in the forties of what was to come. The most notable of these were to be found in the stories of Angus Wilson, who satirized a morally flabby middle class too fettered by its own hypocrisy to adjust smoothly to the forces of change going on around it. Wilson, then, was a transitional figure across the decades.

It may be a sign of health that the two important short story writers to emerge in the forties—Wilson and Sansom—were almost immediately recognized and applauded by reviewers and the reading public alike. Of the two, Sansom came closer to experimentalism in short fiction; Wilson, on the other hand, made strong forays into the class theme. Angst and psychic disorientation are present in Sansom's work directly; in many other writers these psychological states, so characteristic of the postwar period, are filtered through implication and nuance in such a way as to seem too diluted to readers who like elemental emotions served straight. In writers other than Wilson, the class theme is often handled with delicacy and understanding, but in a curiously removed way: readers cannot be sure that the authors really did hear the social rumblings going on around them. Wilson does not paint with water colors and light brush strokes; his satiric etchings are done with acid and a finely pointed instrument.

In sum, it may be said that the period provided us with a number of very good to excellent short stories that deserve to be remembered for their innate interest and their artistry.

John J. Stinson

State University of New York College at Fredonia

THE ENGLISH SHORT STORY IN THE FIFTIES

By the beginning of the 1950s, it was clear that World War II and its aftermath had brought a social revolution to Britain. This revolution might be called the bureaucratization of everyday life. During the war, hundreds of departments had sprung up at all levels of government to regulate and ration everything from potatoes to paper; these departments continued in existence long after the war as Britain fought a new enemy—foreign debt. High prices, shoddy goods, long queues for basic necessities, scarcity, and drabness remained facts of life throughout the forties. Adding to the cumbersome wartime machinery for economy and distribution were the new social programs of the postwar Labour government under Prime Minister Clement Attlee. Nationalizing coal mines, banks, and transportation systems may have produced a more democratic England, but it also created endless tiers of bureaucracy and miles of official red tape. Social welfare services to care for the poor, the unemployed, the delinquent, the criminal, the aging, and the homeless attempted to humanize daily life but often created animosity against those who were seen to be "meddling" in the private affairs of others. To pay for the burgeoning civil service and the social welfare programs that accompanied them, high taxes were levied on the wealthy and middle classes and on every form of luxury and leisure. Not surprisingly, anger and frustration over these measures soured into resentment among the wealthy and the comfortable, often re-creating the very class distinctions that the socialist measures were intended to erase.

Authors were affected by these developments in a number of ways. Established and successful writers suddenly found themselves up against a new enemy of their art—the tax collector. Sales figures for best-selling books that would once have guaranteed their authors comfort and prosperity for life now produced only moderate revenues, the chief beneficiary being the exchequer. Paper rationing, which had killed off dozens of magazines and periodicals during and just after the war, was finally relaxed during the 1950s, but skyrocketing costs for basic materials, labor, and transportation added to the woes of editors and publishers. The diminishing number of outlets for short stories that had begun with the outbreak of war continued apace in the new decade. This in turn created a climate hostile both to new writers and to innovation: faced with the necessity of selling large numbers of books or magazines, few editors or publishers could take chances with new and unproven writers. The market became more closed and more conservative. Established short story writers like H. E. Bates, V. S. Pritchett, Sylvia Townsend Warner, and Rhys Davies could find adequate outlets for their works in Britain or the United States, but the booming literary market that had encouraged these writers in the 1920s and 1930s had disappeared.

Not surprisingly, therefore, the British story of the 1950s appears for the most part to be middle-aged and graying around the temples, for most of its successful practitioners had been born before World War I, some of them before the turn of the century: Warner in 1893, Pritchett in 1900, Davies in 1903, Bates in 1905. Even a relative newcomer and one of the most important and influential writers of the decade, Angus Wilson, could hardly be called a young man, having been born in 1913. This is not to say that youth and innovation were denied all chance to be heard, but conditions were not favorable.

By the time Elizabeth II ascended the throne in 1953, many of the worst conditions of war and postwar life had disappeared or been alleviated. The Festival of Britain in 1951, though in some ways a public relations ploy, suggested an optimistic mood. Dissatisfaction with the pace, if not the results, of socialism resulted in a new government in 1952 with Churchill once again prime minister. Comfort and a measure of prosperity steadily returned as the decade wore on. The cold war, loss of Empire, decline of British power and prestige, and economic leveling produced a short story of grumbling rather than of revolution. To be sure, the so-called angry young men of the decade lashed out in novels, plays, and occasionally short stories (Alan Sillitoe being the most prominent) at the remnants of the class system, the dullness of life in the welfare state, and the absurdity of existence under the threat of nuclear annihilation, but the short story was largely a form for rather quiet social criticism and psychological introspection.

Stories of Social Protest

In some ways, the social protest fiction of the 1950s was a direct outgrowth of war fiction of the 1940s, where often the theme of the story contrasted the valor and sacrifice of soldiers and airmen with the bureaucratic bumbling of officious and incompetent desk jockeys. In the new decade, however, the protest against bureaucracy and meddling socialism often took the form of complaints that life had been reduced to a uniform grayness by the intervention of the welfare state. Among the most vehement was Wyndham Lewis (1892–1957), whose *Rotting Hill* (1951) is a series of barely fictionalized essays against postwar dullness, inefficiency, and stupidity. In an earlier age, Lewis might have expressed his points in philosophical dialogues; denied that outlet, he turns most of the stories in this volume into interminably dull discussions of the failures and disappointments of the modern world. The title story uses the rather obvious metaphor of dry rot to characterize the whole of current society; other selections in the volume are equally contrived to expose decay in the church, the economy, industry, education, and government. As fiction, these stories have little to recommend them, but as barometers of the contemporary atmosphere they have a certain validity.

Other authors who agreed with Lewis's diagnosis of modern life chose more subtle and indirect ways to attack it. J. B. Priestley (1894–1984) published only one volume of short stories in his prolific career, *The Other Place and Stories of the Same Sort* (1953). In one way or another, most of the tales included here deal with the plainness of everyday life. "The Grey Ones" is a kind of modern psychomachian drama in which the Devil and his henchmen are portrayed not as the Seven Deadly Sins but as bowler-hatted bureaucrats whose object is "to make mankind go the way the social insects went, to turn us into automatic creatures, mass beings without individuality, soulless machines of flesh and blood." Priestly's cautionary tales avoid the excesses of Lewis's outbursts, and in stories like "The Statues" and "The Leadington Incident" he creates readable if somewhat transparent fictions on the triviality of modern life and the zombielike nature of modern man. But the allegorical approach has seldom served the short story well (Hawthorne being a conspicuous exception). The short story responds better to authors who concentrate on character or situation to make their points.

One of the most successful stories in the social criticism vein is "Maggie Logie and the National Health" from *The Dying Stallion*

(1967) by Scottish author Fred Urquhart (1912–). Maggie is a sturdy and independent widow thriving by hard work and thrift, content with few possessions and traditional ways until she is corrupted by the National Health scheme into coveting everything from a cupboard full of free pills to a mouthful of false teeth she does not need. The point is anything but subtle, but Urquhart's humor and confident handling of character produce a story at once funny, touching, and trenchant. Maggie, her boyfriend Tam, and the villagers of Cairncolm are lively and full-blooded Scots; the style is firm and racy, enlivened by judicious use of Scots dialect.

Maggie Logie's exploitation of the National Health contrasts sharply with the more usual resistance shown to welfare schemes, particularly among the elderly. Rhys Davies's (1903–78) "I Will Keep Her Company" from *The Chosen One* (1960) captures the mood often evident in stories of the decade. Living alone in a remote cottage are Mr. and Mrs. John Evans, both in their eighties, both determined to retain their home and independence, even in the face of a severe snowstorm. Worried about their health and welfare is Nurse Baldock, whose motives are those of the professional humanitarian and whose approach is to insist that she knows what is best for her clients. Davies skillfully contrasts the simple dignity of Evans as he tries to cope with the tasks of keeping warm and feeding himself with the officious busyness of Nurse Baldock, following a snowplow to Evans's cottage. Her anger at finding Evans and his wife dead suggests that she is more concerned with the Evanses as an intractable "case" than with their welfare. Nurse Baldock means well, but in forcing upon her clients the new values of the welfare state she has failed to take into account the simple human values of those she wants to serve.

A more complex and ambiguous portrait of a well-meaning bureaucrat occurs in Neil Gunn's "The Tax Gatherer" (*The White Hour*, 1950). Gunn (1891–1973) presents a conscientious young man in the tax office caught between the demands of his job, which require him to collect a dog license fee from a poor mother and her children, and the promptings of his heart, which finally impel him to give her a pound of his own money so that she can pay the fine. He is shocked when the woman chooses to spend five days in jail so that the entire pound can be spent on food for her family. Reminded of the folktale of the tinker who made the nails for Christ's crucifixion, he looks over the town and sees its upright citizens as "straight as nails, straight as spikes"; Pilate-like, he washes his hands. Gunn's skillful manipulation of biblical imagery and his cool, indifferent tone create an effective story in which the system abuses both those who serve it and those whom it is intended to serve.

Equally effective, though entirely different in tone, is the portrayal by Ian Hamilton Finlay (1925–) of bureaucratic idiocy in "National Assistance Money" (*The Sea-Bed,* 1958). The central character is a poor artist who confounds the paper pushers at the Labour Exchange by saying that unemployment money will enable him to work (i.e., paint, which is not officially recognized as "work"). At length he is able to explain this paradox, but when he reports that he has sold a picture painted two years previously and thereby earned £5.5.0 "without working," he throws the bureaucrats into a complete tizzy. The only solution, gratefully accepted by the Labour Exchange, is that he resign his rights to National Assistance. "So I completed the forms of resignation, and I left the building a free man." Finlay's absurdist comedy admirably captures the feeling of a world gone mad under an avalanche of official forms, senseless jargon, and arbitrary regulations.

A great many similar stories could be analyzed to show the dissatisfaction among short story writers with the welfare state as it had emerged in the early fifties. Ironically, the very institutions founded to humanize and rationalize life were increasingly seen as creating an inhuman and absurd society. Other aspects of this paradox will emerge in many of the stories yet to be discussed.

Supernaturalism

The ghost story is as old as fiction and in Britain seems especially vigorous. The fifties saw a strong revival of the form among a great variety of writers who could on no other grounds be put into the same category. Whatever the reasons, the decade shows a surprising number of accomplished short stories in which the supernatural is treated as a natural part of the everyday world. Sylvia Townsend Warner's (1893–1978) interest in the subject dates from her earliest novel, *Lolly Willowes* (1926), so the inclusion of "Uncle Blair" in *Winter in the Air* (1956) is hardly a surprise. The story is a dotty British mixture of old girls' school animosities, schemes for a folk museum, local pride and economics, and a girl named Jeanie whose attempts to block the construction of the museum by giving it the evil eye backfire and succeed in killing the project's most vociferous opponent. Although the tale is comic, Warner's belief in the occult is entirely serious.

Muriel Spark shares Warner's belief in the occult, though as a Roman Catholic she uses it for different purposes. Spark (1918–) first came to public notice by winning a *London Observer* short story contest with "The Seraph and the Zambesi" (1951), a satire on the crass commercialization of Christmas set, rather improbably, in Africa. "The Portobello Road" (*The Go-Away Bird,* 1958) is a long story narrated by a ghost nicknamed "Needle" during her life because she once found a needle in a haystack. The story chronicles the lives of Needle and her three childhood friends, culminating in her murder by George when she threatens to reveal his clandestine marriage to a black woman in Africa. When Needle appears five years after the event to George and his new wife, Kathleen, as they shop the markets in Portobello Road, her manifestation can be regarded as a projection of George's troubled conscience. More important, however, Needle's ghost symbolizes the existence of a spiritual dimension to life which she and her materialistic friends have always ignored in their struggles for economic security.

Scotsman Eric Linklater (1899–1974) also frequently ventures into the spirit realm. "A Sociable Plover" (*The Sociable Plover,* 1957) defies neat summary as it skillfully weaves several narrative strands into a carefully plotted and highly successful story about a rare bird, the sociable plover, which comes to haunt writer Torquila Malone as a "fetch," the embodiment of an enemy's spirit. One can never be certain whether the uncanny nature of the bird derives from its supernatural origin or from its power as a projection of Malone's troubled conscience. This ambiguity lends richness of texture to a story in which stark Scottish scenery contrasts sharply with the complex psyche of Malone; his illness defies the ministrations of modern medicine just as the plover's nature confounds the methods of science. This is an eerie and haunting tale of considerable power.

Few other writers use the supernatural with the assurance and conviction of Warner, Spark, and Linklater. For most writers of the decade, supernaturalism is a literary device, useful in exploring states of mind or experiences beyond the ordinary, or as a metaphor for otherwise inexplicable forces or events. In "Jane Dore—Dear Childe" (*Novelette with Other Stories,* 1951) by A[udrey] L[illian] Barker (1918–), the "witchcraft" of Jane Dore is merely a projection of the narrator's guilty conscience and repressed sexual desires. Barker is far more effective in "Domini," a story suggesting the influence of Sylvia Townsend Warner. The narrator is an old woman reflecting on her childhood and on the supposed innocence of children. The story purports to be a factual account of her troubled childhood, detailing the death of her father, the long mourning of her mother, and finally the mother's betrayal in taking up a life of fashion and gaiety with a lover. On the instigation of her playmate Domini, the girl one night removes all her mother's "wicked" dresses from their closet and burns them on the porch of the summer house, thereby unintentionally killing her mother and the lover. This chilling event is followed by an even stranger revelation—that Domini leaves no footprints in the snow. Whether Domini is an evil spirit or a figment of the child's imagination is never entirely clear, nor is it meant to be.

In a similar fashion three of J. B . Priestley's tales employ some form of the supernatural. "The Other Place," in the volume of the same title, presents a dreamlike world of color and life, contrasting sharply to the smudgy and uncongenial life of a British industrial town. In "Uncle Phil on TV" the ghost of Uncle Phil haunts his family until one member confesses to hastening his death by withholding his heart medicine. The most ingenious of these, however, takes a couple who work in film into a time warp that transports them to the eighteenth century, a period of grace, manners, and beauty that contrasts sharply with the drab twentieth century. By this device, Priestly combines the supernatural with social criticism.

In the title story of his slender volume *Satan in the Suburbs* (1953), philosopher Bertrand Russell (1872–1970) presents the Devil in the person of Dr. Murdoch Mallako, whose specialty is giving people suggestions that purport to solve their problems but end in ruining them. The doctor is deliberately bourgeois, tempting his victims to rather sordid little evils. The story, however, has little power, being essentially an amusing parable written in a curiously stiff style with highly artificial dialogue.

In "W. S." (*The White Wand,* 1954), L. P. Hartley (1895–1972) presents a ghost story of a very unusual kind, for writer Walter Streeter is haunted not by a departed spirit but by the soul of the only entirely evil character he ever created in his fiction. The haunting takes the form of postcards that arrive first from Scotland and then from cities progressively nearer the writer's home. Though he receives police protection, Streeter is found choked to death with bits of snow on him, though none has fallen anywhere in Britain. This is a far more subtle, clever, and effective tale than Hartley's "The Two Vaynes," in which a statue comes alive to avenge a murder. Hartley is at his best when delving into the complex psychology of his characters in a style James-ian in incisiveness, yet without James's prolixity. When he applies these strengths to the genre, as in "W. S.," the result is supernatural-ism of a high order.

For all the authors discussed here, the supernatural is a territory to be explored, sometimes for what it reveals about the natural world, at other times for psychological interest, and at still other times for its own sake. Perhaps boredom with the blandness of everyday life or the paralyzing materialism of modern science and the terror of the atomic bomb prompted widespread interest in the supernatural as material for short fiction. Whatever the reasons, the supernatural occurs with great frequency in stories from the 1950s.

Mainstream: Deep and Wide

As noted earlier, the short story of the fifties in Britain continued to be dominated by traditional techniques and themes. The influence of Maupassant and Chekhov continued unabated through the work of many writers but most particularly those who had seemed experimental in the twenties and thirties but were now well-established writers in middle age. Literary historians and critics favor innovation and enjoy the thrill of discovering a new voice; readers are much more likely to prefer the known and solidly established. These tensions make it dif-ficult to assess the continuing fine work of writers like H. E. Bates, V. S. Pritchett, Sylvia Townsend Warner, and Rhys Davies. None of them ventured very far into uncharted waters, and reviewers of their work often exhibit a mild disappointment that such conventional au-thors are still around and still writing in their accustomed ways. By the same token, it was these writers who produced many of the best stories of the decade, and it was they who kept alive public interest in the form by contributing to the magazines that published short fiction.

H. E. Bates continued to be a most prolific author, publishing four collections of stories, five novels, three books of novellas, and several nonfiction works during this decade. Among these are two very fine volumes of stories, *Colonel Julian* (1951) and *The Watercress Girl* (1959). The former collection mixes Bates's lifelong interest with the country-side and its inhabitants with stories deriving from his Flying Officer X experiences. The country stories are marked as always by a strong sense of atmosphere, a delicate awareness of mood, lush, pictorial lan-guage, and vivid characters, most of whom are frustrated or anguished. A contemporary note emerges in stories like "The Lighthouse" and

"The Flag," indicating Bates's awareness of changing social conditions and mores. *The Watercress Girl* is arguably Bates's finest collection of stories, for every one of the thirteen tales is of high quality. All are narrated through the eyes of children, and all demonstrate Bates's uncanny ability to evoke the luminous yet disturbing world of the child. Focusing on fleeting moments or states of feeling, the stories defy quick summary. Richest among them is the title story, which portrays nothing more complicated than a young boy's day among elderly relatives and his encounter at the brook with a watercress girl. Years pass; cottages turn to bungalows sprouting television antennas. A second meeting with the former watercress girl evokes feelings of profound regret for a lost world of dusty roads, clear brooks, and the haunting cry of the watercress vendor.

• • •

By contrast, V. S. Pritchett published only one volume of stories during the same period, *Selected Stories* (1956), a retrospective collection. His new stories, which were appearing primarily in the *New Yorker* but also in *Gentleman's Quarterly* and *Encounter,* would not be collected until *When My Girl Comes Home* (1961). Nevertheless, the appearance of this collection served to remind critics and readers that a formidable talent had produced a large quantity of stories of a uniformly high quality and precision of expression. One never feels, as one sometimes does with Bates, that the author is reworking old material or writing to a formula. Nearly every Pritchett story commands attention and respect, even if the theme is slight or the characters a bit thin. Difficult to define but always present is the famous Pritchett irony, incisive, occasionally devastating, sometimes provocative, never dull or habitual. In *Why Do I Write?* (1948), Pritchett maintained that "society needs writers to enrich its knowledge of itself," but by this he does not mean that the writer is primarily a social critic in the usual sense or that he takes a political stance. Rather, Pritchett favors "the sacred instinct of party disloyalty" and adds "I vastly prefer the cynics to the pious, but I prefer the sensitive to either."[1]

"The Sailor," based on a character Pritchett once knew, illustrates his methods perfectly. In London, the narrator meets a hopelessly lost sailor and offers to buy him a drink. The sailor's refusal on grounds that "it's a temptation" so interests the narrator that he offers him a job as his cook and handyman. In spite of differences, the two suit each other well: the narrator provides security, and country living offers freedom from temptation. On his part, the sailor introduces order and a nautical vocabulary into the writer's life. But even in the country there are temptations, partly from the villagers but mostly from the colonel's daughter, the boozy and loose woman who is the narrator's nearest neighbor. Another factor in the equation is the desire of the narrator to make his sailor free and happy, and to this end he sends him on errands in the hopes that he will learn his way around and also meet people. Inevitably, this leads to temptations that the sailor cannot resist; after a while he is seeking out neighbors to gossip with and shortly thereafter is enticed by the colonel's daughter into listening to records at her bungalow. The sailor returns reeling drunk and after this spends most nights in the pub standing the locals to drinks. When the narrator leaves for Europe, he returns the sailor to London, where once again he sets off in search of Whitechapel.

The story is delightful Dickensian comedy, especially because of the richly eccentric character of the sailor, a man who is anxious to avoid temptation because, like Oscar Wilde, he can resist anything but it. His search for Whitechapel is surely symbolic. The story is also complex in moral exploration, for the puritanical narrator, wanting the sailor to be independent, inadvertently leads him into sin. Meanwhile, the narrator himself faces tempting advances from the colonel's daughter, who is a former mistress. These crosscurrents are reflected in the story's clash of opposites: the sailor's old fashioned concern with temptation contrasting with the story's modern tone; the disorder of the writer's life and the colonel's daughter's with the sailor's Royal Navy order; the childlike dependence of the sailor on others who are in the end nearly as innocent as he. This and other stories in the collection affirm that, in Pritchett, Britain had found another short story writer of the first order.

• • •

In Wales, mainstream postwar writing was ably represented by Rhys Davies. His *Collected Stories,* published in 1955, gave evidence of his strong regional talent, regional not in the sense that his stories are of limited interest but in the sense that they derive much of their power and interest from Welsh national characteristics and geography. His new volume, *The Darling of Her Heart* (1958), continued in this tradition, updating it in some ways. "A Visit to Eggeswick Castle," for example, is a satire on the welfare state, those who support it and those who exploit it successfully. Thematically, it resembles a cross between Wilson's "Such Darling Dodos" and Urquhart's "Maggie Logie and the National Health."

Davies's strength, however, is not social criticism but character and atmosphere, an attribute he shares with H. E. Bates. His characters are often eccentrics, and he is particularly effective in portraying strong women, like Sian Prosser of "The Darling of Her Heart." Mrs. Prosser is sixty, vigorous, and domineering; she will brook no nonsense from her husband and certainly none from "the harlot" who has been turning the head of her youngest son. To underscore her point, she burns her son's bed in a ritual of cleansing, confronts the girl's mother, and then announces her actions to the bewildered and defeated menfolk.

The color and vigor of Davies's characters are matched by the liveliness and clarity of his prose. The Welsh countryside and its small towns come alive in sharp, pictorial descriptions, and he is equally good at evoking the coal-and-slate melancholy of a Welsh mining town in "Afternoon of a Faun." Here he shows uncanny insight into the mind of an eleven-year-old boy whose father suffered from silicosis for years before dying. He copes with the disaster by staying away from home as long as possible and trying to become absorbed in irrelevant activies. Woven into the story are recurrent references to a dead mining horse, tossed on a slag heap, where it symbolizes the wasted life of the boy's father. The best of Davies's stories have a timeless vigor and reality, and even the weak ones are of interest. However, it is hard to escape the feeling that Davies's new stories are too much in the vein of his past successes. There is no question of second-class workmanship, merely the lingering feeling that nothing new is happening.

· · ·

Sylvia Townsend Warner (1893–1978) never published a representative collection of her short fiction, which is unfortunate, for she deserves such a monument to her position in the honor roll of the century's storytellers. Like Bates, Pritchett, and Davies, she has enormous reservoirs of sympathy and understanding, and like them she never allows herself to become sentimental with her characters. They are presented, revealed, even judged and found wanting, but neither despised nor excused. Above all is the quality of her style, elusive to describe or analyze, yet unmistakably Warner. Consider, for example, the opening sentences from the title story of her only 1950s collection, *Winter in the Air* (1956):

> The furniture, assembled once more under the high ceiling of a London room, seemed to be wearing a look of quiet satisfaction, as though, slightly shrugging their polished shoulders, the desk had remarked to the bookcase, the Regency armchair to the Chippendale mirror, "Well, here we are again." And then, after a creak or two, silence had fallen on the dustless room.

Here is the absolute assurance of one who knows the value and weight of every word: *polished* and *dustless* have seldom seemed such sad and sterile words, and the tone of quiet resignation has seldom been given such casual yet solid embodiment. So often in Warner one meets, too, her peculiarly original angle of vision, as if, to use Henry James's metaphor, she had found some window on the world that the rest of us have overlooked, even though it so clearly provides an excellent view. *Things* in her stories have an idiosyncratic life of their own, a quality deriving perhaps from Warner's faith in the occult and her belief in spiritual powers beyond the material and mechanical.

In "Winter in the Air," objects are the keys that unlock emotional doors. Each piece of furniture in the London flat reminds Barbara of something in the recent or distant past; each is connected in her mind with the events leading to her being replaced in her husband's affections by another woman. Quietly, like Hermione of Shakespeare's *Winter's Tale,* she has been forced from married life into becoming a mid-century nun, locked not in a convent but in a London flat after one of those "decent" and "understanding" modern divorces. The furniture is emblematic, too, of the emotionless retreat of her return to single life: "Like the furniture, she would settle down in the old arrangement, and the silence of the room would not intimidate her long; it was no more than a pin-point of silence in the wide world of London." Silence is what this story is all about, the terrible loneliness of a faithful wife who has, she knows not how, lost home and husband.

Warner also has a mischievous side. "A Kitchen Knife" is a domestic high comedy, written with impish cleverness in a style showing masterly control over tone and delight in metaphor. The main characters are a young husband and wife: he is Trevor Gilmore, up from the lower middle classes by just a notch; she is Rachel, of a more genteel and leisured family. After three years of enduring a one-room marriage in the house of Trevor's parents, they finally get a council house of their own, from which Trevor leaves every morning to work in a bank and to which he returns with the visions of meat extract advertisements dancing in his head. Pathetically, he sees a happy marriage as built on kitchen gadgets, plastic salad bowls ("Choice of art shades in pink, blue, or old gold"), patent potato peelers, bean slicers, egg whisks, and grapefruit knives. Rachel, believing that she must be content in her situation, remains so until invited by her old friend Celia Hanson for a Sunday lunch. There Trevor meets for the first time a cultural level higher than his own: real paintings, genuine silver, old china, rural Georgian solidity. Rachel, too, is changed, and she walks out of the house with a real kitchen knife in her purse. Exulting in her thievery and the revelation of the afternoon, she rides home determined to keep her prize: "Though it had done its work already, severing her from her illusions as cleanly as it would trim off the fat from a cutlet, it was still a thing she wanted, a proper kitchen knife." The story is at once extraordinarily funny and sad; there is something in it of Warner's favorite writer, Jane Austen. But it is unmistakably a story of the fifties, with its witty glances at the changes England was undergoing socially and culturally.

Warner published no more collections of stories until *The Kingdoms of Elfin* in 1977, but individual pieces appeared frequently in the *New Yorker,* among them, those that formed a posthumous volume of fictionalized autobiographical sketches, *Scenes of Childhood* (1981). Her writing is in the broad tradition of English belles lettres without being in the least precious or affected. Her work deserves to be more widely known.

Six Scottish Writers

It might be more accurate in some ways to discuss the work of Fred Urquhart (1912–) with that of the writers in the preceding section. Though born in Scotland, Urquhart has lived most of his life in London and Suffolk, and his interests as a writer range far beyond his native land. Nevertheless, as a short story writer and editor, Urquhart is definitely Scots: most of his stories are set in Scotland, and his characters speak a definite brogue. A professed follower of H. E. Bates and Sylvia Townsend Warner, Urquhart belongs squarely in the mainstream of British writing. Like Warner, he enjoys forays into the occult and writes excellent ghost stories, but most of his stories deal with realistic themes and everyday concerns. Women are often his most successful characters, a trait he shares with H. E. Bates.

The Last Sister (1950) is a solid collection with a number of stories of merit. One of these is "Alicky's Watch," a sensitive and thoughtful study of an eleven-year-old boy whose mother has just died. His prize possession is an old watch she had given him two years previously that has now stopped working. The device of the stopped watch may appear in summary a literary trick, but it works very well in context. The boy's absorption in the watch takes place against a background of adult rituals and conversations by which older people cope with the fact of death and properly discharge their duties to the departed. The child has no such props, for adult ceremonies mean nothing to him; so the watch is perfect as an objective correlative for his grief and loss. The fact that he is able to get the watch going again symbolizes that he has emerged from the experience and that his life—like the adults'—can proceed. Another short sketch of unusual poignancy is "Win Was Wild," in which life in a pub serves as a metaphor for the fact that the meek will not inherit the earth. Win, a mousy and retiring woman, has no chance against Rosie, the loudmouth who picks on her.

The most complex of these stories is "Once a Schoolmissy." On one level it contrasts two styles of life, the cautious, conventional approach of retired schoolteacher Emily Perrott with that of her slightly younger and more daring ex-colleague, Elizabeth Riddell. When Emily visits her friend, she discovers once again how shocked she can be by Elizabeth's slovenly ways and loose habits. Beyond this, a visit by the two of them to the home of a mutual friend exposes Emily for the first time to the repressed lesbian urges that she had hitherto successfully denied. The story unfolds in a casual way, each layer peeling back to reveal something deeper and more important beneath it, until the core is reached. Urquhart successfully balances his characters and the reader's sympathies, producing a story with the power to disturb and enlighten.

• • •

Neil M. Gunn (1891–1973) is best known as a novelist, particularly for *The Silver Darlings* (1941). His second and last collection of stories, *The White Hour* (1950), contains a variety of tales: mood sketches, character studies, propagandistic pieces from the war, realistic studies of human relationships, and stories involving the mystical and supernatural. His characters are usually rural Scots or fishing folk; not surprisingly, a number of the later stories deal with the elderly and dying.

From such a variety it is impossible to choose anything typical, but the title story recommends itself by the power of its writing. It focuses on an old woman called simply Granny, who is nearing death and very feeble. She tells her grandson that lately she has been reliving the past in brilliantly clear recollections, followed by periods of intense white light and the feeling of utter loneliness and silence. The young man receives this news without comment or understanding; but later that evening, he goes into the scullery where his wife is finishing the dishes, and there they embrace and kiss passionately. "The old woman did not see the crushing of the pliant body nor the smothering of the wild kissing, but the companionableness of it was with her in a great sweetness, so that the glazed white light from the window softened to a shadowy beauty." The fusion of the two perspectives creates a powerful sensation of revelation and insight, a moment when love and death are seen as opposing yet complementary processes.

"Black Woolen Gloves" is on the surface merely a boy-meets-girl tale centering on a pair of gloves that the girl finds and tries to return to the young man. Gunn transforms this formula by the subtlety and depth with which he portrays the tangled emotions of the two would-be lovers as they move from misunderstanding to misunderstanding, nearly losing each other in the process.

The most profound and complex of Gunn's stories is "Love's Dialectic," set during the war in an office where young women censor the mail. The protagonist is one of these girls, somewhat ashamed of her work, perplexed by the emotions she reads in the letters and by those she herself feels. The bits of psychology and Marxism that form her intellectual equipment are of little help in explaining her feelings; labeling things does not clarify them. In particular she is mystified by her boyfriend's desire on occasion to inflict physical pain, something she believes she provokes because she does not satisfy him. It is only when she tells about one of the letters that there is an epiphany. One witty and well-educated correspondent related the story that in the eighteenth century noblewomen would undress in front of their butlers as if the men were mere articles of furniture. Censors, the writer implies, are similar to the butlers, though worse, because they pry. This story delights her boyfriend and clarifies her own position. In the end, she realizes that her confusions and fears, her attempts to label, are groundless and futile. She recognizes quite simply that she can talk to her boyfriend and that she does love him, and this realization makes her "deliriously happy." Gunn's power to capture the tangled threads of her emotions and to reveal them in all their complex contradictions gives the story a high pitch of tension that overcomes the sometimes murky discussion of the girl's inner confusion.

Gunn, then, is a writer of great versatility and power. He achieves his effects in a variety of ways, but chiefly through a style that is at once dense yet clear. His characters are often simple on the outside, deep and complicated within. His style is much the same: the surface texture presents no difficulties; sentences are clear, the diction simple, the syntax straightforward. But the clash of events and feelings creates another and more difficult structure altogether, often resulting in stories of both sensual and intellectual appeal.

• • •

Eric Linklater (1899–1974) published only one book of stories in the fifties, *The Sociable Plover* (1957), the title story of which has already been analyzed. This is, in fact, the most ambitious and successful of the five stories in the volume, the sixth inclusion being a radio play. In "Escape Forever" Rory More breaks out of prison and uses every resource at his command to avoid being recaptured so that he can punish his former girlfriend and the fat and satisfied grocer she married after jilting him. As long as the story stays at this level, it is exciting, even mesmerizing, for in his fury Rory has the appeal of an evil genius. When he arrives at his destination and sees that his former fiancée and her husband are making each other miserable, he changes his mind and turns himself in, content that they are avenging him better than any punishment he could inflict. This rather lame and inconsistent resolution has the momentary appeal of a good joke; on reflection, however, we see that it does not satisfactorily resolve the tensions of the story.

"The Masks of Purpose" is a fictionalized account of a massacre at Glencoe in 1692. The thesis Linklater pursues is that all parties to the tragedy contributed by disguising their true intentions and doing what was temporarily expedient. He may have been suggesting a parallel with cold war politics. Even so, the story fails to compel attention,

partly because it is told in an artificial and stiff, pseudohistorical style
that is more annoying than impressive.

* * *

Similar problems beset some of the stories in Naomi Mitchison's
(1897–) *Five Men and a Swan* (1957). Of the five historical tales in the
collection, only "The Hunting of Ian Og" can be called a success. The
others are stiff and formal in style and lack energy and conviction, even
when as in "Aud the Deep Minded," there is something of the quiet
dignity of a medieval saga. Mitchison is far more at home with tales
of the supernatural, particularly the title story. The swan is a fairy-tale
figure, an enchanted bird-woman who assumes mortal shape only during a full moon. The five men are fishermen of the *Highland Mary,*
each of whom tries to possess her. Narrated in the matter-of-fact tones
of a folktale, "Five Men and a Swan" follows the effects of each man
who encounters the bird-woman. Whether these effects are due to the
supernatural powers of the swan or to their own inner promptings is a
mystery that gives the story much of its appeal; this tension is reflected
also in Mitchison's style, which combines the casual fluidity of spoken
narrative with the peculiar formality of the style of legends.

The clash of incompatible worlds is also the theme of "Round with
the Boats," though there is nothing supernatural about the problems
facing the narrator, the skipper of a failing herring boat. Forced by
necessity into taking in lodgers during the summer, his family is by
this means able to keep barely afloat, but finally even this is not
enough. Gathering all the courage he can muster, the narrator asks one
of his longtime lodgers, Mr. Anderson, for a loan, thereby ruining
their friendship and even a romance between his daughter and Anderson's son. It is perhaps a commonplace enough story, but the narrator's
simple style and stoic attitude make his tale dignified and affecting.
At the same time, we are given important insights into the lives of
people whose culture is slowly eroding from under them, worn away
by forces they can understand but cannot control.

* * *

The most original in style and vision of the Scottish authors of this
decade is Ian Hamilton Finlay (1925–), who subsequently achieved
considerable fame as a poet, publisher, and artist. In his only volume
of stories, *The Sea-Bed and Other Stories* (1958), Finlay experiments with
a variety of approaches and styles, enlivening whatever he touches with

a fresh and sometimes lyrical style reminiscent in some moods of Dylan Thomas' work. The title story exhibits on the surface nothing very remarkable. It concerns two young boys who are fishing from jetties of rocks protruding into the bay. They have caught nothing. "Suddenly, about an hour later, one of the boys felt that his skin no longer fitted him. His heart stopped beating for a second as he watched the great cod. . . . The cod swam up to the bait and sniffed it without touching it. Then it turned and swam quickly out to sea. It was gone like the shadow of a bird, quickly, soundlessly. The boy let out his breath which he had been holding all the time without meaning to." This is for the boy a moment of revelation; the fish unleashes his imagination, and we know that from this point on he will dream different dreams, see the world in a new light, and follow a vision unlike that of his friend, who is happy to catch real fish, even though they are small and ordinary.

Most of Finlay's other stories are in a similar vein. He writes about ordinary people, most often children, engaged in the most commonplace activities; yet each of them achieves vitality and individuality through the largeness and sympathy of Finlay's vision and style. He chooses each word with care, though without straining after effect, and the result is a highly suggestive and yet simple prose that lifts ordinary people and subjects into extraordinary realms. "The Old Man and the Trout," for example, is in many ways a typical old-man-teaching-a-boy-to-fish story, but from it comes insight into the pain of growing old and dying and an appreciation for both life and death. Similarly, "Straw" portrays the frustrations of an unsuccessful shopkeeper as he searches for a brook that has never been fished; the story includes an accident involving the death of a carthorse. The straw that the horse's owner puts under the dying animal's head to ease its discomfort becomes a powerful symbol of the man's quiet suffering, and indeed of human suffering generally. Finlay has playful and comic as well as elegiac moods, and in "Midsummer Weather" he approaches the surreal in a dreamlike sketch about a mysterious lamb that appears in the narrator's garden and then just as mysteriously dies. Unfortunately, Finlay has since abandoned short stories and turned his verbal powers to other media.

• • •

Another new voice in Scottish fiction is that of Muriel Spark (1918–). Often compared with Evelyn Waugh because of her satiric wit and Catholic faith, Spark is frequently concerned with spiritual hollowness and moral indifference. In *The Go-Away Bird* (1958), her only volume of stories from this period, she focuses attention on individual foibles and failings rather than on social issues, though in "The Black Madonna" she uses Raymond and Lou Parker as embodiments of phony liberal values, which she deftly skewers. More typical is "The Twins," which seems at first to be about the minor misunderstandings and failures of communication that so often disturb adult relationships. It is not until the narrator is leaving her friends for the last time that she realizes that behind the disturbances that have separated friend from friend are the lies and machinations of the twins, children who to all appearances are sweet and innocent. Thus, the story suddenly takes on a theological dimension, becoming a comment on the "Old Adam" and original sin, a concept that is often ignored because of sentimental ideas about the natural goodness of children. "Daisy Overend" treats something of the same idea as it relates to adults, adding to it, however, the observation that the very people who are most callous in their treatment of others are often those most sensitive in regard to themselves.

The most successful of Spark's stories are those that deal with abstract ideas through complex and concrete characters who achieve a life and individuality of their own apart from the stories in which they appear. When Spark becomes heavy-handed, as she does in "You Should Have Seen the Mess," or overly ambitious, as in "The Go-Away Bird," the stories make satiric points without touching deeply at the core of anything. Even the weak stories, however, show careful craftsmanship and a gift for fresh and lively writing. Nor is Spark confined to one satiric key: she can modulate into gaiety in "Miss Pinkerton's Apocalypse" and into solemnity in "Come Along Marjorie," a deeply disturbing story about a woman whose religious integrity verges (in the present climate at any rate) on madness.

· · ·

It is difficult to extract from these six authors anything one could define as an essential "Scottish" quality. The range and energy are enormous, the Scottish story displaying the tendencies, both good and bad, of the British story in general. The Scots, unlike the Irish, have rarely used political weapons to insist on a separate identity, and perhaps for this reason have been treated most often as English writers, without a regional identity. Like the Irish, the Scots frequently capitalize on their colorful language, Celtic heritage, and traditional ways to convey what is unique about Scotland, but rarely is there any insistence that the Scottish character is radically different from the English, at least in the stories analyzed here. The best stories, of course, transcend national boundaries, but paradoxically there is something to be gained from asserting one's uniqueness from time to time. In the fifties, at least, the Scottish story was thriving and in capable hands, even if its identity was sometimes smothered by its neighbor to the south.

The Short Story in Wales

Discussing the short story in Wales during the fifties is problematic, in part because a number of its authors were so fully integrated into the English tradition that they are often not regarded as thoroughly Welsh. Rhys Davies, Dylan Thomas, and Roald Dahl should all be regarded as representing their native land, even though they are discussed elsewhere. Another difficulty is that some authors of the period chose Welsh as their primary language, forcing non-Welsh readers to rely on translations for access to their fiction and somewhat clouding the definition of *British* or *English* in contexts like the present one. Nevertheless, the fifties must be regarded as a time of rebuilding in Welsh short fiction, an almost fallow period during which one era was passing and another struggling to be born.

A glance at the contents of the major anthologies of Welsh short stories illustrates the point quite well. For example, the collection edited by Gwyn Jones and Islwyn Ffowc Elis in 1971 entitled *Twenty-Five Welsh Short Stories* includes a preponderance of stories by authors born late in the nineteenth century or early in the twentieth: E. Tegla Davies (1880–1967), Caradoc Evans (1878–1945), John Gwilym Jones (1904–), and Geraint Goodwin (1903–1941), to name just four. At the other extreme are authors born during the thirties, whose careers blossomed after the fifties: R Gerallt Jones (1933–), Harri Pritchard Jones (1933–), and Eigra Lewis Roberts (1939–). Dylan Thomas and Alun Lewis died in 1953 and 1944, respectively. Thus, historical accident conspired to make the fifties a "lost" decade for the Welsh short story. Moreover, as Jones points out in the introduction to this collection, the period 1930 to 1955 was a "climactic" quarter century; in fact, the climax really came at the end of the forties. In any event, except for the collections published by Rhys Davies, Dylan Thomas, and Roald Dahl, (discussed elsewhere in this chapter), there were very few volumes of Welsh stories published during the decade.

· · ·

One exception to this rule is *Gazooka* (1957) by Gwyn Thomas (1913–81). "O Brother Man" from this volume is a comic tale whose theme, "Behind every piece of virtue on this earth there is a legion of aching hearts and empty pockets," is expounded with deadpan hilarity by its narrator, Mr. Rawlins. A teacher in a boys' school and devoted to helping juvenile delinquents, Mr. Rawlins more than meets his match in a boy named Chaplin Everest, whose kleptomania knows no bounds. Mr. Rawlins's attempts to reform Chaplin through the presumed powers of music result in a series of misadventures and embarrassments that finally lead Mr. Rawlins to the conclusion mentioned above. This is comic writing of a very high order. Like many Welsh writers, Thomas also possesses a fine sense of the absurd and the tragic in life, qualities the Welsh mix with especially effective results. "Where My Dark Lover Lies" is a richly textured and complex story of a young man's disloyalty to his friend and mentor, Morlais Moore. Jilted by a girl, the narrator Waldo Phelps turns his back on his philosopher friend and for a time embraces religion. Failing in the seminary, he returns to his village but still avoids seeing Morlais Moore, taking up instead with the daughter of an undertaker who offers him a bride and a career if he can remain conventional and dignified through a year's apprenticeship. As luck would have it, Phelp's first funeral is Morlais Moore's, which is marred not only by a driving rain but by a refusal on the part of the cemetery keeper to admit the funeral procession. What follows is again high comedy as the mourners take refuge in a nearby pub. Only the adroit maneuvering of Phelps's boss and future father-in-law saves the situation from disaster, but in the process the young man feels he has sold his soul. There is nothing remarkable about this theme, of course, but Thomas's style is rich and original, his control of tone and nuance assured. The following description is typical of his boldness and rhythmic, sensual prose:

A grey little column of thoughtfulness was Morlais Moore, the tenderest thinker we had in all Windy Way where we lived. He moved serenely among us, pale and wonderfully comprehending, a brilliantly lit-up question mark which annoyed all such men as my father who watched life in a more cautious and recessive mood than Morlais. . . . But it was Morlais alone who redeemed those early days from a shapeless squalor, Morlais alone who made me dream of a time when the wind of some great dignity and purpose would fill the sails of all our being and make the planet seem less sullen and alien than it usually did from where we stood in Windy Way.

It is in this manner that Thomas is able to sustain the combination of solemnity and absurdity that marks this very accomplished story.

• • •

Gwyn Jones's *Shepherd's Hey and Other Stories* appeared in 1953, but as some of these plus later stories from the decade are included in the more accessible *Selected Stories* (1974), the later volume will serve as the basis of discussion. Jones (1905–) is Welsh in all the obvious ways: his characters and settings are nearly always Welsh, and he has a keen sense of what is universal and yet unique about his people. Like Thomas, he also possesses a rich comic sense and, like so many others of his countrymen, a fine feeling for nature and vivid awareness of the past.

A number of his stories are in the Coppard-Bates vein of rural writing. "A White Birthday," for example, vividly captures the toughness and bravery of a young shepherd, searching for lost ewes in deep snow while simultaneously thinking of his wife, who is having a child. The juxtaposition may seem a bit obvious, but Jones handles it with subtlety, concentrating his attention on the difficulties of the shepherd and the ewe he finds with one lamb already killed by attacking ravens and another having trouble being born. "Four in a Valley" skillfully unfolds a tale of heartbreak in love while at the same time describing the courtship rituals of a pair of hawks. Ironically, Tom points to the hawks as justification for his leaving Dil: there is no marriage among birds, he remarks. But there is. When a farmer shoots the female hawk, the male faithfully and fatally stays by her side, thus shaming Tom's unnatural attitude toward physical gratification without commitment. Jones has successfully united two ancient themes into a poignant story of love and loss.

In other stories, Jones explores a variety of styles and themes, taking a starkly naturalistic stance in "The Brute Creation," a seriocomic tone in "The Still Waters," and a supernatural approach in "Their Bonds Are Loosed from Above." In these as in previous and later stories, Jones proves himself a capable and flexible writer, a Welsh author whose reputation should extend well beyond the borders of his native land.

• • •

In addition to these authors, others were contributing to the Welsh story by publishing in periodicals and annuals. The journal *Dock Leaves* focused mainly on poetry but published one or two stories in each issue, some by established writers like Roland Mathias and D. J. Williams, others by newcomers. Among the better stories in John Pudney's volumes are two stories by journalist/short story writer Dilys Rowe. "A View across the Valley" (*Pick of Today's Short Stories, 6*) is a sensitive character study and atmospheric piece, and "Six Pairs of Joined Hands" (*Pick of Today's Short Stories, 8*) is a carefully crafted tale on the varieties of female innocence. Nevertheless the dominant impression one gets of the Welsh story during the fifties is that of a vigorous tradition momentarily catching its breath before moving on to a new phase.

Four New Voices

Although the British story in the 1950s received no stimulus as great as that given the American story by J. D. Salinger's *Nine Stories,* it nevertheless saw the appearance of at least four important new writers. Dylan Thomas (1914–53) belongs chronologically to the 1930s and 1940s, and of course his primary fame is as a poet. The notoriety he achieved during the fifties and his untimely death in 1953, however, prompted the publication of two prose collections, *Quite Early One Morning* (1954) and *Adventures in the Skin Trade* (1955). The former is composed almost entirely of pieces that appeared during the 1940s, the most famous of which is "A Child's Christmas in Wales." Fresh and impressionistic in style and vision, these stories conjure up childhood images of such originality and power that they often walk the thin line between poetry and prose. "Quite Early One Morning," for example, has no plot or story line as such; rather it is a collection of reminiscences about a Welsh village waking up, its inhabitants stretching, yawning, and finally greeting a new day. Throughout runs the refrain, "The town was not yet awake." "Holiday Memory" is similar in technique and effect, vividly describing the August bank holiday at a seaside resort as seen through a child's eyes. As always, Thomas's style carries the story along, and he commands the reader's attention by the sheer originality of his language and the aptness of his descriptions. Thomas demonstrates an uncanny ability to find the essence of a moment in a particular bit of description, the universal in a chance scrap of dialogue.

The most traditional of these sketches is entitled simply "A Story," which does have a narrative line though nothing so formal as a plot, and there are two thoroughly engaging characters, Thomas's uncle and aunt, plus an assortment of colorful local personalities. The occasion of the story is the annual men's pub crawl "to Porthcawl, which, of course, the charabanc never reached," though it hardly matters since what happens before the outing and in the various pubs along the way is delightful comedy. Thomas is at his best, here, producing prose of inimitable originality without the difficulties and obscurities that mark many of the pieces in *Adventures in the Skin Trade*. A brief sample will convey the idea:

> But there he was, always, a steaming hulk of an uncle, his braces straining like hawsers, crammed behind the counter of the tiny shop at the front of the house, and breathing like a brass band; or guzzling and blustery in the kitchen over his gutsy supper, too big for everything except the great black boats of his boots.

The annual outing turns out to be a communal drunk, of course, but Thomas transforms it from what might be merely a vulgar booze-up into something that suggests a primeval male urge to break the bonds of stifling femininity and participate in something wholly and essentially male. Riotous, dreamlike, and archetypal, the story succeeds at many levels, making it one of the most satisfying of the decade.

Nothing in *Adventures in the Skin Trade* approximates the success of "A Story," although the title piece has more than a measure of energy and richness, unfortunately unchanneled and occasionally incoherent. Many of the other stories involve fantastic and dreamlike happenings that occasionally achieve levels of symbolic richness and depth but usually result merely in annoying obscurities. These are, as it were, fossils from an earlier age, when experiments in the symbolic and surrealistic were expanding the limits of prose fiction and exploring new layers of consciousness. In the more staid and traditional fifties, they look garish and out of place, though for Thomas scholars they provide an important corollary to the poems.

* * *

A more genuinely new voice of the 1950s belongs to Kingsley Amis (1922–), whose novel *Lucky Jim* (1953) brought its author into prominence and led many to classify him, rather inaccurately, as one of Britain's "angry young men." Amis is primarily a novelist, and his contribution to the short story cannot be called profound or highly original; nevertheless, his use of the form during this decade testifies to continuing, if diminishing, vitality. The stories Amis produced in the fifties were later collected in *My Enemy's Enemy* (1962), and all concern the bureaucratization of life, though Amis also exposes remnants of the class war as it existed in postwar Britain.

In "My Enemy's Enemy," Amis is interested in examining the way in which bureaucracies stifle creative and energetic people and reward those whose chief ability is to hide from responsibility and shift blame. "Moral Fibre" is similar in tone and point of view to *Lucky Jim,* though without the novel's humor. It is narrated by John Lewis, a librarian who resents the efforts of his wife's friend, Mair Webster, to interfere officially in other people's lives. Miss Webster, a social worker, tries unsuccessfully to reform Betty Arnulfsen, who finds life as a prostitute and thief easier and more profitable than the respectability Mair Webster would like to force on her. There is also a suggestion that something like original sin will always frustrate those who take a mechanical and deterministic view of human nature. Reforming Betty's environment or providing a steady welfare check will not change what she is and what she wants to be. Nevertheless, one comes away from these stories slightly unsatisfied, for although Amis is always good at exposing what he does not approve of, he is much less successful at suggesting positive values, and his satire often leaves a slightly bitter taste. In any event, Amis is more important as a social barometer than as a contributor to the story form, though his prominence after *Lucky Jim* no doubt influenced other story writers of his generation to follow his example.

* * *

Doris Lessing (1919–) moved to England just a year before the publication of *The Grass Is Singing* (1950), and during the ensuing decade published three collections of short fiction. Her work touches on two important themes of the postwar world—race relations and women's liberation. Her concern with race relations grows naturally from the fact that she lived from the age of six to thirty in Rhodesia, observing firsthand the effects of colonialism on both whites and blacks. She writes with great sympathy for both sides in the controversy, refusing to condemn with easy slogans what she knows to be a complex situation.

"The Old Chief Mshlanga" dramatizes these difficulties in a particularly effective way, showing that the whites who have the power, even those born in Africa, remain strangers in a strange land. More important, she shows the dehumanizing effects arising from the exercise of power by one group over another, however well intentioned the powerful might be. Lessing does not, however, write moral parables or contrive characters and situations to illustrate preconceived ideas; rather, she creates believable characters and through them shows the effects of colonialism on the human spirit. In "The Old Chief Mshlanga," much is conveyed through the emerging consciousness of a young girl through whose eyes the events of the story are seen. Being herself young and innocent, she is an apt symbol for the great burden colonialism places on both groups, for she perceives, even though she does not fully comprehend, that neither group is allowed to be fully human under a system that prescribes behavior for the conqueror as much as it does for the conquered.

It was probably inevitable that sympathy for one oppressed group, blacks, would lead to sympathy for another—her own sex. Although she has sometimes been criticized for being doctrinaire in her novels, the same charge cannot be made about her short stories. In these she writes with great intelligence and sympathy, acutely aware of changes in modes of feeling. Overall, her theme is the inability of people to connect with one another, especially sexually, though in other ways as well. Her slant, to be sure, is feminist, but it is not antimale. Many of her protagonists are women attempting to find authenticity and identity in a male-dominated world that prefers to thrust certain roles on women rather than allow them to develop as individuals. "The Habit of Loving" from the volume of the same name (1957) is typical in many ways, even though the story is narrated through the eyes of George Talbot, a sixty-year-old theatrical producer for whom loving is, as the title implies, a habit. Essentially, women are necessary to him as an emotional crutch, above all as something to divert his attention from his own mortality.

Many of Lessing's other characters are similarly trapped by lust, confused feelings, social conventions, or circumstances into lives and relationships that are unfulfilling. Mary Brook of "He" is so obsessed by neatness that she drives her husband into the arms of another woman. It is difficult to know in this situation who is the more sinned against. Mary's passion for cleanliness is, after all, part of the role assigned her by the male world, and the story suggests, too, that this compulsive cleanliness masks deeper frustrations that her philandering husband is unwilling or unable to understand.

"Getting Off the Altitude" is set in Africa and concerns the tangled relations of a Mrs. Slatter and her womanizing husband. The story is seen through the naive eyes of a sixteen-year-old girl who witnesses not only the difficulties of the marriage itself but also its effects on her parents. A carefully modulated story of sexual politics, it is typical of Lessing's work in using the limited insight of its young narrator to explore the erotic tensions underlying any marriage.

"Flavors of Exile" is one of the most complex of Lessing's stories. Ostensibly it deals with the problems of growing English fruits and vegetables in a hostile African climate, but it resonates beyond this simple idea and becomes a meditation on unrealized ideals, insensitivity to others' feelings, and clashes between the male and female points of view. In all, then, Lessing resembles writers like Pritchett, Bates, Warner, and Muriel Spark in suggesting an emptiness at the center of modern life. As a diagnostician of modern ills, she is an acute and accurate observer who goes beyond description to suggest a reaffirmation of humanistic values as a starting point for the rebuilding of postwar culture.

• • •

Far more strident in tone is the work of Alan Sillitoe (1928–), who burst on the English literary scene with the novel *Saturday Night and Sunday Morning* (1958) and followed with another success, *The Loneliness of the Long-Distance Runner* (1959). Born in Nottingham of a working-class family, Sillitoe shocked and angered many Britons by the vehemence of his attack on the society that many thought had given justice to the working man. But in Sillitoe's world, the class system is still intact; the police are still the enemy; the main line of demarcation is between "them" and "us." What is more, Sillitoe expressed his discontent not in the irreverent wit of a Kingsley Amis or the philosophical musings of a Wyndham Lewis but in the earthy language of the working man.

In an introduction to an anthology of his work, he wrote that to him a story is best told by a man sitting by a campfire or talking to his friends in a pub or canteen. "I see such a story not as an incident which begins at point A and goes in a line thinly but straight to point B, but rather as a circuitous embellishment, twisting and convoluted, meandering all over the place until, near the end, these irrelevancies can at last be seen to have a point."[2] This is a fair description of his approach and method. Most of Sillitoe's successful stories are narrated in the first person by someone of the working class, and if he does not use Somerset Maugham's device of the narrator talking to friends over the port, he nevertheless imparts a sense of speaker and listener in the casual structure and colloquial style of his fiction.

The best known of his short stories is "The Loneliness of the Long-Distance Runner." Told in the first person by a seventeen-year-old named Smith, it relates circuitously the events and attitudes that brought the boy to his present predicament as an inmate of Borstal prison. As Smith sees his situation, everything depends upon his maintaining his integrity as an unrepentant rebel against the dishonest establishment. In some ways, he reminds us of another Smith—Winston Smith of Orwell's *1984*—only this Smith manages a victory of sorts on his own terms. Having made himself a favorite of the Warden's by excelling at cross-country running, Smith is in a position to do one of two things: win the big race and thus earn for himself respectability and rewards on the Warden's terms, or lose the race deliberately and thereby maintain his own integrity. He sees his choice as a question of honesty:

Sounds funny, but it's true because I know what honest means according to me. . . . And if I had the whip-hand I wouldn't even bother to build a place like this to put all the cops, governors, posh whores, penpushers, army officers, Members of Parliament in; no, I'd stick them up against a wall and let them have it, like they'd have done with blokes like us years ago, that is, if they'd ever known what it means to be honest.

If there is an element of the pathological in Smith's definition of honesty, there is also an unusually high degree of self-awareness and a genuine touch of the existential hero: "And I knew what the loneliness of the long-distance runner running across country felt like, realizing that as far as I was concerned this feeling was the only honesty and realness there was in the world and knowing it would be no different ever." Losing the race means that Smith will endure the rest of his time in prison doing the dirtiest jobs the Warden can assign him, but it also leaves him free of debt. Ironically, in doing this work he contracts pleurisy, which keeps him out of the army but does not prevent him from returning to his life as a thief.

In spite of the nihilism of Sillitoe's vision, his stories bring a breath of new air into the British short story, making many established writers appear rather tame by comparison. "Noah's Ark," for example, bears comparison with H. E. Bates's story of childhood fear, "The Poison Lady," but whereas the Bates story chronicles the growing pains of two young boys against a background of a warm and rich rural setting, Sillitoe's story traces the escapades of two young boys at an urban carnival, where they resourcefully cheat, steal, beg, and deceive in order to enjoy pleasures they cannot afford. Bates's story has its chilling moments, but Sillitoe's vision is nearly Dantean in its lurid colors and manic terrors, and whereas Bates implies that childhood imagination may flourish, Sillitoe's imaginative boy Colin is doomed by a world that has no place for sensitivity and no tolerance for weakness. What Colin and Bert of "Noah's Ark" are as children, Lennox and Fred of "The Match" are as adults. Lennox is the focus of the tale, and his failing eyesight and declining physical powers represent threats to his manhood, which he cannot acknowledge or control. Hence, when Nottingham loses its soccer match to Bristol City, he can vent his frustrations only by bullying his family. In the macho world of the working class, there is no room for weakness. The power of Sillitoe's story is that it probes the human condition through a particular working-class character, giving Lennox a measure of dignity in spite of the pathetic impotence of his domestic violence.

Although Sillitoe is successful in these stories, he has chosen a style and approach that cannot be maintained indefinitely. It is difficult to sustain the fiction that the working class is peopled by tough and articulate spokesmen who just happen to write well-crafted stories. The strain shows from time to time in "The Loneliness of the Long-Distance Runner" and also in "Uncle Ernest." Here the protagonist is a lonely upholsterer who befriends two young girls and in all innocence buys them treats until two detectives notice his activities and order him to stop. Uncle Ernest is a pathetic character to be sure, but the situation is sentimentalized and the police are portrayed as dirty-minded bullies lacking human feeling. Similarly, "Mr. Raynor the School-Teacher" is a heavy-handed exposé of the pathetic sexual fantasies of a religion teacher who vents his frustrations on hapless students.

Other Distinctive Voices

The four writers considered above are genuinely new voices of the fifties, but equally important is the group that first came to public notice in the previous decade but contributed significant short fiction during the fifties. Chief among these is Angus Wilson (1913–), who turned to writing after a nervous breakdown and used the short story as therapy. The result was a much-praised collection, *The Wrong Set* (1949), followed by *Such Darling Dodos* (1950) and *A Bit Off the Map* (1957). In these collections, Wilson focuses his mordant wit and deadly accurate powers of observation on all levels of society and exposes the tendency to live under pretense and delusion, often driven by intolerance and petty self-righteousness. For Wilson, good characters are those who are morally aware, but virtually no one in these stories fits that description.

"Such Darling Dodos" is told through Tony—a Roman Catholic, homosexual, and political conservative who is visiting Robin and Priscilla because Robin is terminally ill. He hopes that "his relatives might surely at last take off their blinkers and stop trying to fit God's Universe to their own little home-made paper schemes," by which he means the agnostic socialism to which they have dedicated their lives. If Tony is sincere, his hopes for Robin's deathbed conversion might be interpreted as genuinely touching, but Tony wears large blinkers of his own, chief among them an inability to acknowledge his own age and therefore his mortality. Surprisingly, Tony finds allies in two university students who visit Priscilla and Robin for tea; they are the new conservatives, who like Tony regard the liberalism and political activism of the older generation as quaint. To them and to Tony, Robin and Priscilla are "darling dodos," but dodos just the same. On the surface, Wilson maintains an objective stance, neither supporting nor condemning either side directly. But Tony damns himself by his selfishness, his absurd clinging to youth, his snobbery and effete aestheticism, and above all his smug self-righteousness. Nevertheless, Priscilla and Robin are far from blameless; having immersed themselves in housing schemes, sanitary drains, and the like, they have pawned their spirits to material things and hence represent the soulless materialism of the modern world. Even Michael and Harriet Ecclestone, the students who come for tea, are not spared; their own vapid complacency hardly ennobles them.

Another of Wilson's themes is social cruelty, the ways in which people accidentally or deliberately harm one another, often for reasons of status or class. "Christmas Day in the Workhouse" depicts the machinations of wartime bureaucrats in an anonymous section working under the direction of Tim Prosser, who abuses his position to seduce as many of the young women as he can. Work is all that unites these people from diverse backgrounds: the central character, Thea, occupies an ambiguous position between the lower-class girls with their vulgar popular tastes and Stephanie, the polished country aristocrat. In a friendship triangle, Joan Folwer aspires to Thea's affections just as Thea craves Stephanie's. Against the background of the office Christmas party, Stephanie betrays Thea, who then spurns Joan. Like most of Wilson's stories, "Christmas Day in the Workhouse" consists mainly of conversation, and Wilson is expert at catching the tones and phrasings of each character. Since most of his people work in shops and offices and spend much of their time talking over tea or drinks, he is a very "indoor" writer. In fact, this is a trait he shares with most writers of the decade; like England itself, the short story became urbanized in this period, largely turning its back on the country and the village.

The suburb, however, provides a fertile area for Wilson's social probing, as in "A Flat Country Christmas." Again the principals are office workers in a complex bureaucracy; promotion is much on their minds. Again, too, work forms the basis of friendship—politics, religion, and the arts being too risky for conversation. On this occasion, a parlor game in which everyone looks into a mirror to describe what vision he or she may find leads to a crisis, for Ray sees nothing—no future—and hence bursts into tears; then, when his wife tries to comfort him, he lashes out angrily at her, embarrassed by his own frailty. These characters and their empty lives are to be pitied; not so the amoral and manipulative protagonists of "More Friend Than Lodger," in which the wife of an idealistic publisher is pursued and seduced (with her open-eyed consent) by an author and con man who without scruple uses everyone within reach.

The chief qualities of Wilson's style are an eye for significant detail, an excellent ear for dialogue, and a sharp wit that pierces the protective armor his characters wear in public and reveals the moral softness beneath. Sometimes he is classed with nineteenth-century novelists of manners, a connection he does more to encourage than to deny. He acknowledges a debt to mainstream English fiction, particularly Dickens, with whom he is often compared. As a conscious practitioner of traditional fiction, he is important in setting an example as a writer and in chastising experiment as a critic. His influence in this regard may be overestimated, since the short story in Britain during the fifties showed little inclination to novelty in any event, but Wilson's success may indeed have assisted in discouraging new techniques.

· · ·

A completely different order of wit and sensibility belongs to Roald Dahl (1916–), who first came to attention with *Over to You* (1946), stories based on the author's wartime experiences in the R.A.F. During the fifties, he produced a considerable body of short stories, collected in *Someone Like You* (1953), and *Kiss Kiss* (1960). The earlier stories are more tame than later ones, relying less on the grotesque and perverse for their effects. "Nunc Dimittis," for instance, is a study in revenge and guilt, narrated by its protagonist, Lionel Lampson, a critic and "man of culture." Upon learning that his current woman friend, Janet, regards him as a bore, he devises a delicious revenge. It seems that the most fashionable portrait painter of the moment poses his female subjects first in the nude, then in succeeding layers of clothing, painting over each layer until the subject is fully dressed. Lampson arranges for Janet to have her portrait thus painted and then, using his skill as a restorer of paintings, removes the top layer of paint, revealing Janet in her underwear. Guests are invited to a dinner by candlelight, and at just the right moment, the candles burn out and the electric lights are switched on, revealing to the startled guests Janet's ludicrous portrait. Janet, however, has *her* revenge, forgiving Lionel publicly and sending him caviar. At story's end, Lionel feels too ill to mix in society.

Most famous of the tales in *Someone Like You* is "Lamb to the Slaughter," which concerns a detective's wife who murders her philandering husband with a frozen leg of lamb and then coolly cooks it and serves it to the investigating officers, who ironically concede that the missing murder weapon must be right under their noses.

Dahl's later stories often have a sharper edge and display a blacker wit. Among the best is "Rummins," part of a series of stories loosely related and collected under the heading "Claude's Dog." Looking for sport, Claude and the first person narrator take their rifles one afternoon and go to Rummins's farm to watch a rat-infested hayrick be pulled down. The narrator recalls the hot June day last summer when the rick was built; it was unusual because on that day, Old Jimmy, a retired carpenter, disappeared at the lunch break and was never heard from again. Suddenly one of the workers grates his knife against something hard, and a moment later a rat-cleaned skeleton is revealed. "Rummins, who knew very well what it was, had turned away and was climbing quickly down the other side of the rick. He moved so fast he was through the gate and halfway across the road before Bert started to scream."

Also interesting is "Georgy Porgy," which concerns a vicar who is phobic about women. This derives from his youth when his mother took him to see the birth of some rabbits and the mother rabbit brutally ate one of her offspring. Convinced by this that the female is the aggressive sex, he devises an experiment with rats that confirms his feeling. Now, as vicar, he tries to stay away from women, but the more he stands aloof, the more they pursue him. Finally, one tries to kiss him, and all he can think of is the predatory mouth of the mother rabbit. In a panic, he nearly kills her.

The best of Dahl's stories achieve a degree of palpable horror or grim irony that is at once entertaining and revealing. Exploring the id leads Dahl into fascinating territory, from which he often derives stories of great cleverness. These can be very effective, but in large doses they appear contrived and slick. The best of Dahl's stories during this period, like "The Neck," "Parson's Pleasure," and "Lamb to the Slaughter," will no doubt continue to be widely anthologized for many years to come, and deservedly so. Many others, however, have merely entertainment value.

· · ·

William Sansom (1912–) first achieved fame during World War II with *Fireman Flower* (1944), a collection of stories based on his experiences as a London fireman during the blitz. These stories succeed in part because of their timeliness but also in large measure for the sheer virtuosity of Sansom's prose. Perhaps no writer has equaled him in the ability to freeze a moment of extreme emotion and describe every aspect of it in precise particularity. In the decade following the war, he published four collections of stories, each containing fresh attempts to extend his thematic and stylistic range.

In *The Passionate North* (1950) he attempts to wed the genres of travelogue and short story in a series of tales set in northern Europe. The title takes deliberate aim at the stereotype of the unemotional northerner, frozen in stiff, indifferent coolness. The collection is only partially successful. Several of the tales, like "The Girl on the Bus," present interesting situations and reasonably effective characters but fall flat at the end. "Happy New Year" is contrived and sentimental. By contrast, "A Wedding" is vivid and memorable, juxtaposing the beautifully serene Swedish countryside with an almost lurid tale of death and madness. "A World of Glass" evokes all the glittering beauty and peace of a picturesque Norwegian village while unfolding a quietly tragic story of a beautiful young woman whose husband destroyed her eyesight in a fit of jealous rage. Ironically, the narrator is telling this story because, after hearing about the girl, he lashed out idiotically and punched a stranger in the face. On two levels, then, it is a story about serenity and violence, love and anger, sight and blindness.

The best story of this collection, however, is "A Waning Moon," set in Glencoe, Scotland. Sansom seems more at home on British soil, where the less exotic scenery enables him to concentrate on the inter-action of characters, in this case a young husband and wife on a caravan holiday. Tired and out of sorts, their peevishness explodes into a sense-less and angry quarrel that rocks their small trailer "like a huge egg in an animated cartoon." Ruth bolts from the caravan and in the dark slips into a quarry lake, nearly drowning. In describing her rescue, Sansom calls once again upon his formidable talent for physical and emotional description to create a scene of intense and vivid power. Brooding in the background are the Scottish landscape and the legends surrounding the Campbells' massacre at Glencoe. In all, it is one of Sansom's most satisfying and effective stories, capturing at once the volatility of marriage and the frailty of human life.

Lord Love Us (1954) represents an attempt to create an energetic new style based on the rhythms of colloquial speech heightened to an in-tensity that approaches the frenetic. In this passage from "Life, Death," for example, the narrator describes his first meeting with the woman he would eventually marry:

Me, I stood there jumboed. Out of my wits awhile I was. Me, with all the skirt I have each day, fat ones, thin ones, young ones, old ones, cheery ones that pass the time of day, crabby ones all price and poke-finger. And never a tremor goes through me till that time. I must've stood there seconds looking after her; I was seized, and I see I only saw my senses when a big brown voice came in my earhole: "Have you got *all* the day?" But then I thought I had.

The sense of personality, of genuine voice, could hardly be stronger; and the language is fresh and invigorating. One is reminded of Dylan Thomas in his sketches of Wales or the later work of Alan Sillitoe with its working-class gusto.

"Life, Death" is the most successful of the stories in *Lord Love Us,* but nearly as effective is "Trouble in Wilton Road," which conveys in strongly rhythmic prose, odd phrasing, and even rhyme the loss and loneliness felt by a man whose wife has left him. It would be difficult to sustain this kind of prose indefinitely. What begins as evocative experiment could easily descend to annoying mannerism. In fact, Sansom did not attempt anything quite so radical again; later volumes, *A Contest of Ladies* (1956) and *Among the Dahlias* (1957), settle into a quieter, more mainstream style, though these volumes are notable for their humor and satire. Sansom's place is still being evaluated, but it seems certain that at least a handful of stories, most probably those like "The Wall" that deal in heightened emotional states, will continue to be studied and admired for a long time to come.

• • •

Born in the same year as Sansom, Elizabeth Taylor (1912–75) writes a prose as cool and deliberate as Sansom's is fiery and energetic. She has often been favorably compared with Jane Austen. Taylor excels at character delineation, often portraying contrasts through the clash of generations or the grating of social class. Like Pritchett, she is often content to probe and reveal, without judging but with a good deal of sympathy. "An Oasis of Gaiety" from *Hester Lilly and Twelve Short Stories* (1954), for instance, contrasts the almost frivolous but engaging 1920s energy of a mother with the comparatively morose and even neurotic musing of her two postwar children. Taylor's objectivity makes it difficult to say which generation she prefers, but preference is not the point—change is. The war itself seems to have draped a pall over people, depriving them of gaiety and even of style.

Among the best of Taylor's stories is "A Red-Letter Day," a title as ironic as the first paragraph of the story, where the author quietly but strategically describes a shabby and "malevolent" landscape and then brings the reader up short with a dramatic contrast: "Then, as the building itself came into view, they could see Matron standing at the top of the steps, fantastically white, shaming nature, her hands laid affectionately upon the shoulders of such boys as could not resist her." The red-letter day turns out to be parents' visiting day at a boy's boarding school, and "shaming nature" is a good description of its theme, for Tony is a mother unable to connect with her son. "In *her* life all was frail, precarious; emotions fleeting, relationships fragmentary." This is dramatized in painful detail as Tony's day with her son drags on, and their path frequently crosses that of Mrs. Hay-Hardy, whose open and joyous relationship with her boys makes Tony painfully aware of her shortcomings. Yet we sympathize with Tony; hers is an all too common failing and is born of emotional confusion, not want of love or caring. She is the prototype of the modern parent—alienated, awkward, divorced, certain of her own failure yet unable to say where she has failed.

The Blush and Other Stories (1958) shows an increase in subtlety and power deriving in part from a greater maturity of narrative technique. Instead of relying on contrast as the basis of her stories' structures, Taylor in this volume explores the interaction of characters. Still cool and objective, she dramatizes the interplay of personalities with great economy and skill; she is a master at creating scenes and conversations that on the outside betray nothing of significance but that resonate with emotional power. "Good-Bye, Goody-Bye," for example, reunites two lovers who several years previously had agreed never to see each other again. Peter's return to Catherine during a beach picnic for her children is presented with such dispassionate objectivity that the two lovers appear on the surface to be nothing more than casual acquaintances reunited by chance. But such is Taylor's skill that the story radiates with tension and pain, while in the background Catherine's children innocently underscore the tragedy of the lovers' thwarted desires. "Summer Schools" is equally effective in portraying the inner struggles of two sisters as they slide inevitably into spinsterhood. These are stories that deserve to be carefully studied and widely known.

. . .

A[udrey] L[ilian] Barker (1918–) has published sparingly and perhaps as a result has received little attention from critics. Her first collection of stories, *Innocents,* appeared in 1948, and since then only two volumes have followed, *Novelette: With Other Stories* (1951) and *The Joy-*

Ride and After (1964). Her subjects are ordinary people, usually of the middle class, but her main focus is on character, not class. Primarily, she is a student of psychology, exploring a variety of states of mind. Like many authors of the period, she portrays her people as wounded though far from pathological. They are limited human beings, trying to find themselves or at least some form of peace. Barker offers no formula for happiness and has no illusions about people, particularly children. If there is a common concern in her stories, it is people's need for acceptance and affection; but she also has a highly developed sense of original sin, which she explores in "The Villain as a Young Boy."

The stories in *Novelette* show a considerable variety of forms and approaches, so that it is difficult to select any one as typical. "Romney" brings together two wounded people, the ineffectual Joe Rigby and his young pupil Harry, an eight-year-old boy living in the shadow of a big brother whom everyone loved and admired and in the "knowledge" that he has killed this older brother by shooting him with a toy gun. Rigby's concern for the child and his eventual discovery of Harry's guilty secret reads in part like a detective story, but essentially it is a story of psychological and moral detection that leads its readers close to the secret workings of love, guilt, and hate. The parallel between Rigby's guilt at not having been fit enough to be a soldier and the boy's feelings of inadequacy in comparison with his brother is skillfully and sensitively handled.

Similar in tone and sensitivity but very different in narrative technique is " 'Here Comes a Candle.' " In a relatively short space, Barker traces the childhood, adolescence, and adulthood of Haidee as she struggles first with the fears and neglect of an aloof mother and a cold governess, then faces the terrors of boarding school, and finally tries to cope with the rejection of her husband and the natural cutting of apron strings as she discovers that her children have grown up. The strong story line and sensitive rendering of character make the story quite effective, but the facile use of the nursery rhyme in the title and again at the end of the story weakens its ultimate effect.

"Submerged" bears comparisons with Sansom's stories and with Doris Lessing's "The Tunnel" for its ability to convey physical sensations and moments of high anxiety. This is combined with a study of a young boy's discovery of adult duplicity and his own sense of moral responsibility, which does not mature as the reader expects. Again, one suspects that Barker is using the limited vision of childhood to suggest a broader human problem. Overall, Barker writes technically good stories concerning characters who engage our sympathies. If she has not received the attention she deserves, it is partly because of her own modest output and partly because she has not put her distinctive stamp on her version of the mainstream British story.

• • •

John Collier (1901–80) has often been described as a fantasist, though the label should not be applied too strictly, for he wrote several kinds of short stories. Two collections appeared in the 1940s and two more in the 1950s, *Fancies and Goodnights* (1951) and *Pictures in the Fire* (1958); *Pictures,* however, contains ony a few stories not found in *Fancies.* In many ways, Collier could be called a moralist and social critic with a macabre sense of irony. The combination can be extremely effective; his better stories are at once entertaining and laden with meaning. Perhaps outstanding in this respect is "Evening Primrose" from *Fancies and Goodnights,* which presents a world of fairylike beings who inhabit shops and stores, emerging only at night. Organized into a snobbish and rigid hierarchy, these creatures parallel and parody the materialistic society of the bourgeois daylight world, even to the point of employing their own sinister "dark men" who turn any nonconformist into a mannikin. Collier's achievement in creating an entirely consistent and believable fantasy world, complete with its own internal structures and physical laws, is impressive; and his sensitive handling of the outcast Ella and the aspiring poet who befriends her is poignant and moving.

Similar in theme is "Witch's Money," though the treatment in this case is realistic. The story traces the corrupting influence of money upon a peasant population that has hitherto been immune from "progress." Collier's peasants resemble their greedy and shrewd counterparts in Maupassant's tales, but Collier is less interested in exploring individual souls than in exposing the baleful effects of excessive money on the social fabric. Old alliances shatter, greed prompts unsuitable marriages between the young and old, and traditional values of simple sufficiency give way to money grubbing and economic development of the tackiest kind. Here again, Collier succeeds in creating a world that is at once exotic and familiar.

By contrast, "Three Bears Cottage" is obvious and predictable. The attempt is to re-create a fairy-tale world, in fact a kind of Eden in which a husband and wife fall victim to their own jealousies and petty selfishness. When the wife keeps for herself the larger and tastier egg at breakfast, her husband seeks revenge by trying to poison her with a mushroom. Unfortunately, the "surprise" ending is all too predictable.

Collier's style often provokes contrary reactions from readers. Always clear, precise, and original, it is nevertheless marked at times by a straining after effect, an excessive cleverness that calls undue attention to itself. The result is that what strikes one reader as clever or even moving may well strike another as *merely* clever or even slick. "Incident on a Lake," for example, in which a henpecked husband finally gets revenge upon his intolerable wife, has all the depth and insight of a mother-in-law joke. On the whole, Collier succeeds better in those tales that avoid the surface cleverness of a mock-heroic style and instead rely for their effects on his ability to portray the unusual and even the bizarre in matter-of-fact tones. "A Touch of Nutmeg Makes It," for example, succeeds in probing the twisted psyche of J. Chapman Reid because the narrator relates the material coolly and objectively, allowing the horror of Reid's murderous obsession to emerge gradually and inevitably. "Mademoiselle Kiki" from *Pictures in the Fire,* however, is essentially a beast fable in modern dress narrated with a mock solemnity that finally defeats the story's satirical purpose.

Outlets for Short Story Writers

It is a commonplace of literary history that the outbreak of World War II brought to an end something of a golden era in the British short story, for the number and quality of outlets for short story writers diminished substantially. No exact count is possible, given the effervescent nature of scores of little magazines that surfaced and disappeared over the decades, but there is no question that the commercial market for stories shrank drastically between 1939 and 1950 and continued to do so throughout the decade. Perhaps the most significant loss was *Penguin New Writing* under John Lehmann's editorship. In an attempt to fill the gap left by defunct periodicals, John Pudney in 1949 undertook to edit an annual collection, *The Pick of Today's Short Stories.* Pudney, himself an accomplished if not gifted author, annually sifted through hundreds of stories submitted by writers of all ages and talent, selecting twenty or so for inclusion. In nearly all cases, these were stories that had not been previously published, so these volumes can in no way be compared with Edward O'Brien's famous *Best Short Stories* series. Moreover, Pudney's taste was considerably less catholic and inquisitive than O'Brien's, with the result that *Pick* volumes rarely include anything avant-garde. A glance at the table of contents of successive volumes shows that the editor favored a mix of established authors and neophytes. Thus, one finds C. S. Forester, Gerald Bullett, Pamela Hansford Johnson, Richard Church, H. E. Bates, and Graham Williams listed with relative newcomers like Angus Wilson, Dilys Rowe, Mordecai Richler, and Mary Lavin. Not surprisingly, most of the names are today unfamiliar; for some, appearing in one of these volumes was their only claim to fame.

There is no evidence that an appearance in *Pick* launched any new career, brilliant or otherwise, but the consistently good quality of these anthologies served the useful purpose of providing serious authors with an opportunity to reach the story-reading public.

Another hardcover annual anthology was launched in 1955 by Macmillan with the intent of providing an outlet for longer stories that magazines could not publish. Called *Winter's Tales,* these volumes have continued to provide an important forum for that most neglected of all fictional forms, the long story. The five issues of *Winter's Tales* that appeared between 1955 and 1959 contained an average of only a dozen stories each. Thus, there was little room for newcomers. Of the eleven stories in the first volume, for example, only two were by relatively unknown writers; the others were written by such well-established authors as Frank O'Connor, V. S. Pritchett, and Osbert Sitwell. This ratio of new authors to established writers shifted beginning with the next volume, but throughout the decade, *Winter's Tales* continued to include stories by proven authors. A study of the contents of *Winter's Tales* and *Pick of Today's Short Stories* gives a good indication of how difficult it was for a young writer to find an audience for short fiction outside the commercial periodicals.

Although commercial magazines were shrinking in number and in space available for fiction, by today's standards authors of the fifties perhaps should have felt themselves fortunate. Such traditional publishers of high-quality fiction as the *Listener, Argosy, Cornhill,* the *Spectator, Punch, Encounter,* and *Time and Tide* continued their commitment to the short story. Nevertheless, for many British writers, especially those more established and well known, it was American periodicals, particularly the *New Yorker,* that provided both the audience and the substantial check that writers need to survive. An important newcomer during the decade was *Playboy,* which attracted many good writers by its rate of payment alone. A more limited but sophisticated audience could be reached through such journals as the *Hudson Review, Sewanee Review,* and *Kenyon Review.* Unfortunately, *Story* magazine ceased publication during the whole decade, and for Welsh writers the loss of the *Welsh Review* in 1948 was only partly compensated for by the appearance of the *Dock Leaves Review* in 1949 (*Dock Leaves* became the *Anglo-Welsh Review* in 1957). Scottish writers were rather better served by the *Saltire Review, Scot's Magazine,* and even the *Glasgow Herald,* which continued to publish stories. The loss of periodicals meant that BBC radio provided an increasingly important outlet for writers wishing to reach a large audience. Whether read by their authors or other readers, stories thus "published" could gain an important kind of exposure.

Overall, the publishing situation in the fifties in Britain could be described as difficult but not impossible. Story writers of talent and dedication could find outlets for their materials in quality periodicals, and these stories could eventually find their way into hardcover collections. But virtually no one during this period could support himself solely by writing stories; even very well-known short story authors relied on journalism or the novel for their livelihood. To be sure, this had been true during the twenties and thirties, but it was even more pronounced in the fifties. Fortunately for some writers, Rupert Hart-Davis decided to devote a considerable portion of its list to collections of stories, taking up some of the slack created by other trade houses who were unwilling or unable to maintain their prewar production.

The effects of these conditions on the British short story were probably more visible in the following decade than during the fifties for the simple reason that a considerable number of older writers like Bates, Pritchett, Warner, and Davies continued to lend their support to the genre. Thus, the decade produced in all a considerable body of high-quality short fiction by both new and older writers. But if it were not in decline, the story had certainly reached a plateau. Perhaps it would not be far wrong to call it the silver age of short fiction.

Dean Baldwin

The Behrend College Pennsylvania State University—Erie

THE ENGLISH SHORT STORY IN THE SIXTIES

In England the 1960s were a time of expansion after the restrictions of World War II and the stringent postwar economy. During this decade foreign travel, particularly on the Continent, became available to a large segment of the population; popular culture, notably the music of the Beatles and the fashions of Mary Quant, spread throughout the Western world; comprehensive schooling promised to abolish class distinctions; the dissolution of the empire foretold a more just world.

Few of these developments appear in the short fiction of the period. Occasionally a story deals with the self-revelations attendant on holidays in Italy or Portugal, but few reflect trends in popular culture; minor class distinctions continue to engross a number of writers, and few, apart from Doris Lessing, who did not take up residence in England until adulthood, explore colonial problems. The failure of the short story to deal with current concerns is the more remarkable when one considers that traditionally British fiction tended to be more social than psychological or mythic.

Nor was the British short story during this decade more experimental in form than in content. There was little sign of the kind of writer that Richard Kostelanetz calls the "breakthrough fictioneer" like Donald Barthelme and John Barth in the United States or Marguerite Duras and Alain Robbe-Grillet in France; Giles Gordon, for instance, did not publish his *Pictures from an Exhibition* until 1970. Most stories seem to have been written by traditionalists rather than revolutionaries, many having an old-fashioned air as much because of technique as because of subject matter.

The short story was plainly in decline: almost every commentator on the genre spoke of the difficulty of getting stories published. The circulation of literary magazines, at its height during the thirties and first postwar years, continued to dwindle in the sixties; although an occasional story was first published in *Queen* or the *Gentleman's Magazine,* only *Encounter, London Magazine,* and *Argosy* were buying stories in any quantity. The writers who managed to make money were supported by the U.S. publishing industry, particularly *Playboy, Esquire,* and most notable of all, the *New Yorker,* which published such writers as V. S. Pritchett, Sylvia Townsend Warner, and Elizabeth Taylor.

Nor was the opportunity for publishing short stories as collections any better; the short story simply was not a good commercial proposition. Various attempts were made to resuscitate the form, however, several annual anthologies with this express intention starting up during the 1950s and 1960s.

Short Fiction in Anthologies

At the beginning of the sixties, there was only one annual anthology devoted exclusively to the short story. *The Pick of Today's Short Stories* transferred from Putnam's to Eyre and Spottiswoode in 1963, moving, said editor John Pudney, because of a change in house policy rather than a change of "heart or even sales." Although a sale of almost five thousand was good for an anthology of short stories, the commercial advantage of publication must have been small, for *Pick* did not survive the change of publisher.

The four volumes issued during the sixties are not particularly distinguished; the editorial policy outlined in number 11 (1960), stating a preference for stories "with a beginning, a middle and an end . . . and entertainment value," may explain why. In general the themes are mundane: the Englishman "going potty" on the outskirts of the empire, the soccer player delighting in practical jokes, the working-class boy at war with the copper on the beat. The names of most of the writers are no longer familiar, although Kingsley Amis, Alan Sillitoe, H. E. Bates, and Brian Glanville are represented. None of the women novelists who earned such large reputations during the sixties, such as Muriel Spark, Doris Lessing, or Margaret Drabble, is included. Certainly this annual anthology contributed little to the development of the form or the theory of the short story, though number 13 (1963) includes the transcript of a discussion of the state of the art between Pudney and Margharita Laski. Here one finds for the first time some indication that the decline of the short story might not be entirely due to the dearth of outlets: Laski suggests that for the writers of the sixties "the technique of short-story writing has got steadily worse since its great days twenty, thirty, forty years ago."

A new series of anthologies began in 1960, although the volumes were not published annually. *Introduction: Stories by New Writers* appeared three times during the decade. Its main purpose was to give promising young writers a start. None had yet published a book, although all had appeared in literary magazines and undergraduate periodicals. Few of them have made a lasting reputation with the exception of Ted Hughes, better known as a poet, Julian Mitchell, and Tom Stoppard, the playwright.

Ted Hughes's stories, the most remarkable in the three volumes published in the sixties, depend more on the poetic integration of theme and mood than on narrative. His feeling for the British countryside is similar to D. H. Lawrence's. "The Rain Horse" evokes the feel of rainsoaked winter fields and "Sunday," of a heavy summer afternoon. But Hughes's work has a further remarkable quality: his description of the deeper states of physical horror have the effect of felt life. The terror of the man returning to the field where he played as a child only to be attacked by a mad horse who appears out of nowhere has the convincing quality of nightmare. In "Sunday" a boy accompanies his father to the performance of a renowned rat catcher who kills the rats with his teeth. Down on his hands and knees like a terrier, the rat catcher is faster than the rodents themselves; when the little corpses are tossed aside, the boy sees the blood on his jaws. Suddenly the fabric of ordinary life wears so thin that we can see the world of myth and ritual operating hideously beneath it, as though the universe were constructed according to Jung. In "Snow" we see the entirely rational processes of a madman, whose hypotheses about his environment have no relationship to it whatsoever. The Antarctic landscape is realistically rendered. In painstaking detail the narrator tells of his attempt to keep track of his whereabouts, but his obsession with carrying his "ordinary kitchen chair" through the blizzard invalidates his interpretation of every detail.

"Can I Go Now?" by Julian Mitchell is another distinguished story in the first volume of *Introduction*. Written in the first person, it tells the story of a teenager who, having witnessed his sister being raped by their father, has to defend himself against a similar attack. The dialect reflects the boy's working-class background, as his sentiments reflect the matter-of-factness of his age and class. The horror of this story comes from the contrast between tone and content. A similar technique produces the chilling effect of Tom Stoppard's "The Story" in the second volume. It too is written in the first person, the protagonist being a reporter who, simply by making a story available to the newspapers, provokes a suicide. Although he clearly feels some responsibility, he never fully deals with it. The story only implies its main point: journalists, like everyone else, are responsible for the consequences of their actions.

In the third volume, Roy Watkin's "Christine" is the most technically accomplished. In the form of a sequence of diary entries, it traces the descent into degradation of a schoolteacher who, learning that one of his pupils is being molested by her father, recognizes that he is himself attracted by her sexual vulnerability. He escapes raping her only because the neighbors report the father to the police. This story, too, gains its effects because of the contrast between the tone and the content, although here the teacher is aware of the underlying issues: unable to deny himself the pleasure of arbitrary power over the defenseless, he continues to remind himself of his horror of fascism.

· · ·

In 1969, in part because of the lack of "serious publications devoted to the short story," Penguin published three volumes of *Penguin Modern Stories*. They include the works of writers in English regardless of nationality; only about half of them are British. In contrast to the *Introduction* series, most of the names are familiar: William Sansom, Jean Rhys (to be discussed later), and Margaret Drabble, for example. The two entries by Sansom are typical of a certain kind of British story: they treat the relations between men and women in faintly ironic terms regardless of whether the relationships are romantic or mundane, focusing on the foibles not of the really rich but of the comfortably off who can afford sojourns at health spas or holidays in Morocco. In Drabble's "Crossing the Alps," a married man and a divorced woman with a retarded child manage to get away alone on a motoring holiday. He falls sick, and she takes the wheel for the six-hour trip across the mountains. The central conflict of the story lies between their feelings and the events of the journey. Although their idyllic vacation turns to disaster, their emotional attachment to each other increases as they gradually come to realize what they value in each other. She appreciates him the more because he remains loyal to an impossible wife; he appreciates her the more because she bears up under the burden of raising a defective child alone.

In *Penguin Modern Stories* also appeared one of the few pieces of experimental fiction published during the sixties. Giles Gordon's story, "Pictures from an Exhibition," having no narrative movement, seems more akin to the work of the Beat poets than to traditional fiction. It describes "Curves in Space" from Nikolai's Galaxy with great attention to spatial detail, but none to narrative and very little to character and mood.

· · ·

In 1964, 1967, and 1969, *London Magazine* published collections of stories chosen from those it had published during the preceding years. However, these volumes are not confined to the British short story, the first containing only slightly more than half by British writers, the last almost none. The first volume includes Ted Hughes's story "The Harvesting," which depends more on the irony of situation than did the three published in *Introduction*; the protagonist, come to the hayfield to slaughter the wildlife fleeing the mower, dies himself. The summer heat, the prickle of the stubble, the terror of the escaping rabbits are vividly rendered. Once more Hughes has caught the feel of the English countryside at a significant moment.

In addition to stories, the second volume contains essays by V. S. Pritchett, William Sansom, and Francis King. All bemoan the lack of support for the short story: outlets are scarce; the pay is bad; the reading public prefers novels. Yet all note the satisfaction the form affords the writer: since technical weaknesses are more obvious than in the novel, which can survive a few errors, a successful short story is correspondingly greater. Pritchett maintains that "the general weakness of [the short story] now is the lack of a distinctive personal voice." Sansom thinks that it requires a visionary mind to confer a metaphoric quality on the subject, making it mean more than it actually says: "It should echo. . . . Short, it should be enormous."

If the number of outlets for the short story had declined by 1950, the case of the long short story was even more desperate. In 1955 Macmillan started an annual anthology to ameliorate the situation, which apparently did improve in the sixties. On the tenth anniversary of the first volume of *Winter's Tales,* the editor, A. D. MacLean, observed that though the opportunities for the long short story were not good, they were better than they had been at the beginning of the series. In number 6 (1960) all the stories were appearing in print for the first time, whereas by number 11 (1965) seven out of the ten had already been published elsewhere. Throughout the remainder of the sixties, the proportion of first publication to reprinting remained approximately the same.

The nine volumes of *Winter's Tales* under discussion here (number 7 was devoted to the Russian short story) give a representative view of the long short story in England, indeed, in English-speaking countries generally during this period, for the work of Irish, Canadian, South African, American, and Nigerian writers is included. A glance over the tables of contents reveals names that were either well known at the time or have since become so, and they appear again and again: V. S. Pritchett, Brian Glanville, Muriel Spark, Margaret Drabble, Doris Lessing. All these writers, with the exception of Drabble, published collections of short stories during the sixties. Yet when one has read the entire ten-year series, the impression remains that neither the subject matter of the long short story nor its formal concerns changed much during the decade. One might suspect that this uniformity reflects the taste of its editor, but number 14, edited by Kevin Crossley-Holland, shows the same tendencies as those by A. D. MacLean.

All nine volumes contain the faithful recordings of eccentric actions of the middle classes and the predictable difficulties between men and women. The more complex stories center on the problems of the outsider: the difficulty of expatriatism, of separation from one's culture. Two stories on these themes from number 6 (1960) are memorable. "Prisoners" by Francis King centers on the problems of a German prisoner of war restricted to farm work but still writing. Christine, his girl, although in love with him, feels imprisoned on the farm with "oil lamps, earth-closet, well water" and a young baby. Their situation is made worse by Michael, the baby's godfather, who lavishes gifts on them; in fact, they have the cottage, poor as it is, only through his intervention. The villagers resent their having the cottage at all when so many British are homeless. Yet in his own way, Michael too is a prisoner, exiled from the country life he had loved as a boy and imprisoned by his childhood memories. "Survivors in Salvador" by Frank Tuohy also revolves around an expatriate, a Polish refugee who finds himself among outcasts, the dregs of the world. As he tries to deliver a package of cocaine, his contact is arrested. Some remnant of compassion prevents him from selling the narcotic to a young woman, and he throws the package away because he realizes it is killing him. Finally he learns to love and to comfort a young native woman for the rape she accepts as the way of the world; she has come to expect nothing of life except victimization.

Another distinguished story, the best of volume 10 (1964), is Jean Stubb's "A Child's Four Seasons." As the title indicates, it is structured around four heightened moments in the life of a child. Because of the events in which she plays an important part, she suddenly perceives life's transience. A school performance of *A Midsummer Night's Dream* is repeated in her own garden so that it can be recorded on film; up to this point, she has considered that "life was immobile." Now she knows that it will change perpetually and menace "everything she treasured." The story poignantly renders a five-year-old's struggle to recognize the existence of mutability, decay, and death.

Jean Rhys's stories, anchored firmly in a specific place and time, are among the best of the *Winter's Tales* series. "Outside the Machine" (number 6, 1960) describes the emotional states of a woman in the English hospital in Paris during the thirties. Rhys captures as perhaps no one else has the feel of despair, the sense of not belonging, the desperation of woman as victim. Inez is clearly not of the same class as the other patients; having barely enough money for her operation, she has to leave before she is completely well. The intensity of her feeling is manifested not by her attitude toward herself, which is matter-of-fact, but by her empathy with a neurasthenic woman who tries to kill herself in the washroom. The other women spurn the would-be suicide; with a husband and two lovely kiddies, what can she be lacking? Inez tries to defend her. When she has to leave the hospital, she discovers that she too has acquired a sympathizer; an old dying woman, seeing through her facade, slips her some banknotes. But Inez faces the outside world with the same weariness: "You can't die and come to life again for a few thousand francs. It takes more than that."

L. P. Hartley's "The Ghost Writer" (number 7, 1961) seems dated because it depends too heavily on narrative. It is an old-fashioned kind of story in which a twist, a humorous reversal, brings about the ending. A critic has employed a number of friends who specialize in subjects he knows nothing about to write his reviews for him. On his retirement he invites them all to a banquet, sending to each an invitation addressed to Henry McManus, his own pen name. A reporter, gaining entry by introducing himself as Henry McManus also, denounces his dishonesty. A titled friend tries to suppress the news item;

in the morning, the critic reads that McManus, clearly the reporter, was killed by a hit-and-run driver. This accident seems altogether too happy; if Lady Frances has taken care of him, as perhaps we should infer, her character has not been developed to make such an action believable.

The most impressive story of these nine volumes of *Winter's Tales* is Malcolm Lowry's "The Element Follows You Around, Sir!" which A. D. MacLean discovered after Lowry's death. The style progresses in the manner of a mad acrobat: Lowry takes incredible risks, developing his sentences, clause after clause, his paragraphs, sentence after sentence, until the structures threaten to break down under the momentum. But he is always in control. He remains so close to the thought process of his protagonist that the reader begins to entertain the possibility that the Captain's world view is plausible, that everything he touches does burst into flame, that he lives in the *Inferno*: "Yes, he said to himself, again, it's as though nature herself is having a nervous breakdown. Why not? Human beings have them." Certainly the story has both the distinctive personal voice considered essential by Pritchett and the visionary mind required by Sansom, which the British long short stories of the decade as revealed by *Winter's Tales* in general do not have.

Short Fiction in Collections

In spite of a general increase in the number of anthologies, the great bulk of the stories published during the sixties appeared in collections' by individual authors. Although these collections vary in theme and technique, in general they belong to the central tradition of English fiction concerned with placing people in the social scheme. Even the writers not primarily interested in social analysis give enough detail of background and setting to establish the social context of their characters. The largest proportion set their stories at home and abroad, reflecting the British experience as a declining world power. A number deal with the social distinctions between members of the middle class, whereas others concentrate on the boundaries between the middle and lower classes. A small group working outside the realist tradition uses imaginary worlds as settings.

At Home and Abroad.   In 1960 Joyce Cary's *Spring Song* was published posthumously. It includes all the stories that appeared under his own name, and with the exception of "Bush River," all were originally published during the fifties, most of them in such American magazines as the *New Yorker, Harper's,* and *Esquire.* In this collection they appear chronologically, though Winifred Davin, the editor, might have done well to arrange them under the headings Irish, African, and English stories.

The Irish stories are about childhood, and the African about young manhood. The English stories, by far the greatest in number, are more varied, though they concern primarily the odd twists of men's relationships with women. The stories in all three categories manifest Cary's vigorous prose style and his attention to detail. The African and Irish stories have a greater clarity, as though made spare by the passing of time until only the bleached outlines of the essential action remain. "Bush River" is one example, wherein Captain Corner in an excess of youthful spirits pits himself and his horse against a river in flood. An Irish story, "Out of Hand," shows the amazement of a child who has driven a second summer governess to the point of breakdown; the gap between his and the adults' perceptions of his behavior is skillfully delineated. Though some of the English stories are very good, as a group they tend to a jolly acceptance of eccentricity rather than the wonder and awe that characterize the African and Irish stories. "A Good Investment," the best of the English stories, and in many ways the best in the book, depends for its effect on a heavy irony. A man, choosing a second wife on a purely rational basis, marries a woman who has always taken care of the needs of her mother and sister. After they are married, he discovers that her family hardly needs to exploit her because she willingly sacrifices herself to them. Too late he realizes that he is in love with her and that there is no cure for her propensity to be exploited.

. . .

Even though they were written over a period of forty years, the stories in Alec Waugh's *My Place in the Bazaar* (1961) have, as he himself points out, "a certain undated homogeneity." All are written from the point of view of the same first person narrator, who, having no part in the events, is generally reliable. His role is to discover and interpret the action. As Waugh points out in his foreword, this technique allies him with "the storytellers of the Orient whom I have seen in Marrakesh and Baghdad, taking their place in the Bazaar, with their audience squatting round them on their haunches." This consistency of relationship among writer, material, and audience gives the collection a certain unity. The stories are arranged chronologically, and as they are all topical, they provide a commentary on the major concerns of British life since the 1920s. "A Stranger" takes place immediately after World War I; an army officer, a loner by nature, persists in fraternizing with a German girl. Demobilized, he returns to Cologne to marry her. Eventually he kills her during a quarrel and turns himself in at the police station next day. He escapes from prison during a general uprising, but his disfigured body is found in a side street. The narrator, however, later overhears him in a shop in Hampstead but, instead of accosting him, prefers to let him remain a man of mystery.

The other stories written in London from 1919 to 1926 are much slighter, turning on surprise endings and sudden twists in plot. Of those from 1926 to 1927, the most interesting is "The Last Chukka," the story of the white man's battle with the Siamese jungle. Though conceptually interesting, it is marred by clumsy technique; the narrator disappears after a few pages, leaving the rest of the story to be carried on in the third person. From the thirties comes "A Pretty Case for Freud," a slight story turning on a psychological surprise; the world of spies and ex–prisoners of war is represented in the stories from the forties and early fifties. From the latter comes Waugh's best known story, published in *Esquire* under the title "The Small Back Room Near Baker Street" and later made into the movie *Circle of Deception*. The main characters, casualties from World War II, are Lily Martin, an interviewer for Military Intelligence, and Douglas Eliot, the man she chose for a special mission behind the German lines. The story takes place in 1950 in Dominica, where Eliot, disgraced because he was captured and broke down under torture, has exiled himself and taken to drink. Propelled by the love aroused the night before he embarked on his mission and, presumably, by the guilt she still feels for setting him up, Lily has come to rescue him. He is never to know that she selected him because he would give the Germans the false information the British wanted them to have. Though much more complex than most of Waugh's earlier stories, it also depends on surprise rather than on psychological development. With its emphasis on narrative and its use of a reliable first-person narrator, Waugh's work is traditional, even old-fashioned.

· · ·

L. E. Jones's *The Bishop's Aunt* (1961) is old-fashioned not so much in technique as in the kind of world he writes about. His stories are not nostalgic: nostalgia is the regret for a gone world, and Jones does not admit that the kind of world he writes of, with values like those espoused by Trollope, has in fact gone. Evil seems pasteboard, almost imaginary, and subject to immediate dismissal by good. The title story is characteristic. Set in Eastern Europe in 1946, its events are contemporary with Sartre's "The Wall." A Red Army general is about to shoot twenty citizens because a soldier in the army of occupation has been assassinated. The mayor and the bishop offer themselves in place of the twenty, but the bishop's aunt saves the day by outmaneuvering the general. The characters would be at home in Barset.

• • •

In *The Admiral and the Nuns* (1962), Frank Tuohy vividly establishes the various settings. The industrial state in the South American interior where the wild dogs roam, the fashionable London gallery where a young woman tries to sell her lover's pictures, the drab surface of Polish life in the early fifties are so completely realized that they come to seem as important a component of the story as the characters. With the exception of "A Survivor in Salvador," first published in *Winter's Tales,* most stories center on the English as exiles either abroad or at home, where alienation takes the form of a change in social class.

The title story centers on the marital situation of an upper-class Englishwoman married to a Pole, a technician in a South American factory. Already the parents of three children and expecting a fourth, they live in squalor. At the British Club's Coronation Dance, Woroszylski gets drunk and tries to rape the seventeen-year-old daughter of one of the members. His wife, fathered by an admiral and educated by nuns, sticks by her husband; as there is nowhere else to go, they leave for Poland. In the narrator's mind, the blame attaches to Barbara: "She was far too stupid to realize how bad a wife she was." He calls Stefan merely a "dionysiac peasant." It is true that Barbara is imprisoned by her own habits of mind, but no more so than Stefan. For reasons that are not entirely clear, the narrator blames her, infected perhaps by the kind of misogyny made popular during the fifties by such works as *Look Back in Anger,* in which Jimmy Porter's abusive behavior toward his wife is condoned as the product of modern, enlightened views on social class.

In this collection, Tuohy's characters are confined more by their actions than by circumstances. In "Two Private Lives," for example, a consul and a press officer are both imprisoned by their erotic aberrations; although they detest each other, they become allies in their womanizing, visiting brothels together. Tripp engages indiscriminately in sexual relations, but the consul's activities focus on his camera, which finally brings him into conflict with the law, since taking photographs in the red-light district seems to be illegal.

Tuohy's longer stories are thoroughly successful, but the shorter ones like "Showing the Flag" depend too heavily on stereotypes or like "In the Dark Years" on telling rather than showing. Tuohy clearly needs length for the subtle development of setting and theme.

• • •

Guy Wilson's collection *The Three Vital Moments of Benjamin Ellashaye* (1962) reveals an uncertainty of tone. He often seems to be attempting some kind of irony, but too frequently his specific purpose is far from clear. In the title story, for instance, a young American with money works through a succession of events in which his idealism is undercut by his naiveté, at last bringing death at the paws of a lioness. It is amusing enough, but the point seems trivial: the perception that naive young Americans traveling abroad make mistakes hardly seems enough to support even a short story.

Then there are the stories like "The Honeymoon" and "For Her Ultimate Good," focusing on the relationships between men and women, the nature of which seems grounded in a Lawrentian worldview. In both these stories the women are humbled by men, Sally reconciling herself to her husband's notion of marriage, Joan returning to a degenerate who has insulted her only to be insulted the more. In the latter story this trauma sends Joan to God and the Church of England, but it is not persuasive enough to overcome the feeling that she, like Lawrence's heroines, is submitting to the superior blood power of the male.

• • •

The stories in Roald Dahl's *Kiss, Kiss* (1963), originally published in the *New Yorker, Esquire,* and *Playboy,* are set either in England or in New York, but setting is never as important as character, which is itself less crucial than narrative. Dahl's stories, modeled after O. Henry, turn on the surprise ending. The surprises involve some kind of revenge, usually of man on woman or woman on man. In "The Way Up to Heaven" the revenge is accidental. Harassed all her life by a husband who dawdles whenever she has a plane or train to catch, a woman rushes off to Idlewild without realizing that he is stuck in their private elevator, where she finds him on her return six weeks later. In "William and Mary" Mary's revenge is deliberate. William dies of cancer, having agreed to let a neurosurgeon try to keep his brain alive in vitro, one eye still attached. When Mary realizes from the "minute black pinpoint of absolute fury" in the eye floating in the basin that William, although totally impotent, is totally sentient, she insists on taking the brain home where he will see her smoking, drinking, watching television—activities he has forbidden during the thirty years of their marriage.

In other stories tricksters are beaten at their own game. In "Parson's Pleasure" an antique dealer posing as an antiquarian clergyman persuades a family of ignorant farmers to sell a rare Chippendale commode; he needs only the legs, he says, to attach to another piece of furniture. Thinking to help him when he goes to fetch his car, they saw off the legs and chop the commode into firewood. A similar mechanism caps the plot in "Mrs. Bixby and the Colonel's Coat." Mrs. Bixby, at a loss for a reason to introduce an expensive mink coat, a gift from her lover, into the household, hits on the idea of pawning it and telling her husband she found the ticket. She refuses to accompany him as she fears the pawnbroker will greet her like an old customer. Unable to wait until her husband comes home, she meets him in his office. When she opens the package, she finds only a mangy two-skin neckpiece. Clearly she cannot complain, even when she sees the receptionist leaving for lunch "exactly like a queen in the beautiful black mink coat that the Colonel had given Mrs. Bixby."

· · ·

The Stories of William Sansom (1963) contains thirty-three stories selected from those published over the previous fifteen years and includes an introduction by Elizabeth Bowen. The stories are conveniently arranged in chronological order, but this arrangement would have been more useful had they been dated.

The dominant aspect of Sansom's fiction is neither plot nor character in the usual sense. His characters are not particularized; they are more like transparent envelopes filled with the emotions called forth by the situations in which they find themselves. The young man trapped on the side of a gasometer in "The Vertical Ladder," for instance, is a pale ghost compared to the vividness of the fear transfixing him, as is Nor-

man Harris in "A Country Walk" compared to the malevolence of the
countryside pressing in on him. Sansom achieves these effects by the
cumulative description of sensation. Bowen points out that the crisis
of each story is "a matter of bringing sensation to a peak where it must
either splinter or dissolve." The setting is a contributory factor to the
sensation; it is intensely felt, from the fertile landscapes of Siena "where
one saw the dark-ribbed patchworks of the Tuscan fields map out to
the horizon beyond" to the frozen countryside of Norway with its "dark
brown wooden stations eaved with dragons' heads." The environment
becomes as animate as the characters, and caught up in the situation,
the reader participates directly in the emotion.

Sansom's virtuosity is such that he can force the reader to participate
in contradictory emotions in the course of a single story. This talent is
especially obvious in the stories told from two points of view, a technique Sansom favors in stories about the relationship of a man and a
woman. Typically, neither character understands the other's emotional
state. The story peaks at the suggestion of violent death—a suicide in
"Episode at Gastein," murder contemplated and rejected in "Waning
Moon," and planned and executed in "Various Temptations."

By the time this collection appeared in 1963, Sansom had been publishing stories for twenty years. His facility in the genre is the salient
characteristic of *The Ulcerated Milkman* (1966), the prevailing tone of
which is a light irony, jolly rather than satiric, a defense against sentimentality rather than a criticism of the world. For instance, the title
story describes the situation of a milkman with ulcers who, although
hating the commodity he makes his living from, has to drink it by the
gallon to neutralize his ulcer. Certainly the characters have moments
of revelation when the world seems larger or brighter, but this expansion of vision does not always carry through to the reader.

• • •

Most of the stories in Ruth Prawer Jhabvala's first collection, *Like
Birds, Like Fishes* (1963), were originally published in the *New Yorker*;
with one exception, they are set in India. That exception, however, "A
Birthday in London," deals with a theme Jhabvala repeatedly returns
to, the psychology of exile. All the characters, Jewish refugees from
Germany, have difficulty in adjusting to the present and glorify the
life they have been forced to leave. They long for the splendid comforts
of the past, the piano lessons at the Berlin Conservatorium, the vaca-

tions at Biarritz or Marienbad. This situation recurs throughout Jhab-vala's work: loss of the past is more disturbing than loss of country. One can be an exile in one's native land if it has undergone profound changes in a short period of time.

This kind of alienation has overtaken a number of her Indian char-acters, especially those educated in England or prominent during the great upheavals of mid-century. Such is the case with Dev Prakash, a poet who hoped to be "the Tagore of today." Exiled for twenty-five years in England, where he has written poems inspired by India, he returns home after Independence and feels even more an exile. But the day the Akademi Award is bestowed on him, he is at last reconciled to his native country, where he feels "this oneness, this love, this union of spirit." The young English wife of "The Aliens" suffers a different kind of alienation, in which her values of industry, frugality, privacy, and reserve are constantly denied by the noisy, irascible, sensual, com-munal life of her husband's upper-class family.

Jhabvala writes from the point of view of male and female, Indian and European. Her characters include irresponsible young men who refuse to take the jobs their families are desperate to find for them. In "The Interview" a young man, accustomed to immediate gratification, will not wait for a job interview because the last one he had was so unpleasant. The protagonist of the title story wishes to live as freely as the birds and fishes. Then there are the quiet, responsible, obedient men, like Ram Kumar in "A Loss of Faith" who supports a flock of female relatives by working for a tyrannical shopkeeper, against whom he perpetrates only one act of revenge. There are gentle, tender hus-bands and fathers, like Babu Ram of "Sixth Child" who, driven from his house by crowds of womenfolk, feels as sorry for his five little daughters as he does for himself. When his wife delivers another girl, he welcomes her in spite of his profound longing for a little boy to accompany him to his shop.

Jhabvala's women are richly varied. The grandmother in "The Old Lady" maintains the peace bordering on ecstasy she has attained through her guru in spite of the attempts of her family, products of the modern India, to involve her in their problems. The young woman in "The Widow," left in control of her husband's possessions because he wished to secure them from their relations, abandons her wealth in despair when an adolescent she conceives a passion for refuses her.

The stories in Jhabvala's second collection, *A Stronger Climate* (1968), most of which were also first published in the *New Yorker*, concentrate on the relations between Indian and European. The first group, subtitled "The Seekers," explores the various ways in which Europeans, attracted by the traditional mystery of India, look for spiritual, intellectual, or social solutions to their own problems. The answers frequently come as some embodiment of passion: Richard of "In Love with a Beautiful Girl," becomes infatuated with a young Indian woman who is interested in him only because he represents the cosmopolitan life of the diplomatic corps. Overlooking her taste for fast cars, he persists in seeing her as an incarnation of India, finding her everywhere, "in the streets, the sky, the air, in flowers and water and trees." In "Passion" a young Englishwoman becomes enthralled by an Indian because he is so ordinary, so typical of the clerk who supports a large family on a small salary. Even his ill treatment, which he thinks appropriate for a fallen woman, does not undercut her feeling for him. Once again it is India rather than the individual Indian that motivates passion.

The young woman in "A Spiritual Call" is similarly infatuated, except that her passion is ostensibly of the soul rather than the flesh. Daphne, following her guru from England, lives with his other disciples in an ashram; Swamiji clearly understands the sexual nature of the hold he has on the women, using it to persuade them to accompany him when he moves the ashram to the estate of a wealthy California widow. In "The Biography," a young Englishman becomes involved with the niece of a great dead leader. She longs for the glories of the old days, when she could hope that at some future time her uncle's ideal of complete emancipation for women could be realized. But history, as a minister says, has made India "no longer a place for Memsahibs." The biographer has found not the uncle's story but the niece's and cannot deal with the failure it implies.

The three stories collected under the subtitle "The Sufferers" concern Europeans beached in India by the tides of history. In "An Indian Citizen" Dr. Ernst, ex–office worker and part-time tutor, does not feel at home either with Lily, a new immigrant, or with Mrs. Chawla, an aristocrat. He is comfortable only with a small group of expatriates, much like those in "A Birthday in London," who are happiest when reminiscing. In "Miss Sahib," a retired schoolteacher who always preferred Indian children to the cold English girls, realizes at a noisy emotional funeral, complete with ritual burning, that she wishes to be buried with some restraint and a dignified prayer or two. In "The Man with the Dog," a Dutchman, caught in India by the war, is taken in by a rich widow, who offends her children by this unseemly behavior. Alienated from their respective cultures, the two of them cling together, she because of passion, he from necessity.

• • •

Doris Lessing published a number of collections during the sixties. Most of the stories in *African Stories* (1964) are reprinted from *This Was the Old Chief's Country* (1951) and *Five* (1953); however, two of her earliest short pieces appear here for the first time. Though slight in themselves, they are important for Lessing's development as a writer, as she herself points out in the introduction to this volume. "I see ['The Pig' and 'The Trinket Box'] as two forks of a road. The second—intense, careful, self-conscious, mannered—could have led to the kind of writing usually described as 'feminine.' The style of 'The Pig' is straight, broad, direct; is much less beguiling, but is the highway to the kind of writing that has the freedom to develop as it likes." Thus Lessing makes clear that she deliberately chose her style, clumsy as it frequently is, in the belief that it had greater possibilities than a more polished one.

"The Black Madonna," reprinted from *Winter's Tales* (number 3, 1957), describes the picture painted by an Italian prisoner of war to adorn the church in the village he has agreed to build for demolition practice. The white Rhodesians are scandalized that he has painted a black Madonna; he is scandalized that the troops will raze the church. Lessing says that this story is "full of the bile that in fact I feel for the 'white' society in Southern Rhodesia as I knew and hated it." The style is, as one might expect, "straight, broad, direct," giving the narrative ample room to include Lessing's observations on Rhodesian culture.

The stories in *A Man and Two Women* (1963) were originally published in such magazines as the *New Statesmen, Encounter,* the *Partisan Review,* and the *Kenyon Review.* They contain most of the themes of her major novels, including concerns that did not clearly emerge till later: the relationships between the individual and the collective, the influence of geography on character, the instability of the personality, the difficulty of the relationships between men and women, the importance of dreams and other nonrational states. This collection contains some of Lessing's finest work, the short story enforcing an economy noticeably absent from her novels. Nonetheless, the best are comparatively long, running between ten and twelve thousand words. The

title story analyzes the difference a baby can make in the family con-
stellation. The story is told mainly from the point of view of a close
friend of the new parents; as her own husband is abroad, the friend's
loneliness makes her more sensitive to the family dynamics. Jack is
uneasy because motherhood has changed his wife. Stella, the friend,
seeing Dorothy with the new baby, remembers the close physical tie
between mother and child, and it makes her miss her husband vio-
lently. It soon becomes plain that Dorothy feels she has abandoned Jack
and that he is an intruder. She tacitly gives Stella and Jack permission
to go to bed together; stirred by events, they curb their feelings only
because they understand how powerful they are.

An equally acute analysis of the relationships between men and
women takes place in "One Off the Short List." This story has a satiric
quality absent from "A Man and Two Women." It reveals the utter
shallowness and egomania of a middle-aged, second-rate writer who
maintains a sense of self by seducing women on his "short list." The
irony is all the greater because the story is written from his point of
view. He manages to worm his way into the house of a fashionable
stage designer; out of fatigue and boredom, she gives in when he demands that she sleep with him. To his horror, he finds that he can't
manage an erection; she, trying to get it over quickly, massages him,
and at the point when he thinks he can enter her, she "made him
come." He is humiliated because he clearly sees that she thought, "Yes,
that's what he's worth."

This collection also contains what is probably Lessing's most famous
story, "To Room Nineteen." It chronicles the decline of a woman who,
at first a contented wife and mother, discovers that the whole edifice
of family life, including four children, a mansion in Richmond, a char-
woman, an au pair girl, even a private "mother's room" at the top of
the house, stands on an insubstantial base. The structure evolved from
the love between her and her husband but now has acquired a momentum of its own, and she, discovering that she has no center, slips away
emotionally. The image of the dark river at the bottom of her garden
fills her thoughts. Wishing to subside into unconsciousness, she takes
a room in a sleazy hotel, spending more and more of her time there; at
last she turns on the gas and settles into bed, waiting for the dark river
to carry her away.

· · ·

Francis King's collection *The Japanese Umbrella* (1964) deals with the
middle-class Englishman in foreign surroundings. The relations be-

tween English and Japanese are complex, though there is a greater variety of character types among the Japanese than the English, who, at least if male, tend to be professors. The title story analyzes an Englishman's growth toward self-understanding. For years he had denied his resentment of the Japanese: even though he spent some years in a concentration camp, he resumed his post at a Japanese university after the war. When, however, he sees the loyalty of the staff and students turn from him to the new German teacher—who will also be giving classes in English conversation—he becomes enraged with them all, venting his spleen on a favorite student he thinks is exploiting him. He bursts out at the ingratitude of the Japanese, the words forcing themselves out "from some previously blind abscess . . . of hatred and contempt."

"A Corner of a Foreign Field" tells the story of an aging Japanese professor who all his life has surrounded himself with things English. An English colleague (whom King names after himself), tries to set him up with the fellowship in England he has always wanted, but he is amazed to discover that Professor Kuroda does not pursue his opportunities. At last the Japanese confesses: he has for so long lived with his idea of England—country of Jane Austen, Wordsworth, George Eliot, Hardy—that he is frightened of losing it by seeing England as it is.

Many of the stories in this collection deal with the difficulties of love relationships when the pair are from different cultures. King's women are more varied than his male Britishers, perhaps because they are defined by their relationships rather than by their jobs: they are daughters, middle-aged wives with youthful lovers, frustrated mothers, missionaries who ruin their careers and their personalities because of love.

The stories in King's second collection, *The Brighton Belle and Other Stories* (1968), many of which first appeared in *London Magazine* and *Harper's Bazaar,* deal with characters who organize their emotional lives in unconventional ways. The subtleties of unusual relationships are analyzed in persuasive terms: the Brighton Belle, a frowsy old earl's daughter fallen on hard times, earns the love of an aging chorus girl who nurses her in her last years; a wealthy old lady realizes, when her black servant leaves because of his shame at a homosexual affair, that she had lived for him just as much as he for her; a teenage boy, overcome by the physical and moral squalor of his family, poisons the lot of them. Two stories are particularly fine, both in content and in technique. The slighter of the two, "The Performance of a Lifetime," shows the way in which the pain of life can be transmuted into the very finest musical performance; "Loss" also deals with the precise relationship of life and art but comes at the problem from the opposite direction. A Japanese scholar, on recovering his manuscript, the work of a lifetime stolen and then returned by his jealous English girlfriend, realizes that every paragraph is shot through with the pain of life denied. The epiphany is described in the most moving detail: the sufferings of his docile undemanding wife, of his children, to whom he had been "a remote and minatory presence," of Eithne, whose body had dwindled, whose eyelids darkened, "whose glossy coil of hair had dried like grass in the midsummer sun."

• • •

The settings of Peter Ustinov's *The Frontiers of the Sea* (1966) are also foreign to many of his readers. The characters vary widely as to nationality; he writes of the Spanish in Spain, the French in France, the English in England, whose eccentricity, contrary to stereotype, lies in their psychology rather than their manners. The stories are amusing but hardly bear a second reading as they depend very heavily on an unexpected revelation or a twist in the plot. Consequently their appeal is not to the emotions; Ustinov shows the characters from the outside for the reader's amusement. The Yugoslavian soprano who lives out her life according to the plots of the more romantic operettas, the French inspector who does not know how to deal with a bunch of swindling elderly assassins, the bride who falls in love with a dog after he kills her husband, arouse no more than mild distaste.

• • •

Lawrence Durrell's *Sauve Qui Peut* (1966) is also set in alien surroundings. The exaggerated world of the expatriate British diplomat is colored by an eccentricity so profound as to render it farcical. This slight collection of nine stories is uniform in style and general approach, all narrated from the point of view of a single character, Antrobus, who is introduced as the narrator in the first sentence of each. In every case he tells an anecdote about some bizarre custom, happening, or escapade, his overt reason for which is to throw ridicule upon the foreigner, while Durrell's intention is to reveal the idiocy, short-sightedness, and insularity of the British diplomatic corps. The anecdotes are amusing—the reactions of the British delegation upon being invited to a ceremonial adult circumcision; the havoc wrought in the hearts of the corps when a pretty widow is appointed ambassador; the difficulties of smuggling out a valuable skeleton under the eyes of a concierge—but the material seems oddly dated as though all the characters have stepped out of the pages of P. G. Wodehouse. The writer of *The Alexandria Quartet* is hardly in evidence. Yet these stories must have wide commercial appeal; they were first published in a variety of magazines on both sides of the Atlantic, from *Playboy* and the *Weekend Telegraph* to *Mademoiselle* and *Argosy*.

• • •

Gordon Meyer also writes about expatriates; the stories in *Exiles* (1966) are set in South America, the remoteness of the locale emphasized by the stylized language. Although the subject matter and the mode of describing it are removed from daily life as we know it—the stories deal with the leisured classes, whose lives revolve around social relationships—there is a fidelity to another level of experience. The psychological penetration is so great that it approaches myth. The subterranean currents that dominate relationships, individual lives, and whole communities flow through these stories, which are carefully constructed, no extra detail or superfluous word remaining. Although the effect on the reader clearly depends on recognition, it is not recognition of the surface of life but of the emotional tides that, for instance, bring a young woman to a single moment's empathy with her hated mother-in-law, or make a daughter fall upon her father's breast in tears, not because of his welcome, but because of the hardness of his heart, which, in spite of his will, softens at her distress. These stories require, and repay, close attention.

• • •

Geoffrey Household's collection *Sabres in the Sand* (1966) shows English men and women against the backdrop of various European societies, as in the title story, or conversely, in "The Furry Dance," Europeans against British society. Either way, he uses recognizable national types: the English colonel who despises the Italians running the prisoner-of-war camp while admiring the efficiency of the Nazis; the English businessman who, finding himself compelled to engage in a duel in Romania, resolves to teach the natives a lesson; the Victorian governess in Hungary who defies the SS when they try to requisition her furniture; the Russian ballerina who attempts to describe her soul. He does use stereotypes, but they are absolutely necessary. A stereotype gives instant recognition, enabling a writer to play off the reader's expectations, which is exactly what Household does. Some of those expectations are fulfilled, some disappointed, but in either case, the prose is so controlled that the writer's intentions are never in doubt.

• • •

The cynicism of Graham Greene's *May We Borrow Your Husband? and Other Comedies of the Sexual Life* (1967) puts these stories in the category he has called "entertainments" to distinguish them from his serious fiction. They were originally published in such magazines as *Esquire, Vogue,* and *Playboy.* With a single exception, all have a first-person narrator, a writer who interprets the material he presents. In the title story he does so at great length, protesting his impotence to alter the course of events as he watches a pair of aging homosexuals in Nice separate a new husband from his bride. That their seduction improves the sex life of the honeymooners only makes more reprehensible the narrator's role of noninterference.

Most of the stories in this collection are trivial, depending on contrived situations and surprise endings rather than on psychological development. "Mortmain" shows the increasing alienation between a newly married pair brought about by the discarded mistress's conniving. After the wedding, she continues to be kind and considerate, including the bride in her thoughtfulness. She uses her key to enter the husband's flat, which the newly wedded pair are to occupy, to turn on the fires for their return. She hides a typed list of useful numbers in the telephone directory. She leaves on the bedsprings a sheet of instructions as to how often the mattress should be turned. The husband becomes infuriated at this solicitude, alienating his wife, who thinks his mistress sweet and helpful. "Beauty," "The Overnight Bag," and "The Invisible Japanese Gentleman" are slight sketches, but "Chagrin in Three Parts" and "Two Young People" are more substantial. The stories are set in Paris, and the pairs of people they depict are seen dealing with their loneliness in different ways. In the first story, a widow and a deserted wife agree to console each other; in the second, two expatriates, both neglected by their spouses, live for one evening as they might have done had they married each other fifteen years before.

None of the above stories has the moral dimension of "Cheap in August." An Englishwoman goes on vacation in Jamaica, half intending to have an affair. Her husband, a meticulous, sensitive American professor, hates "anything gross." At the resort, examples of grossness abound: elephantine women from St. Louis in Bermuda shorts and curlers; tight-trousered homosexuals; a huge man, old, fat, and frightened of dying alone in the dark. The Englishwoman takes the old man as a lover, once only and almost by accident. As they part, he points out that the two of them have a lot in common. She agrees "in order to quiet him," but clearly, in spite of the thirty years between them, her need to fend off time and death is the same as his. This story, though abounding in satirical observations, is fundamentally less cynical than the others in this collection.

The Middle Classes at Home.   Penelope Mortimer's stories, which have been published mainly in the *New Yorker,* concern the middle class. Most of the stories in *Saturday Lunch with the Brownings* (1960) revolve around problems in the lives of professional people. Although the characters rarely act out their pain, it throbs loudly through Mortimer's unequivocal prose. She does particularly well with the mutual exasperation of married couples whose relations are complicated by the presence of stepchildren. The title story describes the sorrow and sense of injustice a woman feels when she perceives that her husband favors his own children, slighting her daughter to whom he took a dislike when, a difficult infant, she accompanied them on their honeymoon. Children, in fact, figure largely in this collection, frequently as victims. "The Renegade," for example, a story with marvelously controlled variations in point of view, shows a daughter suffering the consequences of her father's cowardly retreat from his freethinking position. Mortimer does not let her characters off lightly, nor does she gloss over the more bitter aspects of domestic relations; consequently her irony tends toward satire.

. . .

V. S. Pritchett published three collections in the sixties, the first, *When My Girl Comes Home,* in 1961. With the exception of the title piece, which is some twenty thousand words, all the stories were first published in commercial magazines, the majority in the *New Yorker.*

Pritchett's world is peopled with the middle classes—small shop-keepers, librarians, accountants, solicitors, physicians—although oc-casionally a window cleaner or member of the small gentry appears. All are acutely class conscious, those with pensionable jobs despising those without, the librarians sneering at the workers on the line, the shopkeepers admiring the gentry so much that they never press them to pay their bills. Pritchett's fine ear for the nuances of class distinction is one of the main features of his comedy. This interest in social differ-ences leads to a certain dependence on stereotypes. The finest strokes of Pritchett's humor come from the confrontation between an individ-ual and an alien culture. "When My Girl Comes Home" depends on such a confrontation between the values of a small community in a London suburb and a young woman who has spent all the war years and some thereafter abroad. The Londoners believe that, because she spent some time in a Japanese prison camp, she would need "feeding up" when she came home; instead, traced and brought back by the efforts of Mr. Fulmino and various international committees for repa-triation, she appears on the railway platform with twelve pieces of cream-colored luggage containing, among other luxury items, six eve-ning dresses. The inhabitants of the community have neither a struc-ture of values to interpret Hilda's behavior nor a sufficient understanding of the world to perceive what has happened during her absence. The librarian, who tells the story ten years after these events have taken place, has spent the intervening years trying to come to grips with the phenomenon of Hilda. After Hilda's mother died, she left the suburb with the man who was to write her life story. The community expected the book to be about her exotic adventures during the war, but instead "it was about us."

One of the most common conflicts in Pritchett's work arises between a man and a woman who confuses and undermines him. In "The Wheelbarrow" the handyman-cum-preacher, who is well-versed in the temptations of the world, manages to avoid them, whereas the window cleaner in "The Necklace" does not understand that his wife is a path-ological liar and a thief until he gets to the police station. The narrator of "The Snag," though perceiving the organizing principle of his be-loved's character—"calamity was what she lived by"—does not under-stand that he cannot provide enough calamity to keep her going.

Other stories are more inclined to give a fuller character analysis. "The Fall" shows us the inner workings of an accountant who has lived in the shadow of his brother, a well-known actor; one night he exposes his rich fantasy life by playing a scene in an empty theater to an imaginary audience. "Just a Little More" concerns an old man who still plans a future, his greed for life clearly manifested as an extraordinary interest in food. "On the Scent" shows an ex-military type who, working in a museum and living in the past, recognizes by the smell of toilet water a German spy he trailed during the war. "The Citizen" concerns a middle-aged woman whose father, larger than life, stands between her and a satisfactory love relationship.

The last story in this collection, "The Key to My Heart," is also the title story of Pritchett's next collection, published in 1963. Subtitled *A Comedy in Three Parts,* it chronicles the entanglements of an upwardly mobile baker with the gentry at Heading Mount. The baker's mother, Mrs. Frazer, who plays a small part in the plots of all three stories, is one of Pritchett's most successful characters. Her class and character instantly recognizable, she is nonetheless highly particularized. The goings-on of a family named the Bracketts occupy in her emotional life a place similar to that of soap opera in Middle America. She is mesmerized by the charm of Noisy Brackett, whom she refers to as "the Wing Commander," cashing checks for him when his wife, Sally, keeps him short of money. She is delighted when, in "Noisy Flushes the Birds," he returns to Heading Mount, imagining that "love—the one and only—" is at last triumphant. She is even reconciled to the engagement of her son, Bob, to a Major Dingle's daughter, who is above his station. This engagement excites Sally Brackett's competitiveness. She is well aware of Bob's infatuation and, during the commotion aroused when Noisy makes off with a case of stuffed birds, manages to keep him out all night, effectively breaking off the engagement. In the last story, "Noisy in the Doghouse," Bob finally manages to get Sally into bed. Noisy outwits Bob in a practical joke and, taking advantage of Sally's anger toward Bob, reconciles with her.

All three stories are told in the first person from Bob's point of view; he is a bystander to the main action, which centers on the relationship between Sally and Noisy. Pritchett's great achievement is that Bob sees and reports more than he understands or suspects. Much of the comedy arises from the conflict between the breakdown of the British class structure and the rigidity of class attitudes. Bob's mother, for instance, is so impressed by Sally Brackett's station that she thinks Bob will ruin his business if he insists on having his bill paid.

Most of the stories in Pritchett's third collection of the decade, *Blind Love* (1969), were previously published in the *New Yorker,* with the exception of the title story. Once again Pritchett exploits the longer narrative form to full advantage. It allows him to give enough information about the two main characters' past lives and the difficulties of their developing relationship to be convincing. The contrast and balance between Armitage's visible handicap, his blindness, and Helen Johnson's invisible one, the birthmark staining her shoulder and breast, are gradually developed so that they do not seem forced. Both make errors in their dealings with the other because they cannot see past their own humiliations. Helen cannot tell him about her disfigurement until she plans to leave him; losing her temper because he has taken up with a faith healer, she shouts the truth to him across the dinner table. She has already said, "I love Mr. Armitage as he is," but she cannot believe that Armitage feels the same toward her. In fact, this story is Helen's; she finds her imperfection more difficult to deal with because it is not real except in her relations with men. His handicap undermines his sense of himself much less.

Other stories in this collection depend less on character development and do not have the same depth, although their subjects may be inherently as profound. The central situation in "A Debt of Honor," for instance, is as complex as that in "Blind Love" but, insufficiently worked out, does not seem as credible. Even though we have been told that Mrs. Thwaite was first attracted to her husband by "a sudden hungry jealousy," we find it hard to believe that when he returns to her after nine years she really wishes she had twelve hundred pounds to give him. Similarly "The Skeleton" and "Our Oldest Friend" would benefit by a more thorough development.

"The Speech" contains the best character analysis in this collection. Sally Gray, with her big belly and double chin, appears at first as one of Pritchett's typical butts. But as the story progresses it becomes apparent that she has taken pains to become "Good old Sally." An aging socialist who abjured a personal life to work for idealistic causes—the Spanish civil war, the Second Front, peace campaigns, the Hungarian uprising, and now banning the tests—she assesses her life while giving a speech to a sparse crowd in her hometown where they do not even know how to spell her name. Her voice assumes a life of its own while she comes to terms with the working class she has always spoken for: "You never gave me a minute to read a book, look at a picture or feed the spirit within me. . . . You're ugly, and you've made me as ugly as you are." Her coarse humor prevents self-pity, but enhances the tragedy of her life. This story points at the dark underside of existence; its irony is less surface, more pointed toward the contradictions of a flawed universe.

• • •

H. E. Bates published four collections of new stories during the sixties, but only *Now Sleeps the Crimson Petal* (1961) can truly be said to measure up to his highest standards. The title story chronicles the slow realization of a butcher's wife that the "pheasant and partridge class" is gone forever. Even when the local mansion, standing empty since World War II, is opened up again, the new owner is nothing like the gentry who used to order "barons of beef and saddles of lamb . . . and the choicest cuts of venison." Living alone, he renovates the mansion in an eccentric way, inviting to a weekend party crowds of drunken, fashionable, vulgar people; he is clearly nothing but a jumped-up "sausage and scragender."

The passage of time likewise devastates the colonel in "Where the Cloud Breaks." Retired, he lives in an isolated cottage without a telephone or television set. He owns no watch and has given up the *Times*. His only contact is a spinster lady whose cottage is three meadows away; he has taught her semaphore and attracts her attention by whistling when he wants to signal. They exchange homemade treats and meet several times a week for tea, but the relationship is ruined when her sister gives her a television.

"The Enchantress" is the story of a social climber who works through a series of marriages until at age fifty she is the Countess Pinelli. It is told from the point of view of a young man who was infatuated with her in his youth; as Bertha is presented only from the outside, her thoughts and feelings must be inferred. She is beautiful at ten, at fourteen, at fifty, but her main charm appears to be that she has no attitudes or interests of her own, adopting them like a chameleon from the current man in her life.

Although Bates occasionally places a story in the Pacific or Caribbean, these settings are not so effective as those in the English countryside, which Bates lovingly describes: "In summer time the chalk flowered into a hill garden of wild yellow rock rose, wild marjoram, and countless waving mauve scabious covered on hot afternoons with nervous dancing butterflies." The vividness of detail, particularly in the stories set in the past, makes objects in the environment seem animate, as they might be to a child. "The Place Where Shady Lay,' for instance, is told from the point of view of a young boy whose senses are still fresh: "Strange blue eyes of mould shone from the rotting oranges under the golden lamplight and curious winey odours filled the night air." Learning of the glorious past and ignominious present of Shady Baxter, legendary runner and county boxing champion who was imprisoned for killing a man in a fight, he seeks him out to give him a loaf of bread. He discovers Shady "sleeping rough," covered with brown paper and old sacks. At first sight the animate and inanimate cannot be distinguished: "There was something odd about the sacks. They had a big yellow swede-turnip lying in the centre of them. There was something odd about the turnip too. It sprouted pale-elderberry-colored shoots and the shoots, in turn, were held by a discoloured hand." For this specificity and vividness of detail, Bates draws on the memory of his own Northamptonshire boyhood.

• • •

Noel Blakiston's collections, *The Lecture* (1961) and *That Thoughtful Boy* (1965), deal with the upper middle classes—professors, vicars, gentry with their muniment keepers—who constantly find themselves in situations that are no surprise to us but are to them. "That Thoughtful Boy," for instance, shows the final break between a professor of poetry and the ne'er-do-well son, who, from the father's point of view at least, merely pretends to be a painter and uses that status to flaunt his egoism. This behavior complicates the professor's response, as he has always defended the rights of poets like Byron or D. H. Lawrence to their "overweening egoism." Another example of this kind of irony is "Damn Braces." Here the parents are made uneasy by their three sons' joy in vandalism and torture. The boys' favorite reading is Fox's *Book of Martyrs.* They prefer Domenico Berto, whose nose and ears were severed and cheeks cut open before he was put to death with red-hot pincers. Their favorite games, toward which their parents never show any disapproval, involve imaginative exercises in torment and mayhem. Their father tries to convince himself that by the time they have grown up they will have worked off their destructive instincts and become pacifists, Buddhists, or demonstrators against nuclear weapons.

Blakiston has a fine eye not only for the delusions of parents about their children but also for their delusions about themselves, specifically their hypocrisy in the face of the British class system. A seventeen-year-old, back from his first foray into the working-class world, explains that he likes it, enjoys the people he met, and wishes to get a job instead of going back to his prep school where he will study for Oxford. All his father's comments about the class system, he suddenly sees, are hypocritical. He now realizes that his father despises the working classes—even worse, thinks the way they speak, their behavior in general, is hilariously funny, good only for a laugh.

. . .

Sylvia Townsend Warner, whose publishing career began in the 1920s, is remarkable for her technical mastery. The stories in *A Spirit Rises* (1962), many of which were first published in the *New Yorker,* and *The Stranger with a Bag* (1966) demonstrate the sureness of her touch, the precise understanding of her limits. She has a fine eye for the details of decaying middle-class life: gas brackets, sardine sandwiches, hot-water bottles. Again and again she catches the exact degree of the English preoccupation with food: the locum recollecting the bread sauce, the sister asking "if they are sure they didn't want ham" for tea. Her shifts in point of view are subtle, something not easily accomplished in a short story. She always delivers what she promises. But her irony is meant to distance rather than to satirize; she intends to amuse more often than to involve. Her stories sometimes end with a reversal, as in "A Question of Disposal," where in the last paragraph the spinster imagines that her brothers and sisters are competing for her labor rather than trying to dispose of her. In short, her style is, in Lessing's words, "careful, self-conscious, mannered," designed above all to entertain rather than to involve or to edify.

. . .

Although Elizabeth Taylor's conception of the short story is more robust than Warner's, she has much in common with her. She finds the same kind of situation interesting, the same kind of characters worthy of attention. The moral base of her work is sturdier, but the middle-class world her characters inhabit is visibly similar. She is not as skillful, rarely matching Warner's elegant turn of phrase, and frequently making arbitrary shifts in point of view.

The stories in *A Dedicated Man* (1965), most of which were published in the *New Yorker,* focus on lonely old women, trapped adolescent girls, isolated and alienated females in general. The title story, one of the best in this collection, is really Edith's story rather than

Silcox's, the "dedicated man." A waiter and waitress, they pretend to be married in order to get jobs at a good hotel that has only one bedroom for the two of them; they exist in silent partnership until Edith discovers the existence of Silcox's son, a young man of twenty. The ending is a sudden reversal, though an appropriate one. A different sort of story, "The Thames Spread Out," is organized around the image of the flooding river. Rose, surrounded by the rising waters, and trapped in the upstairs of her love nest, finds the resolution to walk away from the whole relationship when the flood subsides. In "Voices" a woman listens to the women on the other side of a wall and then tries to enjoy her visit to Delphi by imagining what their responses have been. Here, as is frequent in Taylor's stories, the central image connotes isolation.

• • •

The stories in Rumer Godden's *Swans and Turtles,* most of which were originally published in such magazines as *Ladies' Home Journal, Harper's,* and *Collier's,* are prefaced by descriptions of the incidents they are based on and arranged to form a record of the events and ideas important in her life and thought. Her awareness of the appropriate detail makes her particularly successful in evoking psychological states through setting. The house in "Time Is a Stream," with the ha-ha and the green light filtered through the elms, makes real the despair of the aging woman who, unable to look after herself, no longer cares where she lives or if she lives at all; and the cinder path in "You Need to Go Upstairs," suggested through the senses of touch and smell, clearly renders a blind child's determination to be independent.

The most successful stories had their genesis in childhood trauma: Godden and her sister suffered when they were sent to England to learn the manners and accent proper to middle-class girls. The solidity of a prosperous Edwardian household so reassuring to the proprietors is a source of terror to the smaller inhabitants; five-year-old Alice in "Down under the Thames" clutches "her frilled drawers, . . . her knees and fingers desperately clinging" to the mahogany seat that stretches from wall to wall, while the willow pattern china pan looks big enough to drown in. The adults seem as unaccommodating to the children as is the furniture: Aunt Gwenda rips all the stitches out of Alice's embroidery with the injuction *"That* will teach you!" Alice, angry at last in a house where her typical response has been fear, flushes away her rejected traycloth.

A similar reversal occurs at the end of "The Little Fishes." Two sisters find the English boarding school run by Anglican nuns totally foreign; the climate, the bare building without privacy, the emphasis on competition and sportsmanship make no sense to the girls from India, "where people are not in a hurry." The headmistress, whose puffy cheeks swell when she grows angry, calls them "the scum of the school" in front of a visiting priest, who, when the elder sister raises her hand to protest the insult, silently pressures Sister Gertrude to apologize. The contrast between the lush Indian garden the children left behind and the cold, dark school parallels the difference between the loving treatment accorded by family and servants and the bullying of the girls and nuns.

• • •

In setting, tone, and narrative style, Penelope Gilliat's stories seem most similar to the work of Warner and Taylor. Like theirs, most of the stories in *What's It Like Out? and Other Stories* (1968) were first published in the *New Yorker.* The stories are long, but the style is crisp. Gilliat deals in eccentric types: Fred and Arthur, vaudeville comedians who build their turns around scenes from Shakespeare; an incompetent woman doctor who refuses to marry the father of her child because she is opposed to marriage in principle; a customs officer who does not know how to deal with the breakup of his marriage; a professor with a library so weighty it breaks down the joists of his Elizabethan house. Her stories are memorable because of the strength of characterization and the selection of detail.

The Working Class.   John Wain, Kingsley Amis,and Alan Sillitoe, all "angry young men" who published collections during the sixties, are faithful observers of the point where the middle and lower classes intersect, and their purposes are generally more political than are those of the preceding writers. Brian Glanville, on the other hand, mainly a writer of sports stories espousing working-class values, has no political intentions, and those of Jean Rhys, Nell Dunn, and A. L. Barker are implicit rather than overt.

• • •

The two collections John Wain published during the sixties are chiefly remarkable for their variety of form and content. The anecdote, the fantasy, the character sketch are used, as are first- and third-person narrators, male and female, adults and children. Most of the stories in both collections were first printed in such publications as *Harper's Bazaar, London Magazine,* and *Ladies' Home Journal.* In the first, *Nuncle and Other Stories* (1960), alienation and loneliness are pervasive. "A Message from the Pig-Man" deals with the imagined terrors of childhood; in "A Few Drinks with Alcock and Brown" a young man remembers that the first time he kissed his ex-fiancée was "the only real thing in his life." The title story is ironic in structure and theme. A once-famous novelist imagines that marriage to a reliable woman will cure him of his writing block; he discovers, however, that his father-in-law can write and soon comes to the arrangement that the father-in-law's books will be sold under the famous author's name.

Wain's second collection, *Death of the Hind Legs* (1966), shows his firm grip on a recognizable British world or, rather, worlds, for the worlds of the middle and working classes do not really overlap. Wain has a fine ear for the dialects of both classes as well as a profound interest in their psychology. The working-class narrator of "King Caliban," who makes his simple brother a wrestler but refuses any responsibility when he breaks down, is clearly distinguished in thought process, sentence structure, and vocabulary from the middle-class narrator of "Further Education," an Oxford graduate who visits a couple he has not seen in twenty years, only to find that the wife still fascinates him. The differences in thought and manners between the dons and the businessman are skillfully delineated, as are those between Penelope, the mistress who gave up her job to be treated like one, and Elsie, the aging dresser for the Gaiety Theater.

The title story, chronicling the passing of vaudeville, is the most moving story, as "Further Education" is the most profound and "Down Our Way" the funniest. In the latter Wain catches the typical interfamilial tensions of the working class: the battle between men and women and between old and young revealing the constant one-upmanship typical of cockney culture. A journalist in blackface answering advertisements for rooms to let has been refused lodgings in East End homes. Dad thinks up a bright idea: if the phony "darkie" comes, they are to let him the room, pretending to believe his story. To the consternation of the family, Mum rents the room to a West Indian. How, the family demands, will Mum get rid of this unwelcome lodger? One cannot fling out a black just because of his color. Here the story takes a turn. Mum points out that there never was a lodger one did not have to make allowances for, the habits of men being what they are. This one she will make no allowance for; after all, she has not lived fifty years "to end up not being mistress in her own house." Dad looks up from his paper as though he sees her for the first time—and, for the first time, says nothing at all in response.

* * *

Brian Glanville published five volumes of short stories during the decade: *A Bad Streak,* 1961; *The Director's Wife,* 1963; *Goalkeepers Are Always Crazy,* 1964; *The King of Hackney Marshes,* 1965; and *A Betting Man,* 1968. The stories previously appeared in such magazines as *Winter's Tales,* the *Saturday Evening Post, London Magazine,* the *Transatlantic Review*—all publications of quality fiction. And yet one wonders why. Was there really such a large audience for such very trivial stories? They are either long anecdotes about soccer players or sketches of the more obvious character types in England and abroad. Glanville has a fine eye for the stereotypical Italian, the East End football hero, or the upwardly mobile English Jew, but he rarely does anything remarkable with his material. One of his football stories, "The Man behind the Goal" (1968), however, is more engaging. The man in question is a social outcast living in a Salvation Army hostel; his one passion is the theory of soccer. He plays in the park every day, eventually finding a disciple, a lumpish schoolboy, to train. But he fails to train the boy, and being out in all weathers, he finally succumbs to pneumonia. He ends as a wasted derelict in a public ward; the one thing he had to offer the world was useless.

Stories with such depth are rare in Glanville's work, however. His popularity in Britain stemmed from the authenticity of his detail. A sportswriter, he knew his subject thoroughly, but a fiction writer needs to do more than simply report what he knows.

* * *

The stories in Kingsley Amis's collection *My Enemy's Enemy* (1962) were previously published in such magazines as *Encounter, Esquire,* and the *Spectator*; "My Enemy's Enemy" was also selected for *Winter's Tales,* and "Interesting Things" and "Something Strange" for *Pick of Today's Short Stories.* Amis has always been a comparatively intellectual writer, and this collection is no exception.

The most ambitious, "I Spy Strangers," is perhaps too weighted with character, incident, and density of meaning to be immediately engaging. It is a period piece, capturing the mood not only of the army officers and men it overtly analyzes but of the entire nation at the end of World War II. A story of some twenty thousand words, it asks what will become of postwar Britain. The fight between the old conservatives and the new socialists is represented by the struggle between the commanding officer of a regiment stationed in Belgium in 1945 and his junior officers and men. The complexity of the ideological debate is accurately reflected by the variety of political views and the men who hold them. Rank is not a reliable indicator of political position: Major Rawleigh himself is a hidebound old Tory, Lieutenants Hargreaves and Ascher are socialists, and Sergeant Doll is clearly a fascist who thinks it a pity that the Germans and British did not together wipe out the Russians. The political point is underlined by the mock parliament convened by the regiment to pass away the evenings. The major consoles himself that England will muddle through, but the reader knows the England he imagines is not the England of the future.

• • •

Like the fiction of the angry young men, A. L. Barker's short stories concern the working as well as the middle classes. She published two collections during the sixties, the first of which, *The Joy-Ride and After* (1963), consists of only three pieces, each long enough to be a novella. The title story is especially well done. Concise despite its length, it offers a multiplicity of characters, revealing the jealous lust of Rumbold, the bullying of Brind, and the covetousness of Joe, a sixteen-year-old garage hand who wants to get his hands on a car more than he wants to get them on a woman. The incipient violence in the older men's lives manifests itself overtly in Joe, who borrows Brind's car for a joyride with a girl he does not care about; in the dark on a bypass he kills a woman, thus putting himself in Esther's clutches forever. The other two novellas in this collection are equally notable for their analyses of isolation.

Several of the stories in *Lost upon the Roundabouts* (1964) deal with the relationships between adolescents and members of an older generation. The first, "View in a Long Mirror," tells the story of a cub reporter who hangs around the house of an aging actress and her companion after his older colleague, satisfied with his interpretation of the companion's story, has left for a pub. The young man stumbles on a grave in the backyard; the companion, for many years the actress's understudy, tells the young reporter about their relationship. Living together for fifty years, they even aged alike, so that seeing the actress was like seeing herself in a long mirror. But no longer: as the grave's a busy place, "there's a lot to choose between us now."

"The Return" tells the story of a twelve-year-old's liberation from his father's shadow. Coming to the farm where the father grew up, they meet a neighbor who inadvertently reveals that many of the tales the father has told his son of his own capabilities and courage are clear exaggerations, even lies. The son takes his revenge upon the father and collapses in laughter at his triumph. This story is in stark contrast to "The Whip Hand," in which a neglected child creates a superego called Brewer from whom he tries to run away all his life. The last story, "A Question of Identity," analyzes the effects of retirement on a chief accountant. He takes an interest in a young woman who is trying to escape from her family, only to realize that his plans for her future were constructed with him at the center, guiding, instructing, commanding the operation.

Barker's stories deal not with bizarre or eccentric characters but with the inner peculiarities ordinary people usually manage to hide. They are familiar British types from either the working or lower middle class. From the outside, they would be recognizable comic types, but from within they assert their individuality. Her style, broad and direct, is appropriate for the description of her fictional world.

• • •

The title of *Statement against Corpses* (1964) by B. S. Johnson and Zulfikar Ghose seems to describe the intention of the book rather than the contents. The collection is not particularly successful, although the stories are technically adequate. There have been better analyses than these of the psychological difficulties of angry young men educated out of the class into which they were born, of men who never outgrew their schooldays, and of the marital difficulties brought about by the egoism of husbands and the stupidity of wives. The one story that might at first glance seem experimental, "Broad Thoughts from a Home," is clearly derived from the Ithaca section of *Ulysses*. While any attempt to bolster the short story as a literary form is a worthy enterprise, this one cannot have had a very positive effect.

• • •

Nell Dunn's world, peculiarly her own, is the matriarchal world of working-class women. *Up the Junction* (1963) stands out by virtue of its form, its content, its sales record of half a million copies, and the film into which it was made. It consists of sixteen short sketches, four of which were originally published in the *New Statesman*. All are in the first person and the present tense; the immediacy of effect is reminiscent of Jean Rhys's work. Nell Dunn's narrator records the life around her without comment, thus accentuating the horror the reader feels at these tales of deprivation.

These stories show the lives of cockney women, mostly very young ones, but include enough aging women to show the future that lies before them. The stories are unified by the same narrator, and by characters who reappear: thieves, grafters, whores, juvenile delinquents, illegal abortionists, bagwash ladies, tally-men. The difficulty of the young women's lives as they try to eke a living working in a clip joint or to bring up their children in single rooms is effectively evoked; but the women themselves, who take for granted that one goes into the factory on leaving school at fourteen, do not seem to notice how hard their existence is. They have a camaraderie that is proof against the men who exploit them; they know their mothers will always come to their aid—as indeed they do. Sylvie's mother appears on the street in her nightdress to beat up her son-in-law when he attacks her daughter; Rube's mother holds her while she delivers her baby, premature because of a botched abortion. The reader is heartened by the courage of these women, whose lives are certainly worse than the heroines of Rhys's work, yet who, expecting so little, do not seem to notice how badly off they are. They simply survive.

• • •

Behind Alan Sillitoe's fiction lurks a great discontent with contemporary social conditions. But his male characters do not merely dislike the broad social arrangements that determine the overall course of their lives; they take out their frustration on their women. One could feel more sympathetic toward them if they had the same kind of compassion for those they bully as they have for themselves when others bully them. Although Sillitoe occasionally writes from the point of view of a woman, he is not particularly adept at figuring out how women's minds work. "The Good Women" from *The Ragman's Daughter* (1963) is a case in point; Liza Atkins, who spends her days fighting the class war, seems unfocused. Sillitoe captures the working-class temper, but his stories about it are often only character sketches, as, for instance, "The Other John Peel." The stories about class war are so flat that

Sillitoe appears to have lost interest in the subject. In fact, he treats more vividly the relations of men and women; "The Magic Box," for example, shrewdly analyzes a marriage that goes wrong.

Guzman, Go Home (1968), of which the title story and "Isaac Starbuck" had been previously published in *Winter's Tales,* concentrates less on the recording of lower-class types and more on the psychological analysis of characters. The first story, "Revenge," is told in the first person: because of the matter-of-fact tone, it takes a while to understand that the narrator is insane. The first clear indication is when he takes a poker to the wedding presents as soon as his friends have left the reception. At first it seems an extreme but not insane reaction to a social convention he has always despised, but as we are drawn further into the story, we begin to wonder how much of what he says is true. His wife, he maintains, is clearly insane, having done time in a mental institution. After she attempts to murder him by putting sleeping pills in his morning tea, he tells the psychiatrists that he didn't mean to kill himself—it was a mistake. He discovers by accident what the psychiatrists really think about him; even so, the diagnosis of paranoia might be wrong.

This story is much more subtle than Sillitoe's early ones, whose themes were too obvious and didactic, as for instance, "The Loneliness of the Long-Distance Runner." The same kind of subtlety distinguishes most of this collection. "The Road" shows us the course of the battle of the sexes between a waiter and his wife; "The Rope Trick" analyzes the part of memory in establishing the lifelong significance of a single meeting.

• • •

Jean Rhys began to publish in the twenties, but dropped out of sight during the forties and fifties and began to write and publish again in the sixties. Although her style is distinctive, she avoids the impression that technique is all. Perhaps it is because her voice is so much her own, her narrator's focus so close to the consciousness of her main characters, that she avoids a mannered style.

Tigers Are Better-Looking (1968) contains eight stories not previously collected in addition to a selection of stories from *The Left Bank* (1927). Most of them were previously published in *London Magazine*; "Outside the Machine" appeared in *Winter's Tales* (number 56, 1960). Her heroines are all much like Inez: poor not only in money but in spirit and extraordinarily sensitive to the cruelties of social relations. "Till September Petronella" shows a young woman suffering from depression in spite of the fact that, earning five pounds a week, she has more money than ever before. She passes through a series of social situations that do not affect her except to reinforce her belief that human beings are not particularly worthwhile. At last escaping from the country cottage where she had expected to spend a vacation, she returns to London, and out of a kind of depressive boredom exacerbated by her poor opinion of herself, she allows herself to be picked up by a young man. The only thought that makes her cheerful is that she can end it all if she wants to.

Most of the stories are set in the period between the wars. Rhys uses a limited point of view, so that the characters' emotions are felt rather than described, the flavor of the times evoked rather than recalled. Her style is matter-of-fact rather than sentimental: the details of clothing, furnishings, and so forth exist as solid objects in the environment. They are in fact more solid than the people who use them, for neither the heroines of the stories nor the people they mix with have any value. The human race seems a poor affair—aggressive, carnivorous even; and, after all, tigers are better-looking.

Imaginary Worlds.   Although the preceding writers vary in social focus, their settings are part of a realistic world, recognizably similar to the one inhabited by readers. There is, however, a small group of writers who set their stories in imaginary worlds containing supernatural or magical elements, or organized on the principles of the dream or nightmare. L. P. Hartley is a case in point. In 1961 he published *Two for the River* as part of his *Collected Stories,* which, however, contains only stories previously published in other collections.

In general the short story over the last quarter century became more social and psychological, but Hartley's often turn upon the supernaturally macabre or the fortuitous, as in "Someone in the Lift." A small boy persists in thinking he sees a shadowy man through a lift's grille. When told it is Santa Claus, he looks forward to seeing his father in that disguise and imagines that he too will arrive in the lift. Impatient, the boy summons the lift only to find his father's bloody corpse slumped in the corner. A similar sense of events controlled by unseen forces moves through the title story, in which a writer's house is saved by the interference of a swan who seems to be an agent of the river.

• • •

Graham Greene's *A Sense of Reality* (1963) is set in a magical world. None of the four long stories is self-contained; incomplete though not exactly fragmentary, they clearly mean more than they say, like an allegory lacking the key that would make all things plain. Here is typical Greene material: the tortured ratiocinations of a nonbeliever who yearns to take his own disbelief as proof that the church is right; the ironies of a situation in which a leprous clerk's suicide counterpoints a general's illegal gambling. Also dramatized is a science-fiction nightmare common in the work of a number of contemporary writers and filmmakers: the child who, long after Armageddon destroys civilization, discovers with awe and wonder the artifacts left behind.

The longest story, "Under the Garden," develops at great length the memories—or are they dreams he had as a child?—of a man who, under sentence of cancer, expects soon to die. After his interview with the surgeon, he returns to his boyhood home. Reading a story he wrote for the school magazine, he tries to recall the experience on which it was based. Yet he cannot ultimately decide whether he imagined the old couple who lived under the oak tree with their treasure, their golden pond, and the memories of their beautiful daughter, now escaped to the world above. This story is strangely haunting; it absorbs and satisfies.

Behind the surface of all Greene's fiction lies another world, the structures and dynamics of which are very different from the one the reader lives in. Occasionally the veil separating the two wears thin and the one beyond—the real one, the title of this collection implies—appears dimly through it.

. . .

Muriel Spark's world is part of an eternal, not a conditional, universe. A published poet and critic, she did not begin to write fiction until she converted to Catholicism, and her stories are built on the tough intellectual stability the faith gave her. The pieces in *Collected Stories* (1968) were published mainly in the *New Yorker*. Heavily plotted, they rely on coincidence and the supernatural to carry the theme, as do her novels. "The Black Madonna" (a title used also by Doris Lessing) is probably the most successful of these stories. It carries a message of arbitrary justice with religious overtones, implying that this world is controlled from without. A couple who pride themselves on their lack of prejudice find, after praying for a baby in front of a bog oak Madonna, that the child, though beautiful, is black. "The Portobello Road" is told by a ghost who delights in appearing before her murderer. The final paragraph reflects that the young take for granted "the glory of the world, as if it would never pass."

A point made frequently in her novels and repeated in her stories concerns the power of the idea. Sometimes, as in "The House of the Famous Poet," it has metaphysical power, "the abstract notion of a funeral" manifesting as a flying bomb that kills the famous poet and a young woman in his house. A similar theme runs through "The Curtain Blown by the Breeze" although here the idea is realized through psychological rather than supernatural means. Likewise, the twins in the story of that name fit their parents to their own mold; as a visitor is taking her leave, she notices them "giving a remarkable long look at the work of [their] own hands." In the same way the family in "The Pawnbroker's Wife" shape their world to fit their idea of their place in it.

• • •

Nicholas Mosley's *Impossible Object* (1968) consists of eight stories interspersed with short surrealist essays on various aspects of modern life. Most of the stories are in the first person. Gradually it becomes clear that, in spite of the similarity of style and tone from one story to another, there are several narrators. In addition, the same reappear, sometimes as character, sometimes as storyteller. This discovery is made slowly because the characters rarely have names, being identified as husbands and wives, girlfriends, sons and daughters. Two narrators are writers by profession, and the surrealist essays are excerpts from a novel one of them is writing. Both the stories and the books the writers are working on revolve around the subject of love. The writers became characters in each other's stories because of their propensity for voyeurism. For instance, the narrator of "Public House" watches a young couple during a succession of lunch hours; their absorption in each other renders them oblivious of the fact that he watches them. From his observations he builds a complete story about them, noting the argument the woman has with her husband when he follows her to the pub and the reconciliation when the man brings his wife. The narrator at last falls in love with his idea of the woman. Writing a further story about the couple, he feels that he is "a character involved in their story as well as they in mine."

Because this narrator seems to understand the overall situation and because he is the author of the interspersed essays, he becomes the narrative center of the series, the stable foundation of the narrative edifice. Then there are stories told by the man of the couple, some concerning his relations with his wife, some his relations with his mistress, and finally "The Sea," narrated by the mistress, giving the story of a holiday she and her lover take during which their baby is drowned. Here all the themes of violence, madness, eroticism, and moral difficulty that have appeared throughout the series come together. But even as the stories are being laid down layer by layer, their validity is undercut. For instance, in "The Sea" we learn that the electrocution in "Family Game," written by the lover, never really occurred; thus the question arises as to whether the parallel incident, the baby's drowning, ever really happened either.

Although the settings range from a house in an English country village to a hotel in Tunisia, the stories dramatize an interior rather than exterior environment. The journey to the top of the Leaning Tower, for instance, is a clear metaphor for a journey inward, just as the sea describes the mistress's state of mind about her baby's death and by extension about her love affair. "There are some things," she says, "For which we cannot be forgiven." The relations between men and women are a battle in the mind, for as the opening essay proclaims, "Love flourishes in time of war."

The structure of this series of stories is carefully planned and executed. The point of the elaborate structure, however, is not clear. Mosley has deliberately tried to cut fiction loose from its moorings to life, which is the "impossible object" of the title. The telling rather than the story is his main concern. The relationship between writer and material is the most significant aspect of his narrative method; it is, however, a relationship from which the reader is apt to feel excluded.

· · ·

Robert Nye's *Tales I Told My Mother* (1969) takes place in a Freudian world where unconscious actions are overt and the waking life is synonymous with the dreamwork. The reader is at the mercy of a capricious narrator who, afflicted by purely literary passions, takes as his special province imaginary kingdoms, like the Brontës' Angria or the magical world of the Mabinogian. He has more than a touch of necrophilia, his dominant themes being death, sex, and incest. He advises readers about their relationship to the text: "Let us try to have the telling pure, without too much story, then the story will fill it. The storying, that is the point." However, he takes little account of their interests, indulging in capricious changes in point of view, ending stories abruptly with phrases like "that is enough for now about Rufus Coate," or providing pedantic footnotes about literary hoaxes.

In "Howell," Nye attributes to Charles Augustus Howell, "friend of Rossetti, purveyor of smut to Swinburne," a number of actions known to have been performed by others; for example, the recovery of a number of poems from Mrs. Swinburne's coffin. "A Portugese Person" is the intimate story of Currer, Ellis, and Acton Bell. Currer, loving Ellis, kills him by slow decay, willing him to die by the power of speech and burying him at last in the graveyard "with the others." Finally Portugese kills Currer, "the whey-faced hermaphrodite," by castrating him. "Mr. Benjamin" actually concerns a Dr. Copper, who is excited by an antique doll's house inhabited by three Victorian dolls. He becomes trapped in an interminable dialogue with Mr. Benjamin, "of distressing sincerity," a motorcyclist in leathers who spins an elaborate theory about Chatterton's suicide: he "killed himself because he was convinced he had the Pox." Benjamin goes on until the doctor, unable to stand it any longer, grabs him by the throat. Suddenly the doctor's interest in his dolls returns; he invites the motorcyclist to see them, but Benjamin, crying out, "What use to me is love?" rides away, whereupon Doctor Copper can hardly face his dolls.

"Mary Murder" turns upon a sex change in a most unlikely character, Captain Wentworth from *Persuasion,* who squandered his fortune by backing a racing system that favored the outsider in three horse races and then repented and changed into a woman. It arbitrarily turns into a story of blackmail and Victorian domestic poisoning. "The Amber Witch" parodies the detective story: "Who killed Howell? And where did the Wandering Jew fit in? . . . And Captain Rufus Coate, with his unconditional hatred of music?" These questions about characters from other stories occur haphazardly to the narrator. He visits Miss Eponym, the foremost authority on the Brontës, whose voice takes on "a sudden and disconcerting Scots accent." Equally suddenly, the narrative breaks off, and a discussion of Emily's lost manuscript, which appears without warning in the narrator's pocket, constitutes the rest of the story.

Some stories seem primarily literary puzzles, others Freudian nightmares. The product of an original mind of immense erudition, they are undoubtedly clever, but because the characters' feelings are disassociated from events, they have little emotional impact.

• • •

Edward Upward's *The Railway Accident and Other Stories* (1969) constitutes his entire output of short stories, all of them written between 1928 and 1948. In each case there was some time lapse between writing and first publication in *New Directions*; for the title story it was twenty years. This collection was prompted by the interest attendant upon the publication of his new novel *In the Thirties,* the first of a trilogy, in 1962.

"The Railway Accident," written in 1928, shows a modern sensibility in its depiction of paranoia and senseless violence. Unlike "Journey to the Border," there is little to anchor it in the twenties. The narrative sequence is confused, and gradually it becomes apparent that a mad narrator is in control. The paranoia is certainly in Hearn's mind; whether the violence is real or a phenomenon of his crazed brain is not so clear. He interprets events in such a way that he appears to live in a nightmare world; a train journey repeats the crash planned by the architect of a tunnel; a treasure hunter is permanently lamed in a duel. Mortmere, Hearn's destination, is a literary rendition of a mad world that Upward and Christopher Isherwood created while they were at Cambridge. In *New Directions* (number 11, 1949) Isherwood describes it thus: the "fantastic village which we called Mortmere . . . was a sort of anarchist paradise in which all accepted moral and social values were turned upside down and inside out and every kind of extravagant behavior was possible and usual." Upward first published this story in 1949 under the pseudonym Allen Chalmers because he felt that "the kind of literature which makes a dilettante cult of violence, sadism, bestiality and sexual acrobatics is peculiarly offensive and subversive in an age like ours—an age which has witnessed the practically applied bestiality of Belsen and Dachau." It is precisely the lack of emotional effect that relates this story to our contemporary world of terrorists and senseless slaughter; when the story first appeared, people were more horrified by Bergen-Belsen and Hiroshima than they are today.

Neither "The Colleagues" nor "Sunday" has a narrative element: both are sketches with primarily didactic intentions. The first shows two schoolmasters' contrasting points of view. Lloyd is a traditional Britisher, the kind of man who thinks that wars are won on the playing fields of Eton. He emphasizes "endeavour and guts," in contrast to the headmaster, who thinks it ungentlemanly to talk about any kind of work. The story then turns to Mitchell, the new master. He constantly acquiesces in what he despises: refereeing games, supervising Boy Scouts, talking to the gardener. "Resistance," he thinks, "would be romantic." He has a vision of Lloyd on the soccer field as a "baboon or antelope." Seeing it as "genuinely religious delusion," he hopes to have more such delusions, in the belief that madness is his only escape from an impossible way of life.

"Sunday" consists entirely of the thoughts of a man terrified of the task awaiting him at work the following morning: "Tomorrow I shall have used a rotary duplicator for the first time." His ruminations lead him to reflect on history and the encroaching mechanizations of modern life, to envision a future in which "the man who doesn't prefer suicide or madness to fighting will band together with others like himself to destroy the more obvious material causes of misery in the world."

Upward's two main interests, Marxism and madness, are contrasted in "Journey to the Border," first published by the Hogarth Press in 1938. The longest piece of fiction in this volume, it is more novella than short story. It is a kind of pilgrim's progress through madness to political sanity in the form of Marxism. The conversion to the correct political faith takes place through a dialectic between the voice of conscience and the protagonist's surface self. The action is set in a typically British scene, the racetrack, where all classes congregate. The nameless protagonist, a Cambridge-educated but impoverished tutor, has difficulty reconciling his image of himself with his situation. He fantasizes ways of escape, each more delusional than the last; paranoia takes hold and he begins to interpret all kinds of ordinary British phenomena in extreme ways. Thus Upward without any intention of humor introduces caricatures of recognizable British types from the twenties: the squire, the socialist, the fascist, the vamp. Unfortunately for the novella, the hells of Mortmere are more aesthetically convincing than the promised land of a workers' paradise.

• • •

Although there were occasional patches of excellent writing, the British short story of the 1960s on the whole seems undistinguished. At the beginning of the period, most of the frequently published figures had already established reputations, and the most popular—V. S. Pritchett, H. E. Bates, Sylvia Townsend Warner, Elizabeth Taylor, for example—continued to do what they had already learned to do well. Their main outlet was the *New Yorker,* which seems to have favored, at least in this decade, sentimentally rather than satirically comic narratives of eccentric middle-class life. Two gifted writers with distinctive voices, Jean Rhys and Edward Upward, reemerged after long silences. Some new writers, particularly women, attracted attention. Doris Lessing secured a reputation she had gained during the fifties; Nell Dunn rose to prominence. It may be significant that of these only Dunn was born in England, and she set her stories in a social class not her own. All these women brought new material to the British short story, which is sorely needed.

As far as technique is concerned, there were no significant developments. There is, however, one point worth making. The annual anthology *Winter's Tales* shows that long stories were being written in Britain and occasionally published, even though many in these collections were written by writers of other nationalities. This state of affairs was typical of British publishing as a whole, many of the most significant short story collections being written by Commonwealth writers such as Margaret Laurence and Nadine Gordimer, or Irish writers like William Trevor and Edna O'Brien. Furthermore, many issues of *Winter's Tales* included long stories not previously published in magazines. It is apparent that, regardless of what editors wanted, writers liked the extended length and continued to use it regardless of publishability. This situation is true of the story in general: although the lack of public demand might have discouraged British writers from finding new material and new forms, it did not discourage them from writing stories altogether.

Jean Pickering

California State University, Fresno

THE ENGLISH SHORT STORY IN THE SEVENTIES

This chapter focuses on the freshest authors of the 1970s, those who published their first volumes of short fiction between 1970 and 1980. Work of the old guard will be addressed as well, but less intensively. This screening sifts up some fine and exciting young writers, virginal in the sense that until now their short fiction has been virtually untouched by serious scholarship and criticism; at least commentary on their stories has been invisible to MLA bibliographers. Among the finer of these younger writers are Ian McEwan, Jennifer Dawson, Susan Hill, Angela Carter, Gabriel Josipovici, and Christine Brooke-Rose; this screening also culls out the much better known John Fowles, perhaps the finest of the younger generation of British fiction writers.

Some excellent collections of short stories published during the 1970s will be noted but will not be discussed since they contain stories that appeared previously in volume form. These include such major achievements as *The Collected Stories of Graham Greene* (1972), Doris Lessing's two-volume *Collected African Stories* (1972) and her two-volume *Collected Stories* (1978), the *Selected Stories* (1978) of V. S. Pritchett, *The Selected Stories of Roald Dahl* (1970) and *The Best of Roald Dahl* (1978), Kingsley Amis's *Collected Short Stories* (1980), the *Selected Short Stories* (1971) of Glyn Jones and the *Selected Short Stories* (1974) of Gwyn Jones.

The late Cyril Connolly somewhere remarked that given all the fiction that already exists the only excusable motive for writing any more is the ambition to produce a masterpiece. When one first encounters the remark, it may seem harsh, but the more one reads the more sensible it sounds. A number of the writers of the decade clearly have no very lofty ambition, and with a significant number of others, reach painfully exceeds grasp—but at least one admires their effort. Of course, a favored few produce stories that the shades of Kipling or Lawrence or Woolf might respect and even, now and then, read with a slight twinge of envy—particularly if these shades have kept up with trends in contemporary fiction and recent French intellectual thought.

Although discussion is limited to stories published in volume form, it is worthwhile to glance at British periodicals and sample the opportunities they offered writers during the decade. There were, of course, the traditional kinds of magazines interested in traditional kinds of fiction (*Cornhill, Encounter, New Statesman,* the British *Vogue, Harper's Bazaar* and, closely allied to them, the newspapers or newspaper magazines normally, although not always, even more traditional in taste (e.g., offshoots of the *Times,* the *Glasgow Herald,* the *Daily Telegraph*). There were British outlets for innovative fiction, but a disproportionate number of such stories appeared first in book form. Others almost always found first publication in little magazines, a great many of which received support from the British Arts Council; the *Times Literary Supplement* for 22 January 1970 (p. 82), listed funds grants for thirty (some not concerned with fiction): *Adam, Agenda, Ambit, Circuit, Critical Quarterly, Expression, London Magazine, Modern Poetry in Translation, New Measure, New Worlds, New Writers, Outposts, Review, Transatlantic Review, Akros, Gairm, Lines Review, Scottish International Review, Anglo-Welsh Review, Barn, Lleufer, Llwyfan, Poetry Wales, Second Aeon, Taliesin, Y Cardi, Y Gehennin, Y Eurgrawn, U Traethodydd,* and *Zutique.*

Obviously, British outlets for challenging fiction existed, but a surprising number of stories with decidedly disturbing subject matter first appeared in American publications. To choose only one writer, Ian McEwan: "Homemade," his story of preteen incest, first appeared in the *American Review,* and "Disguises," in which a child is emotionally brutalized into transvestism, appeared first in the *New American Review.* For less troubling stories many writers favored such major American magazines as *Playboy,* the *New Yorker, Harper's*; women's magazines like *Mademoiselle* and *Chatelaine,* which often featured feminist fiction; and little magazines like the *Paris Review* and the *Iowa Review.* In short, British writers occasionally made use of the sorts of periodical outlets always open to American writers.

In addition to British magazines there were some annual British anthologies, the most important being *New Stories, Winter's Tales,* and *Scottish Short Stories.* One noble experiment that began in 1969 and continued for about three years was the quarterly publication in paperback form of *Penguin Modern Stories;* in each volume three to five modern writers, usually but not always British, contributed one to four stories each. Of course, one problem of reading a story in an anthology or a collection is the distortion lent the story by those surrounding it. A reader might react differently if he encounters a story by itself. Some wise editors at Covent Garden Press had the courage to experiment with publishing short stories in one-story volumes, each volume limited to a small number of copies, six hundred for Elaine Feinstein's *Matters of Chance* (1980), for example, one hundred numbered and signed by the author. This story, like some others, seems much more rewarding when read alone than when encountered within a collection.

A wonderful variation on print publiction involves readings of short stories to a national audience on the BBC's "Third Programme" (each subsequently published in the BBC's weekly magazine, the *Listener*). Such a project is noteworthy first of all because of its scope—the possibility of reaching a larger audience than any single magazine or book could; perhaps more stimulating is the opportunity to reach those millions of listeners who are out of the habit of reading. Especially rewarding is the fact that such readings expose an entire audience to the story at the same time, perhaps leading to a discussion in a living room or pub or bus, some people venturing, "Did you listen last night——" who would never say, "Did you read in this month's *London Magazine*——." Perhaps most stimulating of all are the formal applications, for in terms of technique radio potentially harks back to the oral-aural mode of the Paleolithic campfire and to narrative possibilities foreign to words dumbly imprisoned on the page. Oral readings in creative writing classes and elsewhere can reveal the most surprising facets in fiction, and those capable of mastering the age-old techniques of composing for the tongue may open long-forgotten echoing chambers in the house of fiction.

At least one major short story writer cannot make up his mind whether to damn the electronic media as a pack of ogres or to consider them as present aids, potential saviors. In *London Magazine Stories,* an anthology published in 1967, V. S. Pritchett offered some doleful comments on the media-dominated economic situation British short story writers currently face:

The financial rewards are disgracefully low in England, even for the well known, the top price for anything good which has taken weeks, perhaps months of work being about £60. It is difficult to get a story longer than 7,000 words published at all; after 10,000 words, impossible. The periodicals on which the writer can rely have almost all vanished, driven out by expensive printing, by television and the hundred and one new diversions of an extravert and leisured society.

Still, Pritchett points out, the number of short story volumes published annually seems to have increased, and he judges the audience to be "painfully small," but "addicted." And happily "the short-story writer has one secret economic advantage over the novelist: he is continually re-printed, broadcast and re-broadcast. He has, like the playwright, established a minor income." This income Pritchett can imagine swelling if television producers can ever manage to "forget what they were taught in the television training schools" and begin to understand that in fact television "is a basically literary medium, for the screen is really a crowded page."

Enough of the media; now to the fiction itself. It is impossible to offer any meaningful generalizations that would be true of all or even of a very large number of the many hundreds of stories read for this chapter, but some quirky patterns do show up. In characterization, for example, one is struck by the number of old people British writers of the 1970s chose to write about; their demographics seem decidedly in advance of Britain's drift toward a population of senior citizens. Especially interesting is the fact that a number of writers seem fond of vital old women, brimful of vim and bearing some strange link to culture: Malcolm Bradbury's Mrs. Prokosch of "Nobody Here in England," for example, ceaselessly celebrating a most questionable tie to George Bernard Shaw. One wonders about the prevalence of such characters now, for it has been over sixty years since Ezra Pound in "Hugh Selwyn Mauberley" described Britain as "an old bitch gone in the teeth." Perhaps the generation that matured under Queen Elizabeth II and that elected and reelected Margaret Thatcher has some as yet unplumbed affinity for conceiving of Brittania as a plucky old woman.

Another interesting feature throughout this body of stories is a penchant for settings removed from Britain itself. One would wager that the majority take place in England, far fewer in Scotland, Wales, or Northern Ireland; still, it is fascinating to realize what a great number are set in the United States, on the Continent—especially France—in parts of the former empire, or in some indeterminate fantasyland.

Some fictional themes one expects to transcend decades or generations, but still the 1970s have their own signature in short fiction. The decade seems unusually preoccupied with questions of primitivism, for example. Traditional and avant-garde writers alike often show a fondness for characters or settings or techniques or questions that strip human nature to some kind of fundamental base; among those most interested in this angle of vision are Susan Hill, John Berger, Wilson Harris, and Angela Carter. Perhaps less surprising are the aftershocks of the feminist quake; a great many writers, men sometimes more than women, seem compelled to chart out their rearranged notions of the present and the proper (rarely proximate on any of the maps) conceptions of women and women's roles. It is a rare writer whose fiction remains unaffected by the women's movement. For the most part the writers in our study seem relatively untroubled by the present menu of horrors facing the human race: nuclear Armageddon, mass starvation, overpopulation, gene splicing, terrorism, communism, militarism. But the saturnine need not feel driven to take up hope; one of the oldest of fictional themes is communication, and thanks to avant-garde Continental theories of linguistics writers of the decade can approach the subject with a massive, wholehearted despair. Structuralists and semioticians instructed the decade that social conditioning and language irretrievably imprison human beings in bondage far worse than that inflicted on the denizens of Plato's cave; we can neither know reality nor with any degree of confidence converse on the subject with our fellow human beings. Avant-garde writers in particular have been concerned during the 1970s to take failure of communication farther than it has ever been taken before.

Any essay dealing with a number of writers must find some balance between the need to conceptually order them and the writers' demand not to be categorized. Perhaps the simpler the system the better. British short story writers of the 1970s will be discussed here in four sections. The first consists of the old guard, established writers who began publishing volumes of short fiction before 1970; the second involves those newer writers who focus on the individual and the individual's fundamental problems; the third concerns newer writers for whom an individual's conflicts with a given society seem to be of first importance; the fourth group, composed of avant-garde writers, tends to conceive of individual and social problems as sometimes secondary, often irrelevant to questions of fictional technique or language or aesthetics or epistemology. Of course, the better writers tend to have a strong claim to belong in several categories or in none, but the latter privilege will be reserved for a single writer, the last to be discussed and the one who may be Britain's finest writer of short fiction since 1970.

Established Writers

The writers in the first category have in common the fact that they all published volumes of short fiction before 1970; most share the fact that they are not English: Glyn Jones is Welsh, George Mackay Brown a Scot, Ruth Prawer Jhabvala was born in Cologne, Germany, of Polish parents, and even the English-born Penelope Gilliatt is a virtual expatriate given the amount of time she spends in America. More important than any of these is Doris Lessing; since World War II the English have had few writers in whom they can take as much pride as in her, though she was born in Persia (now Iran) and lived in Africa— chiefly Rhodesia (now Zimbabwe)—until establishing herself in England in 1949 at the age of thirty.

Among the short story writers of the decade, no matter what their background, Lessing stands especially tall. Since 1970 she has published several collections based on work in previously published volumes: *The Collected African Stories (This Was the Old Chief's Country, The Sun between the Feet)* in 1973, and the *Collected Stories (To Room Nineteen, The Temptation of Jack Orkney)* in 1977, as well as *Stories,* also in 1977. The volume with a special claim to attention in the decade, a collection of stories appearing in book form for the first time (though having appeared in periodicals as early as 1963, as late as 1972), was published in Britain as *The Story of a Non-Marrying Man* (1972) and in the United States as *The Temptation of Jack Orkney* (1972).

Lessing is a card-carrying intellectual as well as a fiction writer of distinction, and her stories can be marvelous when the latter identity firmly controls the former—as it normally does. But there are exceptions. She has in her novels lately made a massive commitment to science fiction and has one story, "Report on the Threatened City," which is a disguised moral tale in which aliens berate the human perversity of clustering in a population center like San Francisco that is doomed to incur major earthquake damage. (One longs for an alien who would persuade her to abandon science fiction.)

It would be misleading to say that she experiments in a variety of forms, but she does dabble in them. Three are sketches based on parks or gardens; a couple of pieces Charles Lamb would have no trouble identifying as personal essays—"Side Benefits of an Honorable Profession" and "Spies I have Known"; all are thoughtful and thought provoking, well written, but none achieving the kind of complete success one would hope for.

On the whole the better stories in the book investigate different aspects of love. In "An Unposted Love Letter" a surprisingly articulate and thoughtful actress struggling with middle age uses unconsummated love as a kind of fuel to raise the level of her performances on stage.

"Not a Very Nice Story" would be easy to condemn as soap opera, but with amazing insight and charity it follows through several decades two married couples who in the most normal and decent way fall into love and adultery both within and outside the foursome; one of the men dead, they end in a kind of respectable though not openly acknowledged polygamy. In this one story Lessing manages to survey an amazing variety of the faces of love. In "Mrs. Fortescue" a rather unlikable adolescent struggles through sexual confusions, especially those involving an older sister, by brutally forcing himself on an aging tart. The intellectual in Lessing enriches these three stories by bringing to them an understanding of the complex vagaries of humans and their emotions but fails her in refusing to acknowledge the grandeur that can flow from what we might call the unintellectualizable. The intellectual seems to resent mysteries and confusions that the pure writer might do better simply to exploit. One recalls the example E. M. Forster makes of George Eliot in his *Aspects of the Novel*.

Each of these three stories fascinates and convinces, but none finally achieves as much as "The Story of a Non-Marrying Man." Here she focuses on a drifter who has dominated a corner of the imaginations of several people; an apparently fine and decent man, he sequentially marries four fine and decent women, leaving each after a year or two or four for no accountable reason. Lessing seems in sympathy with her narrator who would understand the man as seeking a simpler, more Thoreauvian life than is possible with any of the women. Lessing and her narrator understand men rather well, but they do not understand the central figure in this story; what they manage to capture without understanding—the emotional reality beyond any logical motive—makes the story a fine one indeed. In the last of the five love stories, "Out of the Fountain," a middle-aged man of modest circumstances takes some trouble to present to a rich but lazy-minded young girl a pearl of great price. Each is transformed by the experience, she into a young woman who understands she must not settle for the second rate, he into a passionate collector of jewels and bright bits of worthless glass that have in common only their place in his vague desire to honor the girl. They meet only once more, many years later, bedraggled, weakened, sad, each disillusioned at meeting the other, neither quite the proper material to support the imaginative weight each has put on the other over the years. Have their lives been wasted or enriched by the idealism represented in that long ago gift? Lessing has here almost a fable, but one that questions far more powerfully than it answers.

The best story in the volume, the last and longest, begins with Jack Orkney called to his father's deathbed. Over the next few weeks Orkney, a successful middle-aged leftist journalist, reviews his own life, his relations to father, siblings, and children, to his wife, to his activist colleagues, to his most fundamental political, social, and religious beliefs. Here Lessing's powerful intellect is at its best—questing, tentative, honest. Like Ivan Ilyich, Orkney probes the extent to which his life went off course; by the end he seems to have resumed his old life's established patterns, but that life has been altered by "a gift," a compulsion to seek further: "Behind the face of the sceptical world was another, which no conscious decision of his could stop him exploring." Lessing's exploring here leads her toward a masterpiece.

· · ·

Ruth Prawer Jhabvala is a woman of even more confusing background than Lessing. She was born to Polish-Jewish parents in Germany, was educated in England, married an Indian architect, and lived for a good while both in India and in New York. Her identity as an English writer is problematic, but certainly any country would be happy to claim her. India she has claimed for herself.

Virtually all her stories are interesting, but some unfortunately offer the reader little other than exotic settings (e.g., "Two More under the Sun," "The Englishwoman," "In the Mountains"). Others, however, probe beyond the surface to supply a reader with understanding and insight that transcend the vagaries of cultures. "Prostitutes" abandons stereotypes to pierce to one chamber of the heart of human relationships, that chamber in which we so willfully betray ourselves by choosing for our deepest affection the most unworthy; it comes as a shock, yet seems natural, when the story reveals how even those who are paid for their "love" can be prey to the affliction. "Picnic with Moonlight and Mangoes" jerks the reader back and forth between sympathy and contempt for a man paying a severe price for an uncertain degree of guilt involving "advantages" he may or may not have taken of a young woman who came to him looking for a job. The conclusion is one of irony: we see him attempt to sublimate his lust into a kind of religious adoration. But to condemn him, the vacuous young woman, or the bitter, blackmailing father is to deny the human complexity of all three. Each is guilty, each is a victim, all are terribly human. "Desecration," almost more fairy tale than short story, deals with a young

wife idolized by her rich, gentle old husband but who must give herself
to a virile police superintendent who finally values her not at all.

Jhabvala will always be known as a writer of Indian stories, but her
real subject matter is human attachments, the complex vagaries of the
human heart. She sometimes falls into shallow recitals of adultery or
of lost love, but at her best she reveals far more of substance about
human emotion than she does about India.

One of her most entertaining stories is one of the least typical. In
"How I Became a Holy Mother" her normal flashes of wit and irony
become a satirical floodlight focused on the institutionalization of the
Indian yogi or spiritual master: "They are always called something like
that—if not Swamiji then Majaraj-ji or Babaji or Maharishiji or Gu-
ruji; but this one was just called plain Master, in English." The narrator, a twenty-three-year-old ex-model and twice divorcée is, if not a
burned-out case, a thoroughly singed one. The ashram, or holy center,
she finally settles on is like a summer camp for temporary dropouts,
until a bossy Italian countess turns it into something more like boot
camp as part of her project to groom a new spiritual leader to export
to the West. The young disciple has trouble with chastity, so the
countess decides to yoke him with the model who will represent the
female principle: the holy mother. Though satirical, the story leaves
the reader neither enraged nor even troubled, but with a kind of wry
satisfaction that so many flawed people have managed to create a complex of interlocking relationships so satisfactory to each.

· · ·

Britain has regional writers who would like to make their own little
corners of the kingdom as exotic as Jhabvala's India; two of the more
devoted are Glyn Jones and George Mackay Brown. The stories in Glyn
Jones' *Selected Short Stories* (1971) and *Welsh Heirs* (1977) have most of
the virtues and most of the limitations we ordinarily associate with
regional or local-color fiction. We get a strong sense not only of Welsh
village and countryside but of individual homes and hovels, pubs and
marketplaces, churches and farms. The characters tend toward sentimentalized types,and the incidents tend to be unexceptional variations
on events that vainly strive to be archetypal—in dying ridiculously a
sanctimonious old man ironically achieves his aim of reforming some
disreputable neighbors; a runaway boy nearly drowns swimming an
estuary with a golden pony, which itself turns around to swim back.
The final virtue of the stories is the sense of Wales and the Welsh they

communicate; their fatal flaw is that individually each story is so forgettable.

The Scot George Mackay Brown publishes more prolifically than most of his contemporaries, and his stories suffer somewhat as a result. Their style could be more evenly finished, their characters more fully conceived, their treatments finally more significant were he only to write less. The stories range widely in time, from neolithic to posthistoric, covering most of the major cultural eras in between. Most focus on the Orkney Islands, the communities and individuals they shelter, nourish, and oppress. A brief introduction characterizes the stories of *Hawkfall* (1974) as "primarily entertainments," and the description applies equally well to those of *The Sun's Net* (1976) and *Witch* (1977), a selection based on *Hawkfall* and two earlier collections. Brown favors ghost stories, love stories, adventure stories, but almost always rises enough above popular formula to keep the interest of a moderately demanding reader. What Brown almost never does is raise that interest sufficiently to convince the reader that he is involved with real works of art. One near exception is "A Winter Tale" where three narrators— Doctor, Teacher, Minister—relate consecutive versions of a small dinner party all three attend, an almost desperate and imperfectly successful meeting of types somehow alien to the island's ultimate and essential life cycles. Like Jones, Brown seems finally less important for any individual story than for what his work as a whole communicates about a region and its people.

• • •

Among the oldest of the old guard is J. B. Priestley. He titled his volume *The Carfitt Crisis and Two Other Stories* (1975) but in fact describes the title piece and the last, "The Pavilion of Masks," as "two short novels." They sandwich "Underground," a legitimate if weakly conceived story in which Ray Aggarstone, a dastardly man who intends to rob his wife and mother of eight thousand pounds and run away to Rio, finds himself on a subway that refuses to stop at his station; instead it plunges steeply down into the earth where his car will serve as his eternal Hell. Back on earth his body is "found unconscious in the Northern Line train at Hampstead" where authorities determine he suffered a heart attack. The story finally is not much of a fictional accomplishment, certainly not enough to encourage many readers to attempt the companion pieces, which Priestley himself has kindly described on the dust jacket as "high comedies" that were "originally conceived in dramatic form" and as "entertainments embodying some serious ideas." In more detail: *"The Carfitt Crisis* has a contemporary setting. A new kind of man arrives to act as a sort of butler to some conventional, fairly affluent people who are facing a crisis. Because of his self-discipline and training, his lack of vanity and pride, this new man has certain unusual powers. In spite of its picturesque historical setting, *The Pavilion of Masks* is a satirical comedy on the theme of self-deception. All deceive themselves except the professional charlatan, who can manipulate them because he does not deceive himself."

. . .

Of all the writers actively engaged in the short story during the decade, V. S. Pritchett most truly deserves the title of old master. Of course, one expects wisdom, breadth of vision, and irony in stories brought down from a septuagenarian height, but that a man born in 1900 should produce such vigorous, witty, humor-tinged stories is a minor miracle. Of Pritchett's three volumes of short fiction published during the decade, the preferred one might well be his *Selected Stories,* which contains work from 1959 to 1978 from four different volumes; it seems appropriate, however, to concentrate on his two other collections, *The Camberwell Beauty* (1974) and *On the Edge of the Cliff* (1979). On the whole the earlier of the two seems slightly better, though most writers would be pleased to consider either the capstone of a career.

One feels uncomfortable labeling as formulaic some of Pritchett's favorite habits, but the stories of this decade often resolve themselves into love stories of a particular sort. The protagonist is usually a man, rather often a widower and sometimes distinctly old, a man at any rate of a certain degree of dignity, his self-conceit usually vanquishing his irony in a close match (in "The Rescue" the role is played by a sixteen-year-old girl who "likes to see what a young man will do"—there are other variations), but that egotism loses in the final round to the special kind of madness represented by an eccentric female.

A more than minor miracle is the fact that the standard of his stories is so uniformly high, though individual stories do not often strain above that level into true greatness. The title story of *The Camberwell Beauty* does rise to such a level. It beautifully creates for us the tawdry, claustrophobic, insanely competitive, and jealous world of small-time antique dealers, managing a bare living largely through selling old furniture but each devoting his soul to a specialty: Georgian silver,

Caughley ware, ivory. "At the heart of the trade is lust, but a lust that is a dream paralyzed by itself." Only well into the story does one learn that the "beauty" in question is not an antique but in fact a young woman who in adolescence was pirated from one dealer, August, by another, the ridiculous and ugly old Pliny; she is religiously coveted by a third, the narrator who has already failed in the trade. Apparently the first tried and failed to debauch Isabelle when she was his pubescent ward; the intentions of the last are unclear, though he seems to have a goal in the direction of physical consummation; but the second has lived with her for years as husband without being "horrible," as she puts it. Pliny never tries to get her in bed, though, she says, he "takes my clothes off before I go to bed. He likes to look at me. I am the most precious thing he has." The girl has already revealed an unsound mind (when alone she dresses in a cavalry helmet, bangs a drum, and occasionally blares on a horn to keep away potential kidnappers), but she remains, nevertheless, a "beauty." And the object of the desperate attentions of three different men.

The story works beautifully as an ironic peephole into the mentality of the collector but becomes a candidate for greatness when a reader notices the mirror in the peephole and realizes the extent to which the collector's insane lust for possession of a special example of Meissen or Dresden reflects a man's love for a particular woman. In what way, to what extent, does he desire to possess the object of his dreams? To what purpose? To what extent does lust of possession distort any "love"? The question rises from and transcends the story in a way characteristic of only the very finest fiction.

Throughout the two volumes Pritchett manages to compel our belief in a bewildering variety of individual characters: his protagonists range from young to very old men—all seemingly exactly right, whether a retired geologist, an active liberal journalist, a professional nursery-man, a small-time cloth merchant; Pritchett has a genius for creating lives into which a reader can enter. Especially surprising is his ability to create credible women who tend to exist outside the stereotypes normally assigned them by masculine writers. At one extreme would be the seventy-year-old protagonist and title character of "Tea with Mrs. Bittell," but Pritchett manages to make bewitchingly appealing a gallery of women most male writers would automatically reject— women of a certain age, women given to anger and nagging, short stubby women who won't take no for an answer, women who are all bones and given to distraction, in "Our Wife" a woman who is truly "a noise and a nuisance." And though his stories tend to run to triangles involving two men and a woman, his characters seem virtually never to repeat themselves.

Technically Pritchett is fond of the throwaway ending, which tends to define the story as something like a slice of life ("The Vice-Consul," "The Accompanist"), albeit sometimes of extremely eccentric life ("The Last Throw"). His style is an unpretentious joy. At the shore "little families of whitecaps would appear" which "were like faces popping up or perhaps white hands shooting out and disappearing pointlessly. Yes, they were the pointless dead" ("On the Edge of the Cliff"). One character looks "around with that dishonest look a dog has when it is pretending not to hear its master's whistle" ("The Spree"). Another is a poet: "every so often he would go up to his room to sit on the sea wall, and as if he were some industrious hen, he would (as I once said) lay a poem" ("Our Wife").

But Pritchett's final charm lies not in style or in character or form or even in vision; his final charm comes from our sense that we are reading a genuinely classic writer in our own time. He is the real thing.

. . .

Of course, any great man worth his salt must have at least one first-rate disciple, and Pritchett would seem to have found his in Penelope Gilliatt—though she seems to have read her share of Lessing love stories as well. Gilliatt's stories scintillate with old-fashioned narrative virtues: her style is a cornucopia of interesting sentences; her verbal resources inspire respect not far from awe; the eccentrics around whom she tends to construct her stories are virtual guarantors of lively, compelling characters; she is not afraid to be funny or to end a story sadly; she nurtures all her virtues with a constant intelligence that only rarely descends to mere wit.

She is one of the decade's best short story writers, a superbly talented woman who seems almost always to be writing near the limit of her gifts. Then why is she not a writer one expects to rise above the decade and be remembered and read into the next century? It cannot be because so many of her stories are love stories, for some by writers like Chekhov and Lawrence and Singer are about as good as short fiction gets. Why do none of the pieces in *Nobody's Business* (1972) or *Splendid Lives* (1978) approach those standards? Perhaps because she so often limits her stories to narrowly depicting interesting relations between interesting people. A case in point: "Nobody's Business."

An older man and a younger man and woman came to interview the seventyish Prendergasts, Sir Edward, a judge, and his wife, Emily, a prolific writer of low comedy for radio. The Prendergasts offer charming, insightful answers to the most banal queries, revealing that they have enjoyed decades of love, which in their case may be defined as composed partly of deep friendship; of mutual admiration for intellect, talent, sense of humor; of sexual enjoyment; of trust; of the most important of all the old standbys, which the interviewing trio are too blinded with cant or egocentricity to recognize. Like almost all her work, the story glows with intelligence, sympathy, subtlety, wit, understanding—a virtual shopping list of old-fashioned fictional virtues, invaluable traits that make this story like so many of Gilliatt's a pleasure to read. Does it lack anything? It lacks any claim whatsoever to greatness. Why?

Because Gilliatt observes and understands, she does not quest and question. It would be tempting but probably inaccurate to fault her with too much intelligence. Hamlet is not less intelligent than Horatio; he is more open to that which transcends intellect. Gilliatt acknowledges such dimensions at the conclusion when Emily remembers having nearly drowned before Edward all but willed her back to life. A nice enough touch, but Gilliatt asserts the fact rather than fictionally realizing the emotion. Her stories rarely plumb far enough beyond that which she can understand. It seems possible finally to explain what rests at the heart of love stories like "Nobody's Business," "An Antique Love Story," "The Last to Go," "The Position of the Planets," and others. But great stories on such themes thrive on losing the reader in a mystery he may apprehend, may recognize, but can at best acknowledge, never understand. Such mystery may sometimes be an element in Gilliatt's love stories; in the greatest it is virtually the substance.

Nobody's Business seems finally too full of such love stories, their formulas enlivened, almost hidden by wonderfully eccentric characters and a devilishly (or angelically) clever style. One tends to prefer her other, less characteristic stories—"Frank," "Staying in Bed," "Foreigners"—though even in these, love rarely roams far from the center.

Any of these stories could have appeared in Gilliatt's second volume of the decade as well as her first, for *Splendid Lives* delightfully continues to add miniatures to her charming bracelet of eccentrics. As in the earlier book, her most endearing characters tend to be older, relatively self-contained and set in their ways, full of an inoffensive, unthreatening intelligence, idiosyncratically pursuing hobby horses, special interests—not passions, for such characters are generally too well-schooled, too open-minded and tolerant, for genuine passion.

As in her earlier book one gets a heavy dose of love stories, though "love" might require qualification. In reading so many of her stories a reader is powerfully struck by her fondness for a kind of "misageination." The normal pattern is for a charming male eccentric to enthrall an attractive and intelligent woman decades his junior. In her title story, "Splendid Lives," the "Bishop of Hurlingham, aged ninety-two, radical, widowed" and a distant cousin of Queen Victoria, manages to infatuate Ridgeway, a young American leftist who rebounds from divorce all the way to England and, by the end of the story, literally into the arms of the Bishop, a man one would expect to antedate her own great-grandfather. Admittedly, most of Gilliatt's other stories cross ages less drastically, in "The Sports Chemist" and "Flight Fund," for example; and she can imagine old men and old women mutually happy in loving marriage, as in "Phone-In," "Iron Larks," "Catering," and (with reservations about mutuality) "A Lovely Bit of Wood." She can imagine yawning chasms between jettisoned children and their too selfish parents, in "Fleeced" and "Autumn of a Dormouse." But her dominant pattern in these two volumes remains cross-aged love stories, fantasies of which no consciousness-raised male could ever allow himself to be guilty.

The theme of "Catering" is older love rather than cross-aged love. Its untutored lower-middle-class protagonists are perhaps the least glamorous in *Splendid Lives*; still the story rises a notch higher than most of the others. Her couples seem at times glued together by their intellectual facility, but what binds together Mr. and Mrs. Pope remains uncertain. One absolutely believes in those ties, however, when one sees how the two "cater" to each other as well as to others. Mr. Pope willingly shapes a great part of his life to the weekly rituals demanded by his wife's vocation, catering for weddings—a most tedious, most time-consuming, most unlucrative, but, for Mrs. Pope, most emotionally satisfying enterprise. The daughter rebels at the cramping of her own life for the sake of catering and, midway through one such venture, reveals she has had an abortion because she and her steady boyfriend are not ready for marriage. Her parents' steady solicitous catering not only to the guests but to the comparatively selfish daughter and, most important, to each other (he allowed her to keep a child born after an adulterous affair; she voluntarily gave it up when she saw how it bothered him) eloquently speaks to the beauty and good that can be mastered by the humble labors of human decency. The Popes will realize no utopia, but life is inestimably enriched by their catering.

This story is very fine indeed. What is troubling is a reader's nagging resentment that her humane, intelligent, brilliantly written stories seem too insular. "Iron Larks" may tip toward a condemnation of moral cowardice and "Fleeced" may pillory capitalist materialism, but such themes seem finally no more to sum up Gilliatt's real concerns than a bumper sticker sums up a Buick. Too often fondness and infatuation seem the strongest emotions she can fictionally realize. Her intelligence has more facets than a diamond, but the result is more often sparkle than illumination. Gilliatt is far too intelligent to make stupid intellectual commitments to any fad *du jour*. But that saving moderation sadly deprives her stories of most of their intellectual force. Of all the writers of the decade Gilliatt seems among the least capable of writing a really bad story. It is a terrible disappointment that scattered individual stories do not rise above the high standards she sets for them.

Focusing on Personal Crises

Theorists of the short story frequently proclaim that the individual life is the natural subject of short fiction and that of the novel is social life. Such an assertion may or may not be true, but over the last century and a half most of the best short stories have concerned themselves with personal rather than with social crises. It seems easier in short fiction to focus on intimate problems of one character or two or three than to attack more widely ranging issues. In this sense stories in this second category may be less difficult to write than those in the third or fourth; then again they may not.

As there exist genres sometimes called subliterary formulas (detective stories, westerns, and so on) so are there patterns that might be termed serious literary formulas, among them the initiation story (perhaps the most common), the lost-life story (a favorite of Henry James), and the love story. With so many fine stories already written on such natural themes, how can a contemporary writer hope to compete? Ian McEwan competes by pushing his characters into new literary dimensions of psychic pain and depravity. Susan Hill competes by stripping character, setting, experience to an essence as basic and fundamental as the ultimate rhythms of nature itself. Isobel English competes with indirection and subtlety; indeed with her work one sometimes wonders, "What's the point?" The point may be the tragedy waiting just beyond the frail bubble of emotional resolution with which her stories tend to end. Or perhaps the point is an individual's idiosyncratic coming to terms with life. English's protagonists often wind up in a situation that those of us wedded to common sense must condemn as miserable. But immaturity or craziness or some other strange gift often allows such originals an uncommon vision, something like the reflection in a soap bubble. Can a soap bubble be a point? With English it may be.

In the first and title story of *Life After All* (1973), a woman, after losing the grown daughter she has doted on, discovers she is gifted as a medium, develops an ability to see and communicate with those on the other side, and ends planning a party for Celia and their new friends. In "One of the Family," a retarded and emotionally disturbed but finally generous and loving young man named Dan hastens an old woman's death by allowing her cigarettes, a gesture he intends only as a kindness. The woman's grandson, Martin, whom Dan takes to be his best friend, in anger virtually accuses him of negligent homicide. But Dan's mind seeks justification to the point where he can think that "everything had worked out right"; in the end he is warmly addressing Martin as if their intimacy had hardly been interrupted at all.

With one exception these may be the book's strongest stories; like almost all the rest they exclude sentimentality with workmanlike precision; but "Cousin Dot" is something special. Hardly more than three short pages, it alternates prose, reserved for a group of proper, wealthy, and unfeeling relatives, and italicized verse, which represents the perspective of the title character, a harmless, addlepated old bag lady. Despite heavy rain, the relatives keep their door locked against Dot, who realizes she soon will die. Dot befriends a cat on their porch and, before wandering off, leaves with it a valuable jade snuffbox. Meanwhile the relatives scurry around inside, flustered about how long she has remained ("But it's over *five* minutes . . ."), horrified that she might burn down the house with paraffin rags, gratified that it has begun to rain. Dot addresses her friend:

> Pussy, I am going soon
> Round the contours of the moon.

> Dorothy is my real name.
> Cousin Dot is not to blame
> For the hash that she has made
> Of a life not meant to fade.
> But here's a present for yourself
> Better poverty than wealth.

The story ends with Dot gone off to die and the relatives assuming that the jade box is for themselves and considering inviting her to tea after all. The piece has almost more the air of fable or fairy tale than of short story.

Except in "Cousin Dot" English plays no formal games, and despite her sympathy for characters on the dangerous fringes of status, adulthood, or sanity she leaves society to itself—preferring the individual and the individual vision. For her, *Life After All* consists almost solely of private experiences, nothing more, and sadly it seems that only those beyond the pale are allowed to live it.

• • •

Among the more moderately gifted short story writers is Elaine Feinstein, who sometimes unsuccessfully struggles with basic problems of usage (as in the first page or two of "Drought," for example), but more often simply loses battles against unimaginative characterization and a dreary style. In outline the stories in *The Silent Areas* (1980) sometimes sound promising. In "Other People" a long-divorced woman takes in a lodger, and her ex-husband gives her money so she can chuck the man out; she does not, gets the flu, and, perhaps vulnerable, perhaps not, makes love with the man—a thirty-three-year-old virgin who the next morning looks much younger and grander than before. Then, hearing her former husband is marrying his housekeeper, she turns miserable and becomes quite mean to the lodger. In "Ambition" one of her female characters exclaims that she wants "*really* to live. I'm greedy for it; all of it; *all* that isn't ordinary and decent and normal. Because that's how I am." Hardly a clarion call, yet still less soporific than her brother's weltanschauung: "You've always gone on about some special kind of truth that only you have access to. But the only truth is an ordinary decent life." These character types hold throughout much of the volume—smug, tight, Apollonian, stuffy, anal-compulsive men contrasted to women who often feel trapped, slovenly, confused, disordered, miserable.

Feinstein is decidedly more successful with the women than with the men and happiest with characters who migrate from deadness, egotism, sterility to compassion and openness to others. She is not a shallow or superficial writer, but in only one story does she rise high enough above mediocrity to create fiction that deserves to survive the decade. The story, "Hansel and Gretel," a brilliant, troubling, open-ended retelling of the fairy tale, transcends the kind of shopworn wisdom she favors in her other stories. More in this vein could make her a writer of real consequence.

• • •

Mention was made earlier of literary formulas characteristic of this second category, among them the initiation story and the missed-life story. Someone once observed that stories of the first sort ordinarily focus on young people of no real experience who learn that living life can be nasty, whereas the second ordinarily focus on older people of no real experience who learn that *not* living life can be nasty. Even to a trained eye the two literary formulas not infrequently may seem to overlap.

In *The Albatross* (1975) and *A Bit of Singing and Dancing* (1973), Susan Hill's predilection for very young boys and for old women inclines her toward these venerable formulas, and at her best she can work them wonderfully well. The first volume's strongest story, "Friends of Miss Reece," exploits both formulas and both character types: an older woman afflicted with Parkinson's disease who has never really lived and a six-year-old boy whose story opens with a hissed "You're in the way." She dies in a room just down the hall from where he was born; both suffer from relatives with all the material means in the world who selfishly condemn to bitter bleakness those two good souls so similar and so utterly dependent. Susan Hill tells their stories with such insight, sensitivity, intelligence, and impressive craft that one dislikes objecting that their stories are formulaic.

Her affinity for such formulas in fact is one of her real strengths; there is in Susan Hill a stereotypically British fondness for tradition over innovation. One can imagine this generation's great-grandfathers appreciating "Halloran's Child" or "The Custodian" when typical stories by trendier writers of the 1970s would leave them cold or flustered.

The two stories mentioned above, like many of her others, have something of the fable about them. She tends to develop characters through exaggerating certain simplified elements of personality and ignoring others; she has a related tendency to choose introverted characters locked in relatively isolated lives uncomplicated by large families, fancy careers, demanding social ties. If the pared-down characterization suggests fable, more basic still are her themes, which tend to focus on one or another aspect of the fundamental nature of things. The aging mute coffinmaker who dominates "Halloran's Child" is not literally death, but virtually everything about him defines death and our understanding of it. A tacky Victorian Gothic monstrosity of a country home and the retarded boy who inhabits it define the tackiness of an adulterous affair a cynical woman and her lover bring to it in "In the Conservatory." A television set and a lodger in "A Bit of Singing and Dancing" define the small hedonisms that cheer through the escape from mundaneness they provide. In "The Peacock" a bird in a stuffy summerhouse where a frightened woman finds herself trapped helps crystallize the terrifying glory in life from which the timid must flee rather than experience. She seems fond of developing these fables in deceptively simple parallel structures: A = B, make of it what you will.

Frequently characters who seem to have lived (or not-to-have-lived) most of their lives as one of a mismatched pair seem born to have been solitaries, the Mutt and Jeff pair in "Mr. Proudham and Mr. Slight," for example, or Miss Bartlett in "How Soon Can I Leave," who defines herself as independent despite seven years with Miss Roscommon. When the latter describes the relationship in terms of the former's need she provokes a rupture that ends in desperation and death.

The finest of her stories may be "The Custodian." An old man fears he will die before his seven-year-old ward is old enough for independence. The boy's long-lost father comes, lives with the pair for several months, and then desolates the old man by leaving with the boy—who has grown stouter of body and of heart with the younger, stronger man's example. It is a fable rich in meanings, none of them novel, each as central to the nature of things as the passing of generations, as common as the changing seasons, as noble, as painful, as selfish as absolute love.

Hill's stories are uniformly well-crafted, with well-developed characterizations of children and older women and adequate portrayals of others, but she seems reluctant to try to do more. She does have a sense of the essential rhythms of life. She seems at her best when she approaches a kind of near classic simplicity as in "The Custodian"; that basic strength is almost always there, and it is much more impressive when not diluted with little digs at class consciousness or doomed attempts to represent the cogitations of a sixty-year-old mathematician ("Somerville") or of a mentally handicapped seventeen-year-old boy ("The Albatross"). One applauds her attempt to expand her fictional territory while wishing she had tried to expand by abandoning formulas. "The Custodian," which at first seems so much simpler, so much less enterprising, is really much more original, much more compelling; it represents the difference between a Henry Moore and a department-store manikin.

• • •

With Ian McEwan, undeniably one of the decade's better writers, the second category verges toward the third, though not quite crossing the barrier. The paperback edition of McEwan's *First Love, Last Rites* (1975) contains a quotation from the *New York Review of Books* detailing some of the author's subject matter: "Dirt, scum, pus, menstrual blood, pathetic obesity, total chinlessness, enforced transvestitism, early teenage incest, child abuse and child murder." On the cover, it is called "A BOOK OF WICKED AND BEAUTIFUL THINGS." Still, in many ways the stories—despite their invitation to gasps and leers—are determinedly traditional, unrelentingly moral. Indeed, they resemble many of his characters, perverse and monstrous in appearance, reassuringly conventional beneath the surface.

Despite his sometimes radical subject matter, McEwan for the most part refuses to concern himself with novelties of technique or with intellectual posturings. In his most striking stories he focuses on various kinds and degrees of monstrosity and perversion: physical, emotional, sexual, social, cultural. His basic formula, one of the oldest in literature, involves challenging and usually reversing automatic definitions of the good guys and the bad guys. His virtue may be largely a historical one, for his shifting definitions of "us" and "them" occur at a time when a significant body of readers may be prepared to experience a kind of sympathy for certain categories of monstrosity. He tells his stories with imagination, fine humor, psychological insight, and power.

In "Homemade" the adolescent protagonist is old enough to recognize that his culture defines manhood in terms of sexual conquest, normal enough to appreciate masturbation, but sensitive enough to be terrified of initiation via the most readily available hunk of female flesh, Lulu, nicknamed Zulu Lulu,

who—so fame had it—had laid a trail across north London of frothing idiots, a desolation row of broken minds and pricks spanning Shepherds Bush to Holloway, Ongar to Islington. Lulu! Her wobbling girth and laughing piggy's eyes, blooming thighs and dimpled finger-joints, this heaving, steaming, leg-load of schoolgirl flesh who had, so reputation insisted, had it with a giraffe, a humming-bird, a man in an iron lung (who had subsequently died), a yak, Cassius Clay, a marmoset, a Mars Bar and the gear stick of her grandfather's Morris Minor (and subsequently a traffic warden).

He decides, sensibly enough, to rape his ten-year-old sister instead, but after conning her into bed to play Mummies and Daddies he finds himself ignorant of certain subtleties of intercourse: penetration, for example. The sister instructs him, gets bored, falls asleep, and after a lengthy struggle he manages a little pop of an orgasm. He ends the story immensely relieved at having finally achieved real manhood—but averse for a while to the sight of anything at all naked. Despite the sensational subject matter, a reader should have the acumen to perceive that the victim here is not the sister, who seems of tougher stuff than her brother, but the young man who has been turned into an incestuous child molester by a culture that grossly equates adult-hood with intercourse. The boy and his less-wounded sister will prob-ably grow up as healthy as any of the rest of us; the same cannot be said for other of McEwan's protagonists.

In "Butterflies" a young man has endured a lifetime of ostracism because of a physical deformity, utter "chinlessness." Raging for some kind of human contact he leads a little girl on a walk through an urban wasteland—filthy canal, deserted factories, dump, young punks about to roast a cat alive—to a lonely spot where he makes her touch him, ejaculates, and drowns her. The protagonist here is a genuine monster, but one whose monstrosity was created by a society that denies love, acceptance, warmth on the basis of superficial physical features.

Other stories, "Conversation with a Cupboard Man" and "Disguis-es," for instance, concern a theme that is only implicit in the others: betrayal of children by adults generally and by parents in particular. In "Disguises" a sensitive, withdrawn child is raised by an aunt who insists he wear a costume for dinner every night and finally forces him to dress like a garish little girl; the story climaxes at a costume party where all the adult guests seem normal but are cross-dressed; the emotionally brutalized boy seems destined to become one of them.

McEwan's finest is his title story. A couple in their late teens live together blissfully at first, but complications ensue. Her ten-year-old brother spends most of his time in their flat, a refugee from a home desolated by parental warfare. The young couple's sex life slowly decays, in part because of a strange scratching sound in the wall when they make love, a sound he comes to identify with the child he may be making—though he does not want to—in the girl's belly. Metaphors of entrapment, decay, abortion lead the reader to realize that the couple's elders, like those in most of McEwan's stories, have failed to prepare them for a good life. Their society is interested more in trapping them as they themselves have trapped in the river an eel that was seeking only sustenance and killed a pregnant rat that was trying to escape. But the couple finally seem to have managed to struggle free of these patterns. The story's conclusion suggests that they, virtually alone among the volume's protagonists, may discover a way to live a decent life.

McEwan's second volume, *In Between the Sheets* (1979), is a fine collection; still, none of these stories can stand comparison with the three or four best in *First Love, Last Rites*. Here McEwan's subjects are less original, his vision more mundane. The angry wunderkind who created the earlier stories has become a tired young man, less enraged with adulthood's crimes against children, more inclined to nag. The title of his first story, "Pornography," in one sense defines the volume's theme: treatment of human beings as things.

In the first story a clerk in a porn shop dallies too cavalierly with two girlfriends; their vengeance comes when they strap him to a bed and perform an unwelcome and unusual kind of amputation. In "Dead As They Come" a thrice-divorced millionaire engages in a long affair with a department store dummy, finding it preferable to animate women; he finally destroys the manikin in a jealous rage when he's convinced it is betraying him with his chauffeur.

"In Between the Sheets," perhaps the best of the volume as well as the most understated, focuses on a man separated from his wife: "I never satisfied my wife in marriage, you see. Her orgasms terrified me." The story opens with his having a wet dream in which he fantasizes his fourteen-year-old daughter as a substitute for her mother. The daughter and a dwarfish girlfriend spend the night in his apartment and the daughter wakes, as her father often does, in nameless fear of what might be death. He talks her to sleep by telling of the many birthday presents he has bought her: "In the pallor of her upturned throat he thought he saw from one bright morning in his childhood a field of dazzling white snow which he, a small boy of eight, had not dared scar with his footprints." It is a touching story of pre- and postinitiation.

McEwan displays even in his weaker stories a constant loving craftsmanship, a sure hand for balanced details and echoing motifs. He writes often and unhappily of sexual relationships. On the one hand, the women in his stories regularly mutilate the men physically, emotionally, materially—denying their existence as meaningful human beings, depriving them of their children; one even orders a submissive young man to pee his pants in a posh restaurant and, when he complies, introduces him to her parents whom she had seen approaching the table. But the woman too can be as much SM as MS—one nut begs her lover to chain her to his bed for a weekend. McEwan's men are unable to cope with adult women and feel their strongest love—sometimes sexual, sometimes not—for daughters or daughter figures, young, relatively submissive, unjaded, respectful.

Late in the book one of his characters says: "There will always be problems between men and women and everyone suffers in some way." McEwan undercuts characters given to such jejeune pontification, but that banality remains in the mind. The wisdom of this second volume is essentially revelation of the mundane horror spawned in between the sheets and complements the more varied horrors exposed in the earlier and better book.

The Individual in Conflict with Society

One of the enduring puzzles of the short story as a genre is why it took so long for the British to produce writers of the first rank. The Americans, the French, the Russians can offer any number of nineteenth-century classics, but the British—with a list of great novelists stretching from the eighteenth century through the twentieth—have very little to offer in the short story until the twentieth century. One answer is that the novel as a form and the British as a people thrive on an expansive social vision, which tends to choke the short story. It may not be coincidence that the first indisputably great short story writer to be born in England is D. H. Lawrence, whose stories frequently concern social or cultural problems victimizing his characters.

A substantial number of subsequent British short story writers have found the same path, the best among them mastering the tricky technique of suggesting massive social, economic, or cultural forces with subtle details of setting or speech or the unquestioned assumptions of their characters. Perhaps the most forceful postwar expression of this tendency was Alan Sillitoe's *The Loneliness of the Long-Distance Runner* and the books by the angry young men who raced with him. In this regard a surprising and ironic facet of the short fiction of the 1970s is its relative lack of attention to the class system. Snobbery exists and is occasionally pilloried, but the prejudices attacked most enthusiastically are those of race or culture or gender. Anti-Semitism is challenged in stories by Emanuel Litvinoff and by other writers who touch on Jewish refugees, especially children, who landed in Britain in the 1930s. Another important theme for writers informed by a wide social vision is the current state of British civilization—dreadful, they tend to agree, but for a variety of reasons. Malcolm Bradbury condemns a culture too self-conscious, too infected with a social science mentality. Jennifer Dawson rues a society overinstitutionalizing itself, smothering individuality, encouraging the decay of personal responsibility and interpersonal love. John Berger largely turns his back on a sterile civilization that is all but weaned from the natural cycles of life.One of the more interesting aspects of the writers in this category is that only rarely do any two of them seem to be describing the same society or the same remedy.

Malcolm Bradbury's private world is a kind of overacademized Anglo-America, and in *Who Do You Think You Are?* (1976) he offers stellar examples of academic fiction. Story after story is on the one hand well crafted, reflective, witty, on the other, derivative, unoriginal, passionless. Bradbury favors academic haunts both as settings (classrooms, faculty offices, lecture halls) and as characters (beings with human shapes and memories and behavior patterns but with a posthuman lack of viscera).

In "A Goodbye for Evadne Winterbottom," a stuffy psychiatrist briefly evades the clinical imperative, "Thou shalt not get emotionally involved." Evadne, intelligent and oversexed, seduces the narrator into becoming one more in a dizzy chain of therapists who experience a rueful joy in temporarily exchanging their professional ethics for the new morality. The narrator ends by suggesting that Evadne somehow transcends the rest of us mortals in genuine fulfillment and "self-celebration." Still, to at least one reader, Evadne seems more promiscuous than promising as a human being, more a dirty old academic's wet dream (or wet recollection) than a real singing of the body electric.

Evadne represents something of a paradox: while Bradbury makes her the most attractive woman in the book he has also made her finally less human a being. In his other stories he features women at least as sexually aggressive as Evadne but generally more threatening, more powerful, less attractive.

In the title story an academic social psychologist is the protagonist. Edgar Loach tunes in to all the superficial sociopsychological data surrounding him and tunes out anything else in his environment, ignoring, for instance, "the data-less wastes of agriculture and woods" he passes through on his way to serve as panelist on a pilot TV game show. More important, Loach tunes out the natural—that is, the nonsuperficial—in others. The contestants on the program, for example, are reduced to social scientific phenomena when Edgar and the other panelists shred the contestants' roles, hangups, and "cultural referents" in a game show attempt to classify each individual's identity. At an aftershow party the TV group practice the game on themselves. Edgar finds himself reduced to a tipsy whimpering ninny when Flora, the woman who served first as his copanelist and then as his tormentor, offers herself to him as a kind of booby prize. Edgar feels terror: "it struck him all at once that making love with an advanced Freudian was the biggest test of his career." Edgar remains incapable of satisfying either of them until Flora manipulates him into momentarily thinking of her as woman—nothing else. Satisfaction achieved, Edgar later reverts.

Bradbury might achieve a more satisfying story if he could more powerfully, more freely evoke his characters' emotional depths; but imagination, passion, wildness—these he avoids as determinedly as do his databound academics. "Nobody Here in England" succeeds better than any of the others; in Mrs. Prokosch Bradbury has created his only really brilliant character, one who combines elements of his academic and repulsive women, yet still manages to be enormously sympathetic. A dotty, aging woman, she promises a gift of Bernard Shaw letters if a school will allow her to give a lecture. Most of the story focuses on Leo Dennie, "an administrative person" who arranges details of her visit and attempts to learn whether Mrs. Prokosch is a genuine Shaw intimate with letters of some value or merely a con woman. At the climax she sets fire to the pitiful scraps of correspondence—mostly lengthy, passionate letters by her, abrupt postcards from him (they had never met)—and in that act immolates herself on a bed in her room at the faculty club. Surviving the fire is a vial that serves as the story's key metaphor—a vial in which, according to Mrs. Prokosch, Shaw deposited seminal fluid: "We wanted to make a new race. I had the ideal biology for the future." True or not, Mrs. Prokosch *does* have a vigorous wildness that saves her from the desiccated academic limbo in which the standard Bradbury characters languish.

So—who do you think you are? Finally the answer does not seem to matter much. If you are a character in the book, you are probably either a bloodless academic or a vulgar outsider. Either way you probably represent some of the worst in the current sociopsychological conditions of contemporary Western culture.

• • •

Jennifer Dawson's *Hospital Wedding* (1978) comprises stories that are both compassionate and intellectually honest. At times the first condition seems at odds with the second. The paperback's cover quotes a reviewer who enthusiastically wrote that " 'Bleeding Hearts' is one of the sharpest stories about 'liberals' that I have read." Those who read less intelligently, less honestly than she writes may see merely a pair of expatriated liberal Rhodesians who take a displaced African girl into their flat only to find themselves badly confused, exploited, and nearly deprived of their home before the girl decamps. A more sensitive reader might detect a story in which terms like *liberal* and *racist* are gross distortions of complex human attitudes, emotions, relationships. One constant theme in Dawson's work is the destructive power of easy categorization.

Where "Bleeding Hearts" deals with complexities of racial prejudice, "Precinct" deals with class. A Cambridge don prides himself on his lack of snobbery but feels lost when a black worker he tried to cultivate rejects him and even joins in a rude practical joke against him. The don finds himself spiritually broken at the end because of his inability to locate a human middle ground: "Between the devotion of loyal college servants and the threats of an angry revolutionary proletariat, he couldn't find anything."

Dawson's stories often focus on individuals dehumanized by such facile categorizations: the old, the poor, women, the mentally or emotionally ill. She knows, as we all know, that sympathy can erode these barriers. But she has a genius for showing how inhuman well-meaning sympathy that stops short of full love can be. In "The Patient's Place" William Cretley shuttles from mental hospital to Salvation Army to home to who knows where—he has no "place" because everywhere he meets with sympathy, nowhere with real love. Perhaps the most haunting of Dawson's stories is "The Dress," an understated, wrenching story of a Jewish girl orphaned during World War II, one among many who first meets with cheery sympathy from a British sponsor, then is shuffled off to a religious boarding school for unwell children, and finally, virtually forgotten by her sponsor, is exploited as a servant by the school. Many years later she has become a prison officer, refusing any other job or even a promotion because "it would have meant my own clothes." She must wear a uniform and serve as a prison guard, for she has become irretrievably institutionalized.

In "A Spoilt Little Boy" Dawson portrays a small child whose parents "love" him too much to discipline him. Finally, in play, he kills his mother with his father's pistol. Pervading the volume is a hierarchy of human relations with something like abandonment at the bottom and just above it a flaccid sympathy that attends to material needs but fails to become that higher love that can truly help the weak—enabling them to take responsibility for themselves, to become fully human.

Unquestionably the best, most complex, most frightening of these works is the title story, "Hospital Wedding." Here Dawson sensitively integrates and expands her themes into a compelling vision of our culture. The story's nucleus is the attempt by young Dr. Hayward to prevent a lobotomy on Jean Gold, an unattractive forty-year-old institutionalized woman. Orbiting this nucleus are subordinate, but related themes, one being sexism generally: "Men never feel safe with women until they've reduced them to flesh and things." Another is the ominous effect families can have, for "families are more destructive than hospitals." Another is the widespread social approval of one nut's version of urban renewal, bulldozing into rubble structures that some consider homes and that others consider a priceless heritage of centuries past: "the community is an institutionalized invalid already." Lobotomizing, institutionalization—one of the patients sees the implications better than do the doctors. He points to an aquarium. "In ten years' time there'll be no more fish in the rivers. They'll all be in tanks like this. Adaptation. That's the law of survival."

So even nature finds itself an implicated victim. And here arises Dawson's most frightening theme. At first the lobotomy Miss Gold had resisted was described as a kind of "social rape." But in this story

and others Dawson has shown that the ultimate horror of institutionalization is its power to seduce victims into conspiring against themselves. At the climax Dr. Hayward discovers that Jean Gold was
probably a victim of child abuse in her early years; a nonsurgical treatment may save her. But his superior Dr. Dulton has already enticed
Miss Gold into signing the consent form. As the patients and staff
have a party outside on the lawn, Dr. Hayward looks out to see Dr.
Dulton waltzing the willing Jean Gold in his arms. "It wasn't rape
after all. Human dignity was after all an adventitious thing, and it was
a hospital wedding."

Here Dawson brilliantly sums up her major themes—the evils of
categorization and institutionalization, the perils and magnificence of
freedom, the dangers of sympathy divorced from genuine love—in the
metaphor of lobotomy, the denial of human possibility.

• • •

Whereas Malcolm Bradbury and Jennifer Dawson survey a disturbing present pregnant with a horrifying future, Emanuel Litvinoff focuses on a past society dense with problems that nostalgia has largely
robbed of pain. Litvinoff might with some justice declare that the standards by which he should be judged are different from those to be
applied to most other writers of our third category. In a note prefacing
his volume *Journey through a Small Planet,* he describes the East London
borough of Bethnal Green, a bustling Jewish slum where he grew up.
Now, he remarks sadly, "almost every house in it has gone and it exists,
if at all, only in the pages of this book." His aim, one at least as old
as the nineteenth century, is to create stories out of roughly equal parts
of local color and personal reminiscence.

The locality is a London ghetto crammed with refugees from the
Russian empire: the women ground down by poverty and too much
love—of their men, of their children, of their lost homeland; the men
tortured by doomed dreams of great worldly success and too often driv-
en to political fanaticism by personal failures exaggerated by wars and
economic depression. In the first story, "Ancestors," Litvinoff affectionately, sadly pictures a small cell of communists ignorant of the
extent to which their dreams of political revolution are a kind of scab
over unhealing sores in their private lives.

Each of the eleven stories that follows is in the first person, and the
narrator is consistently identified as Emanuel Litvinoff; the mother,
father, stepfather, brothers, and other characters also remain constant.

A purist might insist that the volume consists more of nonfictional personal reminiscence or autobiography than true fiction, but Litvinoff would ignore such caviling; he contents himself with writing well about what he knows—or what remains after the filterings of memory. A child dealing with an absent father, the reluctant acceptance of a stepfather, first stirrings of sexual desire, battles with anti-Semitism, memories of a lovely girl "ruined" by a bounder, a boy whose personality serves as a battleground for the wars of father and grandmother— he turns each into a wry, touching, insightful short story.

In sum, he manages to create a sense of the time and place as he remembers it, and he deserves credit for doing so artfully, with an air of truth. Still, all this finally results in a relatively modest achievement. His troubled young men, bigots, harried mothers, driven fathers come to no more than half-life. His stories illuminate that life on which he wishes to cast light; they do not blaze with a life of their own. Litvinoff succeeds well in what he attempts: a literary re-creation of Bethnal Green between the wars; one can only wish he had set a higher goal.

$$\bullet \quad \bullet \quad \bullet$$

One leaves Britain far behind, though not British problems, in Robin Jenkins's *A Far Cry from Bowmore* (1973), as well integrated a volume of stories as a reader could reasonably want. Each of these conventionally told stories is set in the East—Malaysia, India, Afghanistan. Each offers its special perspective on the volume's thematic keystone—prejudice—and by the final page Jenkins has constructed a solid and impressively complete museum of intolerance.

In "Imelda and the Miserly Scot" the immediate attack focuses on racism. Andrew McAndrick contemplates marriage to a devastatingly seductive Asian, but her dark skin, her facial features, her accent, though irresistible in a mistress, disqualify her to be the wife of a proper British dentist. To give him his due McAndrick does sometimes weaken in his resolve, only to find his racial prejudice buttressed by his cultural prejudice—her ancestors in the Celebese were too recently aboriginal. When even this bastion trembles, the Scot's miserliness remains firm—she would cost him too much in new clothing and other domestic matters. Though she does serve his vanity as much as his lust, he finally determines to rid himself of her. The story ends appropriately when she skewers him on a primitive speared blowgun, an artifact cheated out of an aboriginal chief and kept on his wall for decoration. McAndrick's fatal prejudice reveals itself sometimes as chauvinistic, sometimes as racial, sometimes as cultural, but resolved in his propensity for seeing human beings immediately in categories, ultimately as things to be categorized. This destroys the Scot's soul as fatally as the spear destroys his body.

In his title story Jenkins strives for a masterpiece. Macpherson, a civil engineer on duty in Malaysia, considers himself devoutly religious, liberal toward his children, and sympathetic toward the natives in their conflicts with "civilization." The story stands on a symbolic underpinning that opposes machines to trees, and we see Macpherson ultimately set a consistent pattern of choosing the inhuman and sacrificing the natural. The climax comes in a kind of mini-Conrad inversion. Instead of a big journey to the heart of darkness, Macpherson is badgered into a small river passage to a heart of humanity. The story, however, suffers from calculated intellectualization. Jenkins strives for a good bit more than he achieves, but one applauds the striving.

In many ways more interesting are stories like "Christian Justice," "Jeena," and "Siddiq" in which Jenkins explores prejudice, injustice, and exploitation among the Asians themselves. In "Bonny Chung," the longest story, Jenkins attempts more humor than before and also a broader canvas, dealing significantly in a single story with Indians, Chinese, Malays, Scots, and others—a babel of languages, cultures, races, mores, and prejudices. It is questionable here whether the Asians devote more energy to practicing their own peculiar brands of intolerance or to complaining about the prejudices dominating others' attitudes toward themselves. "Bonny Chung" is a fine conclusion for the volume, however, for all the various brands of prejudice and snobbery of the earlier stories combine here. Finally, *A Far Cry from Bowmore* turns out to be a fairly good book dealing with the subject that animates so many great books—the hell we create for ourselves and others when our socially generated prejudices combine with our egocentricity to prevent us from realizing love.

· · ·

Like Jenkins, John Berger abandons Britain as setting but not as implied subject. *Pig Earth* (1980) is an ambitious and to some extent successful attempt to capture the essence of life as lived by contemporary French Savoyard peasants. Berger highlights his stories with poems and essays, but the heart of the book is the fiction. The book focuses on the peasants' closeness—physical, emotional, psychological—to the basic cyclical processes of life. Such themes are less than novel, but at his best Berger can enrich the stereotype with a specific density that makes his stories memorable. He skirts the great destroyer—sentimentality—not by showing the peasants to be lacking in compassion, kindness, concern but by showing the toughmindedness tempering the compassion, the calculation complicating the kindness, the self-interest inextricably bound in the disinterested concern.

Among the finest is "Addressed to Survivors." A cow that its owner believes to be lost has undertaken a long and treacherous trek to find a bull in a far pasture; on her return the cow falls and rolls one hundred meters, finally stopping short of plunging over a precipice. "She would have hit the boulders at the bottom, a mass of unsellable broken meat and bone." The old peasant woman and her hired man spend the night with the now paralyzed cow, talking and keeping her covered; next day the neighbors help drag the cow to the stable, but she cannot stand. The old woman must call a butcher's wagon to have the cow hauled away, but in a last sympathetic act packs straw against the cow's flank to protect it from the wheel's sharp metal housing. We have entered deeply into the experience of the cow driven by her procreative instincts to seek the bull only to find herself deserted by her legs; now we are moved by the old woman's affection for her cow.

The best story in the book is "The Three Lives of Lucie Cabrol," which realizes the thematic potential of the earlier stories and brilliantly interrelates these themes to produce a narrative fabric that is enduring and aesthetically pleasing. Lucie, we come to realize, represents all that dominates Berger's conception of the peasantry: an indomitable life force; humility undergirding an unpretentious pride that is quaint out of context but admirable within; a beauty hidden to all but the most resolute seeker; patience, determination, and cunning that is capable of transforming a wasteland.

Pig Earth is the first in an incomplete trilogy Berger calls "Into Their Labors." If the later volumes live up to this one, the trilogy will be a significant work indeed.

The Avant-Garde

One might do well to develop a distinction between innovative writers and experimental writers. The former seem relatively more at ease with the traditional story but are concerned to guide its evolution in a way that permits new subjects, themes, techniques, angles of vision, and forms to grow out of the old. The experimental writer is more revolutionary, jaded with the conventional, determined to create a wholly new fiction on the ashes of the old. The experimental writer often calls his works "fictions" rather than "short stories," in part to mark the break, in part perhaps to demand a new critical perspective. The problem with "experiments" is that in short fiction they seem almost always to fail. But even in failure experimentation can pave the way for fictions that do succeed. Major writers like Christine Brooke-Rose and Gabriel Josipovici have the skill to meld what they require of the experimental and the traditional in order to create innovative fiction that triumphs. Excesses of experimentation make us all the readier to welcome the brilliant antemodernism of a writer like Angela Carter who outflanks many experimenters by circling back through tradition to a mode outmoded enough to seem radically new.

Given the attention that British writers in all four categories pay to America, it is surprising that their innovative fiction seems to owe much less to American postmodernism than to Continental movements, particularly the French New Novel and fashionable intellectual trends: structuralism, poststructuralism, and semiotics.

Although avant-garde writers pride themselves on going off in different directions, one concern they currently share is communication. Some reduce the topic to technical gamesmanship; others conceive of the subject as the most crucial of our time, one to be analyzed and experienced with all the sophistication and power that fiction can bring to bear.

• • •

Angela Carter is the least experimental among the innovators. Although she titled her first book of "stories" *Fireworks: Nine Stories in Various Disguises* (1974), a purist might argue that most pieces in the book are essays or sketches on the one hand or tales on the other. "Souvenir of Japan," "The Smile of Winter," and "Flesh and the Mirror" are the former; well written, intense, original as they are they still seem less interesting and less significant than such stories or tales as "Penetrating the Heart of the Forest," an interesting retelling of the Edenic myth with God as something of an absentminded botanist, or "The Executioner's Beautiful Daughter," a psychoanalyst's playground of bestiality, repression, murder, and incest set in a fantasy land of benighted souls.

"Reflections," the second best story in the volume, seems a psychedelic compound of Lewis Carroll, Kafka, Einstein, de Sade, and Urmyth. A man discovers a shell that could not exist; a rifle-wielding girl forces him to an interview with an androgyne who compels him to enter an antiuniverse through a mirror. The story's mystery and magic for the most part work their spell marvelously. The story's motifs can be juxtaposed in enough possible interpretive combinations to puzzle any devoté of the Rubik's cube, a triumph of fantasy.

But by far the best in the volume is "The Loves of Lady Purple." On the surface it is a version of narrative material closely akin to Pinocchio and Pygmalion; Carter's sensual, polished style makes that surface level pure delight. The plot is rather simple. An old Japanese puppeteer accompanied by his nephew and a mute young orphan girl wanders the world with his puppet show, which highlights Lady Purple. This six-foot puppet enchantress weaves her way through a playlet, which has her at twelve seducing and then murdering and robbing her benefactor, building a notorious career as the most passionate, depraved, and cruel of prostitutes, and finally ending as a poor, crazed necrophiliac. The professor dresses her in finery one evening, and kisses her—a kiss she returns before biting his neck to drain him of blood and then setting fire to everything and running to the Transylvanian village's only brothel.

Carter enriches this dramatic but uncomplicated narrative line with her patient, sensual style, but the real power in "The Loves of Lady Purple" lies in the sophistication with which she allows compelling meanings to grow out of the tale; the three most powerful might be called feminist, structuralist, and semiotic.

A feminist will have no trouble reading Lady Purple as woman forced into a role as sexual object, as puppet, as thing. "Her actions were not so much an imitation as a distillation and intensification of those of a born woman and so she could become the quintessence of eroticism, for no woman born would have dared to be so blatantly seductive." But she becomes woman as avenger, wantonly, cruelly destroying the men who come to use her, though herself paying a heavy price for her revenge—never being able to retrace her path back through the role of sexual object to human. Recognizing the pattern of dehumanization, Carter implies, may not be enough to enable us to break it.

From a structuralist perspective the story frightens with its compelling, almost offhanded way of demonstrating how repeated patterns of thought and behavior can create a kind of closed, artificial reality utterly condemning those trapped within it. From this perspective, sexism stands as one of many symptoms, the grand disease being the human compulsion to borrow conceptions of reality from preestablished patterns. As "there can be no spontaneity in a puppet drama" so there can be no ultimate freedom in a universe where each human being's every thought and action depend on immaterial strings of class, sex, culture, family, and, most important, conceptual programming. When the puppet comes to life she can have no thought other than seduction, murder, prostitution—she can only act off the literal stage what countless repetitions on the puppet stage have patterned into her. Is the freedom any one of us seems to enjoy any less illusory than hers?

In reflecting language itself, the story offers yet a third vision equally bleak and disheartening. It is hardly an accident that Carter's oriental puppeteer provides a vocal commentary to his puppet show in a language that no one in his Transylvanian audience can comprehend, nor that the only one who could understand the language—his nephew—is deaf, nor that the seven- or eight-year-old girl who accompanies them is dumb. Their milieu is that of the fairground, the universal fairground where "the huckster's raucous invitations are made in a language beyond language, or, perhaps, in that ur-language of grunt and bark which lies behind all language." Uncle and nephew communicate only by sign language; but all the puppet show communicates itself through a variety of signs—the puppets' costumes, the backdrops, the props, the lighting, and perhaps most of all the "balletic mime" of posture, motion, gesture with which the puppeteer articulates his puppet. But when puppet overcomes puppeteer, he finds himself exactly where, semioticians argue, users of language find themselves—powerless in the grip of that which we naively believe ourselves to control. To a semiotician, soulless language controls its users every bit as much as Lady Purple when she first turns on her would-be master and then as she races to the brothel where deceptive whores are as available to any man's body as are words to any man's tongue. But here, in the reader's world beyond the story, words control more absolutely than whores, and final meanings are as elusive as a wooden puppet's soul.

The stories in Carter's second volume, *The Bloody Chamber* (1979), explore manifestations of the bizarre subterranean forces binding male and female. Her title story provides perhaps the clearest example. As narrative "The Bloody Chamber" suffers from obvious and significant flaws—some apparently careless, others merely silly—of which an intentionally cartoonish deus ex machina ending is most crucial. But

Carter obviously has little interest in mere narrative. Her heart she puts into a sensual, almost succulent prose style that of itself serves as all the raison d'etre anyone could fairly require. More important than heart, though, is the mind manipulating the imagery, incidents, and characters far below the sometimes cloying prose style where lies dark, mythic apologue—satisfyingly deep if not quite bottomless.

The title story, a reimagining of "Bluebeard," takes the form of a reminiscence beginning with the narrator as a ripely virginal bride of seventeen. Once in her husband's castle, she discovers first his cache of sadoerotica and later follows a forbidden path through a "long, winding corridor, as if I were in the viscera of the castle" to a bloody torture chamber where her husband, a marquis, has brutally murdered all his previous wives. The husband, of course, knew she would disobey his prohibition against entering the room and bids her prepare for decapitation. At the last moment the girl's mother inexplicably arrives on a charging steed and puts a bullet through the marquis's head.

On a superficial level Carter offers a kind of feminist Gothic romance, attacking the male as destroyer of the female and exalting the macho woman. But she has too much intelligence, integrity, and native curiosity to be satisfied with such reductionism. Her real interest lies in an attempt to understand the nature of the narrator's desire for the marquis. What strange fancies reign over this seventeen-year-old girl? On their wedding night her husband in the throes of orgasm reveals a face that both disturbs and attracts her. She learns that night something of the truth of her husband's favorite poet: "there is a striking resemblance between the act of love and the ministrations of a torturer." The story's second bloody chamber is her own postvirginal vagina, bleeding from their wedding night.

The third and most interesting bloody chamber is the girl's mind. Her psychic innocence is as easily ruptured as her virginal membrane. She admits that in her "innocence [lay] a rare talent for corruption." This was the latent bloom that drew her husband, and she acknowledges, "I was not afraid of him; but of myself."

Almost more apologue than myth, "The Bloody Chamber" allows the protagonist to plumb her own desires, her own sexuality, and to escape from the masochism inherent in desire for such a husband as the marquis—a man she would not claim to love, only to desire. She is unable to save herself, but is saved by the older woman, the mother, and is finally rewarded not with her husband's vast fortune (she gives almost all of it away, in part to found a school for the blind) but with a different male consort, one who depends on her, whose function is not to dominate her but to tune her piano, one whose blindness, myth critics would insist, represents symbolic castration.

Stories in the volume tend to fall into two categories; in theoretical terms the group containing the less successful is paradoxically the more intriguing. First there is the more artistically successful group of stories: "The Erlking" describes a scruffy, bizarrely seductive male nature being; "The Snow Child," a fable hardly more than a page and a half long, attacks the destructive nature of male sexual fantasies; "Wolf Alice," especially noteworthy, creates a sensitive rapprochement between two lonely, abandoned souls, a feral girl and an old male vampire-ghoul; in "The Lady of the House of Love" a predatory vampiress sacrifices her life for love of a young man. In this first group Carter draws on various characters and motifs from folklore that she transforms willy-nilly into her own lightly plotted but powerfully evocative and original tales. Here she indulges her gift for descriptive writing, bizarre fancy, and luscious imagery—and for painfully observed, truthfully told analysis of the peculiarities of normally abnormal human emotion. Very few other writers have dealt so insightfully, so tellingly, with the proposition that eroticism, love, and happiness have absolutely no necessary interconnections.

In the second and technically much more fascinating group, Carter disdains merely borrowing motifs and rewrites stories wholesale: "The Courtship of Mr. Lyon" offers a tame-enough retelling of "Beauty and the Beast"; "The Werewolf" and "The Company of Wolves" give contradictory versions of "Little Red Riding Hood"; and her "Puss in Boots" strains itself through successive screens of a self-conscious style, commedia dell'arte, and burlesque that sometimes make slapstick seem sophisticated. Not one of these retellings succeeds as it ought; yet each achieves a noble near success. Her venture can be seen as an attempt to recapture the narrative essence of fairy tales for jaded adults; her retellings are in a sense restorings of material that was our inalienable birthright as children but that we have squandered through sophistication. Carter means for "The Werewolf" to pierce to the heart of an adult's subconscious fears as powerfully as "Little Red Riding Hood" can pierce a child's, and she nearly succeeds.

Too many talented avant-garde writers whine in the same narcissistic chorus—their theme, the impossibility of writing contemporary fiction. Carter has scouted one way out; to the newest of storytelling problems she has applied the oldest of all storytelling solutions: do not tell a story, retell one.

Other British writers of the decade have stumbled into similar strategies: Wilson Harris reimagines Amerindian myths and legends; Melvyn Bragg's "A Christmas Child" almost literally translates Christianity's oldest story into contemporaneity; Elaine Feinstein makes a shattering success of a "Hansel and Gretel" that may owe less to the folktale than to magic realism. But Carter seems more gifted than any of them and, in her "restorying," to have found a method she may, with luck, ride to greatness.

• • •

Wilson Harris shares certain qualities with Angela Carter; he feels a compulsion to retell traditional stories; he is an original and intrepid writer with grand ambitions and an inspiring vision of the powers of literature. The fatal problem is that what he writes can be virtually unreadable. He has produced two slender volumes of short fiction, *The Sleepers of Roraima* (1970) and *The Age of the Rainmakers* (1971). These companion volumes depend on an attempt to involve a sophisticated twentieth-century mind in a reexperiencing of tribal myth. The first book focuses on the fierce Carib tribe, a people apparently closer to extinction than the whooping crane but who reportedly once raged like Vikings through the islands and much of the territory bordering the sea named for them. The first story focusing on these people, as Harris tells us in a prefatory note, "is an invention based on one of their little-known myths—the myth of *couvade*." Harris weaves this story from a boy who is one of the last of the Caribs, his grandfather's tales, dreams, sunglasses fallen from an airplane, longings for his lost parents, themes of metamorphosis and eclipse. At the heart of the story, as of Harris's method, lies a profound paradox: metamorphosis means the death of what was, but only in metamorphosis may that which was conquer and survive inevitable change. It seems that the boy's people may survive only by identifying themselves with a tribe they hate and fear; similarly, in order to retain imaginative life, the tribal myth of *couvade* requires metamorphosis into a short story, "Couvade."

Both of these books demand extremely resourceful reading. In fact, Harris's style is much more that of dense free verse in justified lines than that of anything worthy of the term *prose*. He steadily compounds his style with repetition, catalogs, antitheses, double words and phrases, awkward poeticisms; but the base of this unstable compound is abstraction. The function of myth is to transform platitudes into profundities by means of narrative magic. By drowning his style in abstractions Harris tries to claim a profundity he has not earned, and the result is travesty.

His second volume sometimes seems to parody Timothy Leary and at other times, the linguistically befuddled Prof. Irwin Corey. Here as in the earlier volume Harris prefaces his fiction with notes of a page or two in which he backgrounds his mythic material (here of declining South American tribes other than the Caribs) and outlines his intentions: the reader is repeatedly frustrated in hopes that authorial execution might equal authorial intention, but in this second volume Harris seems to fall even further than in the first.

· · ·

These first two writers practice a kind of innovation through retreat. The next two are at the cutting edge of the avant-garde.

The stories in Gabriel Josipovici's first collection, *Mobius the Stripper* (1974), fall into three categories. The first contains relatively conventional stories that finally achieve no very high level of success: "Colourings," "Seascape with Figures," "Refuse." The second group consists of innovative/speculative pieces equally mediocre: "It Isn't As If It Wasn't," "This," The Reconstruction." The third group, easily the most successful, contains stories as innovative and speculative as any in the second group and also on occasion manages to spur real interest in character and situation, to generate real emotional depth. Josipovici has a significant range, but the normal mode of his stories is monologue or juxtaposed blocks of dialogue with relatively little else.

"The Voices" is a curious, eerie piece, a kind of semiotic or epistemological fable that works rather well. The protagonist struggles both with an irrational fear of trees and with a congeries of voices, apparently family voices, which he hears or believes himself to hear. The boy apparently fears the trees' lack of final definition, rather as the voices' struggle with the evanescence of words and of dreams, with the ultimate inconceivability of communication or even of thought. "Little Words," a metafictional story, focuses on the relationship between a little girl and the grandmother whom she learns not to fear; the girl and grandmother share a love of toffee, which sticks tightly to things—like certain little words—and share a quality of imagination that distinguishes them from others in the family. In the conclusion the grandmother, whom the child may have aided in a most lovely suicide, insightfully (and deconstructively) ponders the nature of the stories she tells.

The volume's title piece, "Mobius the Stripper: A Topological Exercise," is a charming though finally rather bloodless metafictional exercise. A mobius strip, usually formed from a strip of paper with the ends joined, is a kind of ring with a single twist. Each page of the story has a dark horizontal line midway down to divide what seems to be one story on top from an apparently unrelated story below. It comes as no surprise that ultimately the content of the lower story merges with that of the upper story to give us a conceptual Mobius strip, a theoretically circular and therefore endless story, but one in which the surface reverses, and meaning alters, with each circuit. The upper story involves Mobius, a fat man who considers his performances in a nightclub as a kind of metaphysical exercise, a stripping of himself to essentials. The lower story involves a would-be writer severely blocked until a girlfriend insists that he go to see Mobius strip at a local club. Even on a first reading, the story invites some intriguing speculations on relationships between body and mind, between Mobius's physical (or metaphysical) stripping and the psychic exercises of the writer; on the congruence of lives (situations, interior and exterior pressures, conceptions of self, of others, of art) so apparently dissimilar as those of Mobius and the writer; on notions of audiences the two face, and so on. But perhaps the story's most telling question involves notions of the creative process and the relationship between one's art and one's life. The second time through the narrative Mobius strip we see how the writer creates the character of Mobius out of the writer's own most intimate (most stripped away) psychic experiences. The writer believes that actually creating a story might radically alter his life, and if so, then the reader might imagine Mobius not merely as a product of the writer but as an active agent of change; thus the Mobius narrative twists yet again. Other twists remain.

What is truth, how might it be sought, how portrayed? The story engages such ideas through a marvelously apt formal structure. If the characters themselves exerted anything like as much attraction as the speculative questions, "Mobius the Stripper" would be not merely a fascinating metafictional exercise but something much more important, a story worthy of enduring.

On the whole, Josipovici's second collection, *Four Stories* (1977), maintains a consistently higher level of success. The volume opens with "Contiguities," a brilliant and most original fiction, one that manages to experiment without abandoning emotion. Prefacing the story, the volume begins with an epigraph from the notebooks of Paul Klee: "White, in other words, is ever present and must be crowded out step by step." For what might we take white as a metaphor? Meaningless-ness? Death? Emotionlessness? Emptiness? Perhaps the void.

Klee is no realist, but one who draws significance from abstracted lines and shapes playing against each other and against the void. Josi-povici favors a similar kind of abstraction and similarly opposes it to void. It is not always possible to be certain whether a Klee figure is a bird or fish or snake or woman or neither one nor the other; the am-biguity can be alternately irrelevant and enriching. "Contiguities" is a brief story, about eleven pages divided into forty numbered sections. The protagonist is "you," apparently standing in a room with "the other" who may be anyone or nothing—a friend, a psychiatrist, a fig-ment of "your" imagination. The other encourages "you" to speak and sometimes "you" will speak and sometimes "a voice" seems to speak for "you" as if "you" were speaking unawares. The reluctant speaking and remembering are composed of similar abstractions but focus on "he" and "a woman." Again, they might be anyone—presumably in-cluding "the other" and "you"—and one could perform an amateur Rorschach by analyzing the identities a reader projects on to them; but to at least one reader "he" is an abstraction of fatherhood—hat firmly placed, coat tightly belted, waking, breakfasting, arranging his tie to a clock's mirroring face, eternally climbing the omnipresent stairs life endlessly places before fathers, and "the woman" must be the mother, weighted by memories and by photographs, which she must tear and toss into the ever-flowing river beside which she walks.

Josipovici composes his story largely of silences, aversions to speak-ing, obliquities, and an echo chamber of repetitions (like the sights of the bus journey: "so monotonously repetitive")—the repetitions that composed the lives of "he," of "the woman," that have become mem-ories backdropping "your" life. "You" spend a great deal of the story like Melville's Bartleby, staring at walls, silent. "You" even say, "I don't prefer"—but Bartleby seems to perish, a lost soul, whereas "you"—and it may be only a reader's projection—seem to reach a kind of catharsis of insight ("your" last spoken words: "I say I. I") and of outsight (the last words of the woman bringing coffee to the smiling man: "I bring it to him").

Again the Rorschach: at least one reader chooses to see a story of someone, "you," struggling against self to define a sense of "your" mother and father, and in this struggle defining an attitude toward life, one touched by loss, incommunicativeness, despair, rote living, but finally illuminated by some unspeakable triumphing over time, boredom, loss, change, denial, loneliness—an unspeakable that in "your" sense of the woman offering coffee to the smiling man marks a towering triumph over all the void.

"Second Person Looking Out," a relatively spare and abstract work, seems to be a metafictional fun piece. On the surface, an individual apparently follows his guide to some strange mansion with seventeen rooms, each room containing three movable windows; no guest ever views quite the same outside landscape that any other guest has seen. The path to the house winds amazingly, and sometimes the house seems quite near, at others much farther away or even to disappear. On leaving the house, one must follow rows of stones tied with string, but retreat and take another path whenever a stick of bamboo has been placed across the path. The story itself has three sections, the first told first person, the next third person, the last second person. Sometimes the protagonist on the path abruptly finds himself not only in the house but having been there for some time already, and as abruptly he may find himself on the path preparing to visit for the first time the house he has just left. All this involves charming enough reality games, games that are admittedly far from the high standards of those Alice plays through the looking glass—but then what such games are not?

A reader inclined to look beyond the surface can discern a metafictional apologue. In justifying the countless perspectives from which fiction may be written, Henry James said that there are many windows in the house of fiction. Josipovici calculates the number exactly, fifty-one, but his coup lies in observing that none of the windows is fixed, and none is ever the same for any two viewers. James's model allows us to assume any number may look from the same window onto the same landscape. Josipovici's insists that no two may ever see quite the same perspective. The story introduces a number of other fascinating questions, among them: What is it to be inside the house as opposed to out? When is one involved in a fiction, when not? What is the relationship between one outside the fiction (a reader?) looking in (at characters? at the narrative consciousness?) and between a "second person looking out"? Is this second person looking out the author anticipating the reader? Who knows?

Josipovici's third and fourth stories are almost as successful. "Death of the Word" and "He" both involve grief over a specific individual's

death, but strain that grief through conceptual puzzles involving communication, fiction, the creative process, imagination, the nature of
human experience.

Despite a reader's necessary reservations about specific elements in
some of his stories, Josipovici seems to challenge the frontiers of short
fiction with a surprisingly consistent degree of success in blending significant thought and emotion. Would that more among the innovative
and experimental writers of his generation demonstrated even fraction-
al amounts of his talent.

• • •

The most relentlessly unconventional writer of the decade (and most
relentlessly boring) is Giles Gordon, whose first collection bears the
same name he gave to a series of prose experiments, *Pictures from an
Exhibition* (1970). Gordon's fictions (he would surely not call many of
them stories, nor would anyone much concerned with precision) invari-
ably sacrifice traditional fictional virtues for the sake of experimentation. In the "Pictures," less fiction even than expressionistic sketch or
prose poem, Gordon seems to try to represent a human consciousness
in the act of perceiving and then reacting. A great many of his other
pieces lean a little further toward traditional narrative: "The Window,"
"The Deserter," "Distractions," and others are primarily extended
monologues, sometimes apparently metafictional, sometimes meditations on being or identity or failed communication. Some are surrealistic, hallucinatory ("Two Women, Two Eyes"), others nearly traditional, though with cartoonish characters and situations; "The Enemy,"
for example, is almost an antiwar fable.

The most successful piece is essentially a sketch, "The One You
Aren't Allowed to See." Structured on a Christmas theme, superficially
broken and disconnected, repetitious, semilyrical at times, mock-en-
cyclopedic, it questions relations of myth, truth, legend.

Farewell, Fond Dreams (1975), though marking some improvement,
still is for the most part terribly dull, narcissistic, carelessly written.
Throughout these pieces Gordon consistently gives the impression of
being completely committed to innovative writing as long as it does
not require too much time or thought or discipline and as long as he
can insist that all standards are irrelevant except his own. The only
successful fiction in the book is the title piece. "My wife has left me"
it begins, and in the following twenty-four pages Gordon offers the

reader uncharacteristically well-written prose—evocative, sometimes sensual or troubling or touching. Gordon compounds the narrative of many motifs for which he betrayed great fondness in earlier pieces: lost voices, confused identities, deconstruction, attacks on authority and on convention, attempts at humor, the waking process, detailed notation of physical surroundings, projection of various hypotheses to explain what is really going on.

Couple (1978) is an easily dismissed pair of experimental fictions (twelve pages in all) about "relationships." *The Illusionist* (1978) is a grabbag. Some stories seem based on dreams or daydreams and impressionistic reports of actual incidents. "Once Upon a Frog" depends on an extended metaphor involving the frog-prince fairy tale; "The Jealous One" features a murderous cat in the role of rejected lover. The volume's primary mode, though, is metafiction, with pieces like "The Sea" and "The Artist" dealing with rationalizations about creativity. The most characteristic and most disappointing is the title story, "The Illusionist." One expects a volume's title piece to be in some sense definitive; in its cardboard characterization, lifeless style, and banal ideas the story does serve as a distillation of the volume.

• • •

Clearly, to write experimentally and at the same time to write well represents no inconsiderable challenge. It is puzzling how Christine Brooke-Rose can so consistently maintain such a high standard in such a variety of stories without producing one or two that are undeniably major, not to say great. More than most of her British contemporaries, she seems willing to take chances, to plumb the peculiarities of her private vision, and to stretch her technique till it can contain that vision. All this is enough to make her consistently better than the great bulk of writers in the decade; yet here and there a somewhat less gifted writer will turn out a stronger story than any in *Go When You See the Green Man Walking* (1970). How can this be? When the question involves work of the first quality, more than one writer has said that it is not enough to write well—though every writer must strive to control every controllable tool to achieve that end—a writer must also be lucky. Perhaps Brooke-Rose is simply missing that final aleatory boost. Perhaps (it is impossible to feel certain) her better stories finally tip a millimeter more toward the merely private rather than the personal, more toward the unique than the universal.

Yet ironically a more public story like "They All Go to the Mountains Now" can satisfy less than a more private story, "Medium Loser and Small Winner." Each involves meditation on the protagonist's inability to meld satisfactorily, permanently, to a loved one. In the first story two lower-class Italians reminisce on their "young and sexy days" when the men maneuvered their way in and out of women tourists vacationing at the beach. Salvatore realizes that he has decayed as has the resort town, the no longer fashionable beach, all his contemporaries. So shall we all. The other story involves a woman constantly romanticizing life and seeking out men who will mistreat her, a woman driven apparently by a compelling sense of her own emptiness. The first takes fewer chances, veers closer to closed stereotypes of character and situation and theme—high prices for allowing the reader more fully to recognize and identify with the psychic territory. "Medium Loser and Small Winner," with its powerful theme, ventures risky but finally successful technique, its characters and situations ranging further from the predictable. Yet the weaker story, "Mountains," captures a degree of universality that eludes the stronger story, eludes it just enough to keep "Medium Loser and Small Winner" from being a benchmark for the decade.

Brooke-Rose's favored form is first-person meditation. If the meditations tend to proceed slowly, nevertheless they do proceed. Again and again her more general subject matter will at first seem to be human relationships, individuals who fail to become genuine lovers; but pared down, the stories concern an individual rather than a pair, most often the individual's struggle to come to grips with life after either losing a partner or never having had one in the first place. In "On Terms" a jilted woman experiences such a loss of identity as to seem to herself a ghost, haunting herself, her former lover, their private places. In "The Religious Button" the woman has had no lover, a lack that drove her to believe she had been immaculately seeded with a female messiah, before she discovered herself desolate, lost, and unpregnant. This woman, like the unhappy minister's wife in "The Chinese Bedspread," finds that the road to happiness and fulfillment follows a tortuous path out of the self, toward others. In "The Troglodyte" a woman leaves London for a fantastic version of Spain; she chooses to live alone in a primitive cave "partly in order to get away from the dubiousness of my friends." But even those in the caves refuse to allow her to be a spinster. The male proprietor of her cave, doubtful about her life choice, moves in, and she suffers a while as his drudge before contemplating a return to London. Again and again it seems more important to come to terms with oneself than with someone else; indeed a relationship sometimes is the setting for individual adjustment rather than the prize.

If Brooke-Rose varies technique in each of her stories, she does have penchants, some recalling Robbe-Grillet, although she is able to stimulate where he so often merely bores. For one thing she favors repeating certain passages until they serve almost as a refrain, at their best absorbing new meanings from successive contexts and radiating that ever-renewing, ever-strengthening richness again and again. At their worst the repetitions have a predictable effect. Another favored technique involves exquisitely precise physical descriptions of surfaces, objects, angles of juxtaposition. Too often she weds the former technique to the latter in unions unblessed. She sometimes writes of active interpersonal conflict but much prefers meditation and monologue to narration and dialogue. Her characters do occasionally act, and often they have been rather active before we encounter them, but more often we are vouchsafed thought rather than action. Sometimes the reader feels like the lone, forgotten passenger stowed in the tender car of a magnificently designed locomotive, the bemused engineer rocking along at two or three miles per hour. She has a style built for performance, not speed; her sentences bear careful reading.

Her stories usually are set in some place that transcends our ordinary sense of actuality; at two extremes are "The Foot," which she sets in the mind of the ghost-pain inhabiting the phantom limb of a beautiful young woman whose leg has been amputated above the knee, and "George and the Seraph," which takes place in some evanescent dimension where an invisible angel locates itself at the Platonically ideal Point of No Return.

The settings, the technical daring, the weighting of concern more with the individual than with society, the fondness for fantasy, imagination, the unordinary would—were it a question of longer fictions—place her in the tradition of the romance rather than the novel. Some have tried to discover an equivalent distinction between tale and story; if such a line of demarcation exists, her short stories would almost all be aligned on the side of the visionaries rather than the mimics.

It is a mark of her talent that one of the most rigorously realistic can be the most haunting. In her title story, "Go When You See the Green Man Walking," a woman in a strange country watches a prostitute from her hotel window and then adorns herself in makeup and filmy silk—but no underwear; she takes a voyeuristic night walk, turns down a proposition, allows another man to masturbate in front of her, finally returns to her room, and goes naked to bed alone. The woman is the more haunting as we know so little about her. Is she merely a freak? Or is she Everywoman? Everywoman's fantasy? Has she achieved something in her dark, insular peregrination? Has she put something behind her? Has she become different, or only found a way to allow herself to remain the same? Whoever or whatever the character may be, her inventor is a talented short story writer, among the most intelligently innovative of her generation, courageous enough to dare originality, sensitive enough to coat her intricate webs with the adhesive of human awareness and understanding, elements that cling tenaciously to the reader. She may sometimes echo the New Novel in technique or Beckett in phrase or theme, but she can generate dreams of her own, powerful ones, vital ones: "without the fantasy I would cease to exist."

Her protagonists may be in tenuous circumstances, but the fiction of Christine Brooke-Rose is not. Her volume of stories is one of the finest Britain produced in the 1970s.

• • •

Only one writer remains to be discussed, and he is the most important not because he manages to combine much of the best in those already surveyed, which he does, but because he produced arguably the decade's finest single collection of short fiction, *The Ebony Tower* (1974).

John Fowles notes that the "working title of this collection of stories was *Variations,* by which I meant to suggest variations both on certain themes in previous books of mine and in methods of narrative presentation." The ties to previous books seem more important to Fowles generally than to this book specifically and may be ignored; the variations in narrative method as such seem not particularly interesting. The first, "The Ebony Tower," is a novella that draws inspiration from medieval romance; the second, "Eliduc," is a translation of a lai; the third, "Poor Koko," is a first-person story by a narrator much more reliable for his facts than for his interpretations; in the fourth, "The Enigma," Fowles offers a kind of deconstructive tribute to the detective genre; the last, "The Cloud," relies on the parallel structure of an original fairy tale.

But one may detect a much more significant kind of variation dominating *The Ebony Tower.* First the basic theme. The four original fictions that make up *The Ebony Tower* (setting aside his translation of Marie de France's "Eliduc") present a series of focal males wedded to a kind of smug traditionalism. Each encounters temptation in the form of an intellectual or philosophical scheme that offers, or threatens, to draw him into an alien conception of reality, meaning, and value. In three cases a bright, discontented woman embodies this new perspective; in the fourth a man with no very strong claim to heterosexuality is trapped in his bedroom, bested, and bound by a virile young punk who voices the alien perspective.

The variations? Each of Fowles's fictions develops in a different way the basic pattern outlined above. Each story offers a different definition of the central male smugness; each introduces a different definition of the intellectual perspective offered by the figure of temptation. It can hardly be coincidence that the temptations take the form of major intellectual-aesthetic-philosophical currents that have successively dominated Fowles' imaginative turf: England and France. The first piece debates abstraction and representation, the second features Marxism, the third structuralism, and the last semiotics.

Fowles opens his book with the title novella, certainly among the finest works of literature in any category produced in Britain in the decade. David Williams is in his thirties, the happily married father of two children, building a modestly flowering dual career as abstract painter and art critic. He arrives at an estate in Brittany to interview Henry Breasley for a book on the latter's work. Breasley, now in his seventies, throughout his scandalous life has held steadfastly to representational art against the onslaught of abstractionism and has wound up a randy old man finally becoming accepted as a significant figure in contemporary art. Breasley maintains a menage à trois featuring two attractive young women. Anne, whom he calls "the Freak," is the less important and serves his now very inconstant desire for intercourse and his constant sexual vanity. More significant to him is Diana or "the Mouse," who rarely shares his bed, but has significant potential as an artist, helps him in his studio, provides intellectual stimulation, and generally mothers him.

Diana is torn by devotion to the old man, who wants to marry her, and by her own desire to be independent and rejoin the great world outside the estate, a world she feels intellectually equal to but fears her inability to thrive in emotionally. Diana and David become increasingly close until one evening lovemaking seems inevitable; first he refuses and then, moments later when he has reconsidered, it is she who denies him. The next morning she refuses to see him before he must leave to meet his wife in Paris.

So far the story may seem more the stuff of afternoon TV serials than of art, but Fowles has some complicating aces up his sleeve. One involves a series of parallels to medieval romance generally and especially to Marie de France's "Eliduc," which shares the Brittany setting, which Breasley himself introduces as a parallel, and which Fowles places immediately after "The Ebony Tower" in his collection.

Marie de France's thematic treatments of honor, faithful and faithless love, betrayal, self-denial, self-sacrifice,and conjugal joy cast complex patterns of shifting light and shadow over all of "The Ebony Tower." Why does David, much the lesser betrayer, lose all the happiness Eliduc gains? Why does Diana finally shut the door opened so wide before? A natural impulse after his rejection of her? Has she decided he is not the man she thought he was? Has he convinced her his responsibilities to his wife and children take precedence? If it is the latter and she honorably refuses him and chooses to maintain her confinement on the isolated estate, then perhaps Diana ironically reprises the self-denying wife of Eliduc.

The haunting overtones of medieval romance Fowles enriches with the characters' discussions of aesthetics and their implications for life. Breasley rants and raves against abstractionists, David being one, for choosing geometry, sterile ideas, disembodied theories and betraying the sensual, emotional, physical foundations of life. For Breasley such painters are villains and cowards, as are all people who place abstractions above life.

The amoral old reprobate has lived always by impulse, intuition, and selfish need and finally become a much finer painter than David as well as ensconcing himself in domestic arrangements in a little kingdom David deeply envies. "To someone like David, always inclined to see his own life (like his painting) in terms of logical process, its future advances dependent on intelligent present choices, it seemed not quite fair."

Diana herself began as an abstractionist and still much admires David's paintings, but under Breasley's influence has begun to see its sterility and the far greater potential of representative art. She seems at a similar turning point in her emotional life. She senses a need to abandon the womblike estate, but still, "I don't have much faith in my instincts." She compares herself to a "virgin," a "nun" in her fear of the outside world, of strangers.

In the moment late in the novella when they kiss, David "knew it was a far more than sexual experience, but a fragment of one that reversed all logic, process, that struck new suns, new evolutions, new universes out of nothingness." Before he had known only "being"; now he knows "the passion to exist."

But as he had first rejected her offer of herself, now she rejects him, and despite this overwhelming love for Diana he is cursed to return to his wife. He senses he is being punished: "his real crime: to dodge, escape, avert." Breasley stood up to life where David proved coward. "One killed all risk, one refused all challenge, and so one became an artificial man." In art and life both, "safety hid nothingness." David's reward: "Castration. The triumph of the eunuch." David finally senses himself terminally locked in his own ebony tower: "He was crippled by common sense." He was "a decent man and eternal also-ran." Unfortunately, the "abominable and vindictive injustice was that art is fundamentally amoral," David concludes, and apparently so is life. It is with an overwhelming sense of personal damnation that David greets his wife on the last page and she asks about him: "He surrenders to what is left: to abstraction. 'I survived.' "

If one accepts Fowles's world and Breasley's condemnation of abstraction, if one reads "Eliduc" honestly, if one sympathizes with David's final sense of damnation, a clear pattern emerges. On one side rest the ebony tower, logic and common sense, self-abnegation, artistic abstraction (in literature and music as well as the visual arts), medieval conceptions of faithfulness in love, and contemporary commitment to marital fidelity. On the other side, in Fowles's world, stand life, passion, self-realization, representational art, a commitment to individual rather than conventional codes of behavior, and love irrespective of marriage.

Why the unhappy ending? Fowles seems canny enough to realize the perils of venturing utopias; he realizes it can be more convincing as well as more emotionally powerful to depict the purgatorial horrors of ebony towerism. His particular genius shows itself to best advantage in "The Ebony Tower": an ability to generate a fertile intercourse between challenging intellect and profound emotion.

Fowles's shorter fictions are less brilliant than "The Ebony Tower," but still major stories. In "Poor Koko" a sixty-six-year-old writer in a borrowed rural cottage is robbed by a young burglar with Marxist tendencies. Despite the old man's fears, the incident involves no physical violence and the two even engage in more or less polite discussion of various topics before the younger binds the older man, promises to call the police the next morning so they can rescue him, and then silently proceeds to burn the results of several years' labor—the old man's notes and manuscript draft of a critical biography of Thomas Love Peacock. The writer passes through shock and rage at this wanton, apparently senseless destruction but finally interprets it as a telling confrontation between representatives of two alien generations: "I am convinced that the fatal clash between us was of one who trusts and reveres language and one who suspects and resents it." He concludes: "What was really burned was my generation's 'refusal' to hand down a kind of magic."

Perhaps that is that. But in "The Ebony Tower" Fowles celebrates commitment to life and action and devalues abstraction; the narrator of "Poor Koko" seems lost in the latter. Early in the story he mentions that "a friend of mine once maintained that there is a class of experiences we should all have had before death if we wished to claim to have lived fully." Even if the notion of some kind of catalog is ridiculous, still in fact the only bit of "life" the narrator offers the reader is a bit of adultery during World War II: "but the husband was safely in North Africa during the whole of our brief liaison." The narrator is a man who seems to have exchanged letters for life, and what kind of letters? His masterpiece is a study appropriately titled *The Dwarf in Literature,* and his ultimate work (despite the fact that London has already "vetoed my small project") is to be a critical study of a man whose name is synonymous with vanity. What kind of book is it? He admits that "certain draft passages merely used Peacock as an excuse for irrelevant diatribes against my own age."

The intruder is not only much more manly and active but—despite the narrator's final self-serving misjudgment—a man of words as well. The young man reads the papers, has made some study of Marx, lauds Conrad (what a contrast to the narrator's Peacock!), and in fact seems to have a ravenous appetite for the written word: "I see books lying around sometimes. Novels. History. Art books. I take 'em home. Read 'em." He is not a slave to objects or to ideas and is hardly an uncritical Marxist: "Okay, so they've screwed a lot of things up. But at least they're trying." He is a man of his word—offering no violence as he promised not to; phoning the police once he is safe—and man of a certain courtesy, even offering to brew up tea or coffee for his victim.

The most telling question is the motive for burning the manuscript. The narrator, as mentioned above, can interpret it all only in egocentric terms, lending himself a power in imagination that he surely missed in fact. Perhaps the intruder's motive was to give the older man what so many other Fowles men are given—a questioning of his own reality. But like certain other Fowles characters the narrator seems too desiccated, too entrenched to profit from the opportunity.

In "The Enigma" a young police sergeant tries unsuccessfully to puzzle out the disappearance of a moneyed, conservative MP until he meets the girlfriend of the subject's son. Basing her theory on hunches, guesses, intuition, she suggests that the MP tired of a life in which all the main threads of his existence had been, were still, and probably would be determined by an abstract system (involving class, family, party, etc.) that treated him precisely as an author treats a character: "So in the end there's no freedom left. Nothing he can choose. Only what the system says." Several other references to writing, novels, authors, and characters ("Let's pretend everything to do with the Fieldings, even you and me sitting here now, is in a novel") reinforce Fowles's theme, a very fashionable theme since the rise of the structuralists. Fowles's ideas here are modish rather than original, but his power lies in the brilliance with which he can realize them for readers fonder of fiction than of avant-garde theories.

The final story, "The Cloud," employs semiotics as the penultimate story employs structuralism. The central figure, Catherine, withdraws emotionally from the others with her on a picnic—perhaps partly in reaction to her loss of a man who may have committed suicide or may simply have left her, but more it would seem because the quality of her mind is so different from the minds surrounding her. She has read Barthes and become disillusioned with language and with all other sign systems by which human beings communicate, or try to. She speaks little to the others, and when she does, she seems misunderstood. She distresses herself further by attentively reading such nonverbal signs as those sent her by Peter, a divorced TV producer who has brought a girl along but makes eyes at Catherine nevertheless. She retreats to a secret place in the woods and tells a niece an original fairy story about a princess alone in the woods for years who can have either clothes or a palace, but never both at the same time; the princess's parents—inevitably misinterpreting her via these ambiguous signs—force a separation, and she wanders, still awaiting her rescuing prince. At the end all the picnickers leave Catherine behind, apparently awaiting her own prince who can pierce to the heart of meaning hidden behind all her enigmatic signing. Late in the story Peter stumbles on her, and she wordlessly signals for him to rub suntan oil on her body, which he does, becoming finally aroused. But she will not look in his face, and we do not know whether or not they make love. When he has left her to rejoin the others, Peter jokes about rejecting "necrophilia." He was obviously incapable of fully interpreting her signs, of rescuing her. The story ends: "The princess calls, but there is no one, now, to hear her." To truly "hear" her would be to rescue her. But semiotics admits of no rescue. Again Fowles has brilliantly interpreted a fashionable abstraction into emotionally gripping fiction.

Perhaps the "variations" of the rejected title refer most importantly to the various intellectual systems Fowles translates into passionate experience. He deserves our gratitude as well as our affection and our respect, for in a sense Fowles is our own interpretive prince.

He is also characteristic of the best in British short fiction since 1970. Despite some tendencies toward innovation and experimentation, the bulk of the writers, like Fowles, favor more traditional modes. Like writers who focus on the individual, he can treat the age-old themes of initiation and lost life and love. Through his style, his character development, his sensitivity to the atmospheres of places, he can make such old themes seem surprisingly new. Like writers who deal with individuals in conflict with society, he is alive to broad social, cultural, and historical patterns. He sidesteps questions of racial prejudice but attends to other forms of injustice through his undogmatic Marxist burglar and through women characters wounded by sexism. More important to Fowles, though, are wider cultural and historical trends—those shifting modes reflected in Breasley's life, for example, and the damning web of social patternings that imprison the disappeared MP. Most impressive of all is the way Fowles makes accessible avant-garde stories. He can create fiction capable of being deconstructive without completely self-destructing. Where other writers often seem self-indulgently bemused, even a little confused by the ideas of structuralists and semioticians, he can make their ideas seem not merely interesting but vitally important, even viscerally gripping.

Fowles finally seems the best of the British writers to have begun publishing volumes of short fiction since 1970, a worthy successor to such masters as V. S. Pritchett and Doris Lessing; but close behind him are such writers as Christine Brooke-Rose, Angela Carter, Jennifer Dawson, Susan Hill, Gabriel Josipovici, and Ian McEwan. They make up an honor roll for a decade in which any country could take pride.

Walter Evans

Augusta College

Notes and References

The English Short Story: 1945–1950

1. Denys Val Baker, *Little Reviews Anthology: 1949* (London: Methuen, 1949), p. vii.

2. In reviewing the novel *The Weak and the Strong* by Gerald Kersh, the anonymous *TLS* reviewer (13 October 1945) writes: "A breath of hot air from the 1930's, Mr. Kersh's new story is uncommonly welcome in these inclement days. No wars, no charters, no atomic bombs, no international responsibilities, nothing but a good emotional turmoil—what a relief it is to re-enter the hothouse of pure fiction!"

3. *Times Literary Supplement*, 20 January 1945, p. 29.

4. W. Somerset Maugham, "The Short Story," in *Points of View* (New York: Greenwood Press, 1968), p. 194.

5. H. E. Bates, *The Modern Short Story: A Critical Survey* (London: T. Nelson & Sons, 1941), p. 207.

6. A statement Sitwell supplied to the editors of the British *Who's Who*; it appears in several editions.

7. Ronald Mason, *Modern British Writing*, ed. Denys Val Baker (New York: Vanguard, 1947), p. 281.

8. Quoted by Michael Williams, "Welsh Voices in the Short Story," in *Little Reviews Anthology: 1949*, ed. Val Baker, p. 103.

9. Bates, *Modern Short Story*, p. 209.

10. Gwyn Jones, Introduction, to *Twenty-Five Welsh Short Stories*, selected by Gwyn Jones and Islwyn Ffowc Ellis (London, 1971), p. xii.

11. E. Glyn Lewis, "Anglo-Welsh Literature," in *Modern British Writing*, ed. Denys Val Baker (New York: Vanguard, 1947), p. 152.

12. Quoted in Cecil Price, *Gwyn Jones* (Cardiff, 1976), p. 18.

13. Gwyn Jones, Introduction to *Selected Short Stories* (London, 1974), p. xi.

14. Ibid., p. xi.

The English Short Story in the Fifties

    1. *Why Do I Write? An Exchange of Views between Elizabeth Bowen, Graham Greene, and V. S. Pritchett* (London: Percival Marshall, 1948), pp. 16, 34, 36.

    2. Alan Sillitoe, Introduction to *A Sillitoe Selection,* ed. Michael Marland (London: Longman Group, 1968), p. 128.

Bibliography

Selected Bibliography of English Short Story Collections, 1945–1980

Amis, Kingsley
Collected Short Stories. London: Hutchinson, 1980.
The Darkwater Hall Mystery. Edinburg: Tragara Press, 1978.
Dear Illusion. London: Covent Garden Press, 1972.
My Enemy's Enemy. London: Victor Gollancz, 1962; New York: Harcourt, Brace, 1963.

Baldwin, Michael
Sebastian and Other Voices. London: Secker & Warburg, 1966.
Underneath and Other Situations. London: Secker & Warburg, 1968.
Bananas. Edited by Emma Tennant. London: Quartet-Blond & Briggs, 1977.

Barker, A[udrey] L[ilian]
Femina Real. London: Hogarth Press, 1971.
Innocents: Variations on a Theme. London: Hogarth Press, 1947; New York: Charles Scribner's Sons, 1948.
The Joy-Ride and After. London: Hogarth Press, 1963; New York: Charles Scribner's Sons, 1964.
Lost Upon the Roundabouts. London: Hogarth Press, 1964.
Novelette and Other Stories. London: Hogarth Press, 1951; New York: Charles Scribner's Sons, 1951.

Barstow, Stan
A Casual Acquaintance. Edited by Marilyn Davies. London: Longman, 1976.
The Desperadoes. London: Michael Joseph, 1961.
The Human Element and Other Stories. Edited by Marilyn Davies. London: Longman, 1969.
A Season with Eros. London: Michael Joseph, 1971.

Bates, H. E.
Colonel Julian and Other Stories. London: Michael Joseph, 1951; Boston: Little, Brown, 1951.

The Cruise of the Breadwinner. London: Michael Joseph, 1946; Boston: Little, Brown, 1947.

The Daffodil Sky. London: Michael Joseph, 1955; Boston: Little, Brown, 1956.

The Fabulous Mrs. V. London: Michael Joseph, 1964; Penguin, 1970.

Now Sleeps the Crimson Petal and Other Stories. London: Michael Joseph, 1961; Penguin, 1962; as *The Enchantress and Other Stories.* Boston: Little, Brown, 1961.

Seven by Five: Stories, 1926–1961. London: Michael Joseph, 1963; as *The Best of H. E. Bates.* Boston: Little, Brown, 1963.

Sugar for the Horse. London: Michael Joseph, 1957.

The Watercress Girl and Other Stories. London: Michael Joseph, 1959; Boston: Little, Brown, 1960.

The Wedding Party. London: Michael Joseph, 1965.

The Wild Cherry Tree. London: Michael Joseph, 1968.

Bentley, Phyllis
Love and Money. London: Victor Gollancz, 1957.

Berger, John
Pig Earth. London: Writers & Readers' Cooperative, 1979; New York: Pantheon, 1980.

Beyond the Woods: Eleven Writers in Search of a New Fiction. Edited by Giles Gordon. London: Hutchinson, 1975.

Blackwood, Caroline
For All That I Found There. London: Duckworth, 1974; New York: Braziller, 1974.

Blakiston, Noel
That Thoughtful Boy and Other Stories. London: Chapman & Hall, 1965.

Bradbury, Malcolm
Who Do You Think You Are? London: Secker & Warburg, 1976.

Bragg, Melvyn
A Christmas Child. London: Secker & Warburg, 1976.

Brooke-Rose, Christine
Go When You See the Green Man Walking. London: Michael Joseph, 1970.

Brown, George Mackay
A Calendar of Love. London: Hogarth Press 1967; New York: Harcourt Brace, 1968.

Hawkfall. London: Hogarth Press, 1974.
The Sun's Net. London: Hogarth Press, 1974.
A Time to Keep. London: Hogarth Press, 1969; New York: Harcourt Brace, 1969.
Witch. London: Longman, 1977.

Burgess, Anthony
Will and Testament: A Fragment of Biography. Verona: Plain Wrapper Press, 1977.

Carter, Angela
The Bloody Chamber. London: Victor Gollancz, 1979; New York: Harper & Row, 1979.
Fireworks: Nine Profane Pieces. London: Quartet, 1974; New York: Harper & Row, 1974.

Cary, Joyce
Spring Song and Other Stories. London: Michael Joseph, 1974; New York: Harper & Brothers, 1974.

Chaplin, Sid
The Bachelor Uncle. Manchester: Carcanet Press, 1980.
On Christmas Day in the Morning. Manchester: Carcanet Press, 1978; New York: Persea, 1979.
The Thin Seam and Other Stories. Oxford: Pergamon Press, 1968.

Collier, John
Fancies and Goodnights. Garden City: Doubleday, 1951.
Pictures in the Fire. London: Rupert Hart-Davis, 1958.

Coppard, A. E.
Collected Tales. New York: Knopf, 1951.
Dark-Eyed Lady: Fourteen Tales. London: Methuen, 1947.

Dahl, Roald
The Best of Roald Dahl. New York: Vintage, 1978.
Kiss, Kiss. London: Michael Joseph, 1960; New York: Knopf, 1960.
More Tales of the Unexpected. London: Michael Joseph, 1980.
Over to You: Ten Stories of Flyers and Flying. London: Hamish Hamilton, 1946; New York: Reynal & Hitchcock, 1946.
Selected Stories. New York: Random House, 1970.
Someone Like You. New York: Knopf, 1953; London: Secker & Warburg, 1953: Michael Joseph, rev. ed., 1961.
Tales of the Unexpected. London: Michael Joseph, 1979; New York: Vintage, 1979.

Twenty-Nine Kisses. London: Michael Joseph, 1969.

Dunn, Nell
Up the Junction. London: MacGibbon & Kee, 1963; Philadelphia: Lippincott, 1966.

Durrell, Lawrence
The Best of Antrobus. London: Faber & Faber, 1974.
Sauve Qui Peut. London: Faber & Faber, 1966; New York: Dutton, 1967.

English, Isobel
Life After All. London: Martin Brian & O'Keefe, 1973.

Factions: Eleven Original Stories. Edited by Alex Hamilton & Giles Gordon. London: Michael Joseph, 1974.

Feinstein, Elaine
Matters of Chance. London: Covent Garden Press, 1980.
The Silent Areas. London: Hutchinson, 1980.

Fielding, Gabriel
Collected Short Stories. London: Hutchinson, 1971.
New Queens for Old. London: Hutchinson, 1972; New York: Morrow, 1972.

Finlay, Ian Hamilton
The Sea-Bed and Other Stories. Edinburg: Castle Wynd, 1958.

Fowles, John
The Ebony Tower. London: Jonathan Cape, 1975; Boston: Little, Brown, 1975.

Gilliatt, Penelope
Nobody's Business. London: Secker & Warburg, 1972; New York: Viking, 1972.
Splendid Lives. London: Secker & Warburg, 1977; New York: Cowan McCann, 1978.
What's It Like Out? and Other Stories. London: Secker & Warburg, 1968; as *Come Back If It Doesn't Get Better.* New York: Random House, 1969.

Glanville, Brian
A Bad Lot. London: Penguin, 1977.
A Bad Streak and Other Stories. London: Secker & Warburg, 1961.
A Betting Man and Other Stories. New York: Cowan McCann, 1969.
The Director's Wife and Other Stories. London: Secker & Warburg, 1963.
Goalkeepers Are Always Crazy. London: Secker & Warburg, 1964.

The King of Hackney Marshes and Other Stories. London: Secker & Warburg, 1965; New York: Cowan McCann, 1969.
The Thing He Loves. London: Secker & Warburg, 1973.

Glaskin, G. M.
A Small Selection of Stories. London: Barrie & Rockliff, 1962.

Godden, Rumer
Swans and Turtles. London: Macmillan, 1968; as *Gone: A Thread of Stories.* New York: Viking, 1968.

Gordon, Giles
Couple. Knotting, Bedfordshire: Sceptre Press, 1978.
Farewell, Fond Dreams. London: Hutchinson, 1975.
The Illusionist. Hassocks, Sussex: Harvester Press, 1978.
Pictures from an Exhibition. London: Allison & Busby, 1970; New York: Dial, 1970.

Graham, Winston
The Japanese Girl. London: Collins, 1971; New York: Doubleday, 1972.

Graves, Robert
Collected Short Stories. New York: Doubleday, 1964; London: Cassell, 1965; as *The Shout and Other Stories.* London: Penguin, 1978.

Greene, Graham
The Bear Fell Free. London: Grayson, 1935; Folcroft Pa.: Folcroft Editions, 1977.
The Collected Stories of Graham Greene. London: Bodley Head–Heinemann, 1972; New York: Viking, 1973.
May We Borrow Your Husband? and Other Comedies of the Sexual Life. London: Bodley Head, 1967; New York: Viking, 1967.
Nineteen Stories. London: Heinemann, 1947; New York: Viking, 1949.
A Sense of Reality. London: Bodley Head, 1963; New York: Viking, 1963.

Gunn, Neil
The White Hour and Other Stories. London: Faber & Faber, 1950.

Hanley, James
The Darkness. London: Covent Garden Press, 1973.

Harris, Wilson
The Age of the Rainmakers. London: Faber & Faber, 1971.
The Sleepers of Roraima. London: Faber & Faber, 1970.

Hartley, L. P.
The Travelling Grave and Other Stories. London: Barrie, 1951.
Two for the River. London: Hamish Hamilton, 1961.
The White Wand and Other Stories. London: Hamish Hamilton, 1954.

Heseltine, Nigel
Tales of the Squirearchy. Carmarthen: Druid Press, 1946.

Hill, Susan
The Albatross. London: Hamish Hamilton, 1971; New York: Saturday Review
    Press, 1975.
A Bit of Singing and Dancing. London: Hamish Hamilton, 1973.
The Custodian. London: Covent Garden Press, 1972.

Household, Geoffrey
Sabres on the Sand. London: Michael Joseph, 1966; Boston: Little, Brown,
    1966.

Howard, Elizabeth
Mr. Wrong. London: Jonathan Cape, 1975; New York: Viking, 1976.

Humphries, Emry
Natives. London: Secker & Warburg, 1968.

Introduction: Stories by New Writers.
London: Faber & Faber, 1960.

Introduction 2: Stories by New Writers.
London: Faber & Faber, 1964.

Introduction 3: Stories by New Writers.
London: Faber & Faber, 1967.

Jacobson, Dan
Inklings: Selected Stories. London: Weidenfeld & Nicolson, 1973; as *Through the
    Wilderness.* London: Penguin, 1977.
A Way of Life. Edited by Alex Pirani. London: Longman, 1971.

Jenkins, Robin
A Far Cry from Bowmore. London: Victor Gollancz, 1973.

Jhabvala, Ruth Prawer
An Experience of India. London: Murray, 1971; New York: Norton, 1972.

How I Became a Holy Mother. London: Murray, 1976; New York: Harper, 1976.
Like Birds, Like Fishes, and Other Stories. London: Murray, 1963; New York: Norton, 1964.
A Stronger Climate: Nine Stories. London: Murray, 1968; New York: Norton, 1969.

Johnson, B. S., and Zulfikar Ghose
Statement Against Corpses. London: Constable, 1964.

Jones, Glyn
Selected Short Stories. London: Dent, 1971.
Welsh Heirs. Llandysul, Dryfed: Gomer, 1978; Chicago: Academy Chicago, 1979.

Jones, Gwyn
The Buttercup Field and Other Stories. Cardiff: Penmark Press, 1945.
Selected Short Stories. With an introduction by the author. London: Oxford University Press, 1974.
Shepherd's Hey and Other Stories. London: Staple Press, 1953.
The Still Waters and Other Stories. London: Peter Davies, 1948.
Twenty-Five Welsh Short Stories (and Islwyn Ffowc Elis). With an introduction by Gwyn Jones. London: Oxford University Press, 1971.

Jones, L. E.
The Bishop's Aunt and Other Stories. London: Rupert Hart-Davis, 1961.

Jones, Merwyn
Scenes from Bourgeois Life. London: Quartet, 1976.

Josipovici, Gabriel
Four Stories. London: Menard, 1977.
Mobius the Stripper. London: Michael Joseph, 1974.

Kavan, Anna
I Am Lazarus. London: Jonathan Cape, 1945.
Asylum Piece. London: Jonathan Cape, 1941.

Kersh, Gerald
Clean, Bright, and Slightly Oiled. London: Heinemann, 1946.
The Terribly Wild Flowers: Nine Stories. London: Heinemann, 1962.

King, Francis
The Brighton Belle and Other Stories. London: Longmans, 1968.

Hard Feelings. London: Hutchinson, 1976.
Hurt and Humiliated. London: Longmans, 1959.
Indirect Method. London: Hutchinson, 1980.
The Japanese Umbrella and Other Stories. London: Longmans, 1964.

Lehmann, Rosamond
The Gipsy's Baby and Other Stories. London: Collins, 1946; New York: Reynal & Hitchcock, 1946.

Lessing, Doris
African Stories. London: Michael Joseph, 1964; New York: Simon & Schuster, 1965.
The Black Madonna. London: Panther, 1966.
Collected African Stories (I. This Was the Old Chief's Country, II. The Sun between the Feet). London: Michael Joseph, 1973.
Collected Stories (I. To Room Nineteen, II. The Temptation of Jack Orkney). London: Jonathan Cape, 1978.
Five. London: Michael Joseph, 1953.
The Habit of Loving. London: MacGibbon & Kee, 1957; New York: Crowell, 1957.
Nine African Stories. London: Longmans, 1968.
Stories. New York: Knopf, 1978.
The Story of a Non-Marrying Man. London: Jonathan Cape, 1972; as *The Temptation of Jack Orkney.* New York: Knopf, 1972.
This Was the Old Chief's Country. London: Michael Joseph, 1951.
Winter in July. London: Panther, 1966.

Lewis, Wyndham
Rotting Hill. London: Methuen, 1951.

Linklater, Eric
Sealskin Trousers and Other Stories. London: Rupert Hart-Davis, 1947.
A Sociable Plover and Other Stories and Conceits. London: Rupert Hart-Davis, 1957.
The Stories of Eric Linklater. With a prefatory note by the author. London: Macmillan, 1968; New York: Horizon Press, 1969.

Litvinoff, Emmanuel
Journey through a Small Planet. London: Michael Joseph, 1972.

McEwan, Ian
First Love, Last Rites. London: Jonathan Cape, 1975; New York: Random House, 1975.
In Between the Sheets. London: Jonathan Cape, 1978; New York: Simon & Schuster, 1979.

Mankowitz, Wolf
The Blue Arabian Nights: Tales of a London Decade. London: Valentine Mitchell, 1973.
The Day of the Women and the Night of the Men: Fables. London: Robson, 1977.

Manning, Olivia
Growing Up. London: Heinemann, 1947; Garden City, N.Y.: Doubleday, 1947.
A Romantic Hero and Other Stories. London: Heinemann, 1967.

Maugham, W. Somerset
Creatures of Circumstance. London: Heinemann, 1947; Garden City, N.Y.: Doubleday, 1948.

Meyer, Gordon
Exiles: Stories by Gordon Meyer. London: Alan Ross, 1966.

Milne, A. A.
Birthday Party and Other Stories. New York: Dutton, 1948; London: Methuen, 1949.

Mitchell, [Charles] Julian [Humphrey]
Introduction. With others. London: Faber, 1960.

Mitchison, Naomi
Five Men and a Swan. London: Allen & Unwin, 1958.
Images of Africa. Edinburg: Canongate, 1980.

Modern Scottish Short Stories.
Edited by Fred Urquhart and Giles Gordon. London: Hamish Hamilton, 1978.

Modern Short Stories: 1940–1980.
Edited by Giles Gordon. London: J. M. Dent, 1982.

Monsarrat, Nicholas
Depends What You Mean by Love. London: Cassell, 1947; New York: Knopf, 1948.

Mortimer, Penelope
Saturday Lunch with the Brownings. London: Hutchinson, 1960; New York: McGraw Hill, 1961.

Mosley, Nicholas
Impossible Object. London: Hodder & Stoughton, 1968.

Naughton, Bill
The Bees Have Stopped Working. Exeter: Wheaton, 1976.
The Goalkeeper's Revenge. London: Harrap, 1961.
The Goalkeeper's Revenge and Spit Nolan. London: Macmillan, 1974.
Late Night on Watling Street and Other Stories. London: MacGibbon & Kee, 1959; New York: Ballantine, 1966.

New Stories, 1945–46.
Edited by John Singer. Glasgow: William Maclellan, 1946.

No Scottish Twilight: New Scottish Short Stories.
Edited by Maurice Lindsay and Fred Urquhart. Glasgow: William Maclellan, 1947.

Nye, Robert
Tales I Told My Mother. New York: Hill & Wang, 1969.

Penguin Modern Stories I.
Edited by Judith Burnley. Middlesex: Penguin, 1969.

The Pick of Today's Short Stories.
Edited by John Pudney. London: Putnam, 1949–.

Plomer, William
Four Countries. London: Jonathan Cape, 1949.

Powys, T. F.
Bottle's Path and Other Stories. London: Chatto & Wyndus, 1946.

Priestley, J. B.
The Carfitt Crisis. London: Heinemann, 1975.
The Other Place and Stories of the Same Sort. London: Heinemann, 1953.

Pritchett, V. S.
Blind Love and Other Stories. London: Chatto & Windus, 1969.
The Camberwell Beauty. London: Chatto & Windus, 1974; New York: Random House, 1974.
Collected Stories. London: Chatto & Windus, 1956; as *The Sailor, Sense of Humor, and Other Stories.* New York: Knopf, 1956.
It May Never Happen and Other Stories. London: Chatto & Windus, 1945; New York: Reynal & Hitchcock, 1947.
The Key to My Heart: A Comedy in Three Parts. London: Chatto & Windus, 1963.
On the Edge of the Cliff. London: Chatto & Windus, 1980; New York: Random

House, 1979.

Selected Stories. London: Chatto & Windus, 1978; New York: Random House, 1978.

When My Girl Comes Home. London: Chatto & Windus, 1961.

The Punch Book of Short Stories.
Ed. Alan Caren. London: Robson, 1979.

Raven, Simon
The Fortunes of Fingal. London: Blond and Briggs, 1976.

Roberts, Kate
A Summer Day and Other Stories. Cardiff: Penmark Press, 1946.

Russell, Bertrand
Nightmares of Eminent Persons and Other Stories. London: Bodley Head, 1954.
Satan in the Suburbs. London: Bodley Head, 1953.

Sansom, William
Among the Dahlias. London: Hogarth, 1957.
A Contest of Ladies. London: Reynal, 1956.
The Equilibriad. London: Hogarth, 1948.
Lord Love Us. London: Hogarth, 1954.
The Passionate North. London: Hogarth Press, 1950; New York: Harcourt, Brace, 1953.
Something Terrible, Something Lovely. London: Hogarth, 1948; New York: Harcourt, Brace, 1954.
South: Aspects and Images from Corsica, Italy, and Southern France. London: Hodder & Stoughton, 1948; New York: Harcourt, Brace, 1950.
Stories. London: Hogarth, 1963.
The Ulcerated Milkman. London: Hogarth, 1966.
Three. London: Hogarth, 1946; New York: Reynal & Hitchcock, 1947.

Scott, Paul
After the Funeral. Andoversford, Gloucestershire: Whittington Press, 1979.

Sharp, Margery
The Lost Chapel Picnic. London: Heinemann, 1973; Boston: Little, Brown, 1973.

Sillitoe, Alan
Down to the Bone. Exeter: Wheaton, 1976.
Guzman, Go Home and Other Stories. London: Macmillan, 1968; New York: Doubleday, 1969.

The Loneliness of the Long-Distance Runner. London: W. H. Allen, 1959; New
   York: Knopf, 1959.
Men, Women, and Children. London: W. H. Allen, 1974; New York: Scribners,
   1974.
The Ragman's Daughter and Other Stories. London: W. H. Allen, 1976.

Sitwell, Osbert
Death of a God and Other Stories. London: Macmillan, 1949.

Smith, Iain Crichton
Burn is Aran (Bread and Water; includes verse). Glasgow: Gairm, 1960.
An Dubhis an Gorm (The Black and the Blue). Aberdeen: Aberdeen University,
   1963.
The Hermit. London: Victor Gollancz, 1977.
Maighsirean is Ministrearan (Schoolmasters and Ministers). Inverness: Club Leab-
   har, 1970.
The Red and the Black. London: Victor Gollancs, 1973.
Survival without Error. London: Victor Gollancz, 1970.
An t-Adhar Amaireaganach (The American Sky). Inverness: Club Leabhar, 1973.

Spark, Muriel
Collected Stories I. London: Macmillan, 1967; New York: Knopf, 1968.
The Go-Away Bird and Other Stories. London: Macmillan, 1958; Philadelphia:
   Lippincott, 1960.

Stewart, J. I. M.
Our England Is a Garden. London: Victor Gollancz, 1979.

Stories from the London Magazine.
Edited by Alan Ross. London: Eyre & Spottiswoode, 1964.

Strong, L. A. G.
Darling Tom and Other Stories. London: Methuen, 1952.

Sykes, Christopher
Character and Situation. London: Collins, 1949; New York: Knopf, 1950.

Taylor, Elizabeth
The Blush and Other Stories. London: Peter Davies, 1958; New York: Viking,
   1959.
A Dedicated Man. New York: Viking Press, 1965.

Hester Lilley and Twelve Short Stories. London: Peter Davies, 1954; New York: Viking, 1959.

Thomas, Dylan
Adventures in the Skin Trade. London: Putnam, 1955.
Quite Early One Morning. Norfolk, Conn.: New Directions, 1955.

Thomas, Gwyn
Gazooka. London: Victor Gollancz, 1957.

Tindall, Gillian
Dances of Death. London: Hodder & Stoughton, 1973; New York: Walker, 1973.

Treece, Henry
I Cannot Go Hunting Tomorrow. London: Gray Walls Press, 1946.

Trocci, Alexander
Four Stories. In *New Writer 3.* London: Calder & Boyars, 1965.

Tuohy, Frank
The Admiral and the Nuns. New York: Scribner's, 1962.
Fingers in the Door. London: Macmillan, 1970; New York: Scribner's, 1970.
Live Bait. London: Macmillan, 1978; New York: Holt Rinehart, 1979.

Twenty-Five Welsh Short Stories.
Edited by Gwyn Jones. London: Oxford University Press, 1971.

Upward, Edward
The Railway Accident and Other Stories. London: Heinemann, 1969.

Urquhart, Fred
The Collected Stories. 2 vols. London: Rupert Hart-Davis, 1967–68.
A Diver in the China Seas. London: Quartet, 1980.
The Last Sister and Other Stories. London: Metheun, 1950.
The Laundry Girl and the Pole. London: Arco, 1955.
Proud Lady in a Cage: Six Historical Studies. Edinburg: Harris, 1980.
The Year of the Short Corn. London: Metheun, 1949.

Ustinov, Peter
The Frontiers of the Sea. Boston: Little, Brown, 1966; London: Panther, 1978.

Val Baker, Denys
Little Reviews Anthology, 1945. London: Eyre & Spottiswoode, 1945.

Wain, John
Death of the Hind Legs and Other Stories. London: Macmillan, 1966.
King Caliban. London: Macmillan, 1978.
The Life Guard. London: Macmillan, 1971; New York: Viking, 1972.
Nuncle and Other Stories. London: Macmillan, 1960; New York: St. Martin's
    Press, 1961.

Warner, Sylvia Townsend
The Museum of Cheats. London: Chatto & Windus, 1947; New York: Viking
    Press, 1947.
A Spirit Rises. New York: Viking, 1962.
The Stranger with a Bag. New York: Viking, 1966.
Winter in the Air. London: Chatto & Windus, 1955; New York: Viking, 1956.

Waugh, Alec
My Place in the Bazaar. London: Cassell, 1961; New York: Farrar, Straus,
    1961.

Waugh, Evelyn
The Holy Places. London: Queen Anne Press, 1952.

Welsh Short Stories.
Edited by George Ewart Evans. London: Faber & Faber, 1959.

West Country Short Stories.
Edited by Lewis Wilshire. London: Faber & Faber, 1949.

Wilson, Angus
A Bit Off the Map and Other Stories. London: Secker & Warburg, 1957; New
    York: Viking, 1957.
Death Dance: Twenty-Five Short Stories. New York: Viking, 1969.
Such Darling Dodos and Other Stories. London: Secker & Warburg, 1950; New
    York: Morrow, 1951.
The Wrong Set and Other Stories. London: Secker and Warburg, 1949; New
    York: Morrow, 1950.

Wilson, Colin
The Return of the Lloigor. London: Village Press, 1974.

Wilson, Guy
The Three Vital Moments of Benjamin Ellashaye and Other Stories. London: Chatto
    & Windus, 1962.

Winter's Tales.
London: Macmillan, 1955-; New York: St. Martin's Press, 1955-.

Wodehouse, P. G.
Nothing Serious. New York: Doubleday, 1950.
Selected Stories. New York: Modern Library, 1958.

Selected and Annotated Bibliography of Secondary Sources

1. Books

Adler, Renata. "Doris Lessing." In *On Contemporary Literature.* Edited by Richard Kostelanetz. New York: Avon, 1964, pp. 591–96. A helpful introduction to Lessing's early fiction, with some attention devoted to the short stories.

Allen, Walter. *The Short Story in English.* New York: Oxford University Press, 1981. Discusses over eighty short story writers, from Sir Walter Scott to Joyce Carol Oates, including the major British short story writers. A readable introduction by a man who knows the territory well.

Atkins, John. "L. P. Hartley." In *Six Novelists Look at Society.* London: John Calder, 1977, pp. 77–111. A sociological approach to Hartley's fiction, generally unfavorable but interesting.

Bates, H. E. *The Modern Short Story: A Critical Survey.* London: Michael Joseph, 1972. An intelligent discussion of the ways in which the short story developed and changed shape. Includes lengthy discussions of the major international figures, plus briefer discussions of many others. Of particular note is Bates's discussion of the Welsh short story. (This work is a new edition, entirely unchanged from the 1941 edition except for a new preface. In the preface Bates recants his earlier optimistic forecast for the British short story and concludes that the genre seems to have lost its vitality.)

Beachcroft, T. O. *The Modest Art: A Survey of the Short Story in English.* London: Oxford University Press, 1968. With minor exceptions a perceptive, useful study of the short story from the beginnings in parable and ballad, through Chaucer, and up to Sillitoe and Lessing.

Bien, Peter. *L. P. Hartley.* London: Chatto & Windus, 1963. An early, but thorough, evaluation of Hartley's fiction, including the short stories.

Boardman, Gwenn R. *Graham Greene: The Aesthetics of Exploration.* Gainesville: University of Florida Press, 1971. Traces the map as a central metaphor in Greene's fiction, though focusing primarily on the novel.

Bowen, Elizabeth. Introduction to *the Stories of William Sansom.* Boston: Little, Brown, 1963, pp. 7–12. Bowen maintains that a "Sansom story is a *tour de force*," that he "has experimented with extension" in a successful way, especially in the short story, which is "the not only ideal but lasting magnet for all that is most unique in the Sansom art." Bowen makes an important line of defense against Sansom detractors when she maintains that he is "not writing *for* effect, he is dealing *in* it, and masterfully."

Brewster, Dorothy. *Doris Lessing.* Boston: Twayne, 1965. The most thorough early discussion of Lessing's fiction, both the novel and the short story.

Burkhom, Selma R. *Doris Lessing: A Checklist of Primary and Secondary Sources.* Troy, N.Y.: Whitson, 1973.

Calder, Robin Loren. *W. Somerset Maugham and the Quest for Freedom.* London: Heinemann, 1972. Traces, among other things, the image of bondage and freedom in Maugham's novels and short stories.

Chaplin, Lila. *William Sansom.* Boston: Twayne, 1980. Chaplin finds Sansom's talents more suited to the short story than to the novel, his ability lying more in his "watchful eye" than in "the depth of exploration of human psyche." Notes that Sansom's early stories—brief, epigrammatic, and quick in their movements—"were in harmony with the nervous, fragmented life of the 1940's."

Coombs, H. *T. F. Powys.* London: Barrie & Rockliff, 1960. A general introduction to Powys's work. The critical comment is generally sensible but leans toward the impressionistic. Chapter 4 is devoted to fables and short stories.

Cordell, Richard A. *Somerset Maugham: A Biographical and Critical Study.* Bloomington: Indiana University Press, 1961. A perceptive discussion of Maugham's short fiction is found in chapter 5. Of Maugham's method: "Too often he has been content to illustrate the unaccountability of man's behavior when we wish that, like Gide or Lawrence or even Sherwood Anderson, he would *endeavor* to account for it."

Craig, David. "Sillitoe and the Roots of Anger." In *The Real Foundations.* New York: Oxford University Press, 1974, pp. 27–85. A Marxist interpretation of Sillitoe's fiction.

Daiches, David. *The Present Age in British Literature.* Bloomington: Indiana University Press, 1969. Especially useful for its nearly two hundred pages of bibliography.

Faulkner, Peter. *Angus Wilson: Mimic and Moralist.* New York: Viking Press, 1980. The most thorough discussion of the Wilson canon. Focuses on the satiric impulse in the short stories.

Fisher, Margery. "Henry Treece." In *Three Bodley Head Monographs: Henry Treece, C. S. Lewis, and Beatrix Potter.* London: Bodley Head, 1969, pp. 7–104. A descriptive account of Treece's writings placed against a brief biographical background. Contains a bibliography compiled by Antony Kamm.

Fitz Gerald, Gregory, ed. *Modern Satiric Stories: The Impropriety Principle.* Glenview, Ill.: Scott, Foresman, 1971. An anthology with a lengthy introduction by Fitz Gerald. Satiric short stories are classified and discussed according to types: satiric allegories, antiutopian and science fiction satires, satiric realism, satiric monologues, and satiric parodies. Stories by Pritchett, Wilson, and Maugham are included.

Gindin, James. *Postwar British Fiction: New Accents and Attitudes.* Berkeley:

University of California Press, 1962. Although mostly concerned with the profound social changes in Britain that are reflected chiefly in novelists of the fifties, Gindin also notes the moral commitment shown by such writers as Angus Wilson, John Wain, John Bowen, and Doris Lessing.

Halio, Jay L. *Angus Wilson.* Edinburgh: Oliver & Boyd, 1964. One of the books in the Writers and Critics series, this brief study was the first of Wilson to appear. Halio's discussion is characterized by good sense and an easy balance. Chapter 2 is devoted to the short fiction.

Jonas, Klaus W., ed. *The Maugham Enigma: An Anthology.* New York: Citadel Press, 1954. Contains observations on Maugham's short stories by Richard Cordell, Gerald Sykes, Malcolm Cowley, and V. S. Pritchett.

Jones, Edward T. *L. P. Hartley.* Boston: Twayne, 1978. Contains brief but helpful commentary on the short stories.

Lehmann, John. *A Nest of Tigers: The Sitwells in Their Times.* Boston: Little, Brown, 1968. A relatively informal account of the three Sitwells and their careers. Lehmann observes that some of Osbert's short stories seem "to have strayed from his autobiography."

LeStourgeon, Diana E. *Rosamond Lehmann.* New York: Twayne, 1965. A perceptive discussion of Lehmann's writing. LeStourgeon notes that the stories found in *The Gipsy's Baby* share many of the qualities found in Lehmann's novels.

Magill, Frank N., ed. *Critical Survey of Short Fiction.* Englewood Cliffs, N.J.: Salem Press, 1981. A seven-volume reference work on the short story, consisting of long essays on general topics and shorter entries on individual authors. Two of the essays are William Peden's "Short Fiction in English, 1910–1950" and Leonard R. N. Ashley's "British Short Fiction in the Nineteenth and Twentieth Centuries." Coppard, Dahl, de la Mare, Greene, Kavan, Maugham, Pritchett, and Sansom are included in the individual authors section; Bates and Warner are not.

Malkoff, Karl. *Muriel Spark.* New York: Columbia University Press, 1969. An interesting study that contains relatively brief discussion of the short fiction.

May, Charles E., ed. *Short Story Theories.* Columbus: Ohio State University Press, 1976. Intelligent discussions from important, previously published books and essays. Contains a section from Bates's *The Modern Short Story* and also a useful selected and annotated bibliography.

Michel-Michot, Paulette. *William Sansom: A Critical Assessment.* Paris: Societé d'Edition "Les Belles Lettres," 1971. A meticulous book in its details concering Sansom's life and publications. Assessments of individual works are multifaceted though not always penetrating. Michel-Michot argues convincingly that the short stories are superior to the novels.

Miller, Henry. Introduction to *Seven by Five* by H. E. Bates. London: Michael Joseph, 1963. Miller comments on Bates's skillful use of nature and treatments of women, plus his humor and "obsession with pain." He concludes that the novella was best suited to Bates's talents.

Mulkeen, Anne. *Wild Thyme, Winter Lightening: The Symbolic Novels of L. P. Hartley.* Detroit: Wayne State University Press, 1974. Contains some discussion of the short stories—more positive than most commentary.

Naik, M. K. *W. Somerset Maugham.* Norman: University of Oklahoma Press, 1966. A balanced and sensible assessment of Maugham's achievement as a short story writer is provided in chapter 8 where Naik finds that in the short stories Maugham seems "to present a more just and sympathetic picture of life than is given in most of his plays and novels." Naik candidly notes Maugham's limitations and concludes that "the list of things which Maugham could not do in the field of the short story is a long one"; feels, nonetheless, that his claim to the title "the English Maupassant" is justified.

O'Connor, Frank. *The Lonely Voice: A Study of the Short Story.* Cleveland: World Publishing, 1963. O'Connor observes that the short story tends to flourish among "submerged population groups," thus the preeminence of the American and Irish short story, among others. One of the most famous studies of the short story.

Olshen, Barry N., and Tony A. Olshen. *John Fowles: A Reference Guide.* Boston: G. K. Hall, 1980.

Price, Cecil. *Gwyn Jones.* Cardiff: University of Wales Press, 1976. A short introduction to Jones's work, containing a bibliography to 1976.

Pryce-Jones, David. *Graham Greene.* London: Oliver & Boyd, 1973. A revision of the 1963 edition, this study extends the discussion to 1971 and the bibliography to 1972. More on the novels than the short fiction.

Sanders, Charles. *W. Somerset Maugham: An Annotated Bibliography of Writings about Him.* De Kalb: University of Illinois Press, 1970.

Stanford, Derek. *Muriel Spark.* Fontwell, Sussex: Centaur Press, 1963. A relatively early study that contains still perhaps the most helpful commentary on the short stories.

Vannatta, Dennis. *H. E. Bates.* Boston: Twayne, 1983. The only book-length discussion of Bates's fiction, short and long.

Wilson, Edmund. *Classics and Commercials.* New York: Farrar, Straus, 1950. Contains a discussion of de la Mare's ghost stories, among others.

Wobbe, R. A. *Graham Greene: A Bibliography and Guide to Research.* New York: Garland, 1979.

Wykes-Joyce, Max. *Triad of Genius. Part I. Edith and Osbert Sitwell.* London: Peter Owen, 1953. A leisurely study containing much information.

2. Periodicals

Bradbury, Malcolm. "The Short Stories of Angus Wilson." *Studies in Short Fiction* 3 (1966):117–25. Bradbury finds that there are two main streams of influence upon Wilson: first, "those of novelists like Jane Austen, or George Eliot, or Forster, or the central figures of Leavis' Great Tradition," and, second, that of Dickens. The comic modes in Wilson are complex, the comedy of manners being mixed with the grotesque, caricature, and an inclination toward the absurd.

Butcher, Margaret K. " 'Two Forks of a Road': Divergence and Convergence in the Short Stories of Doris Lessing." *Modern Fiction Studies* 26 (Spring 1980):55–61. Butcher argues that Lessing's own contention that her short fiction falls into two groups—"the story which reflects the process of thinking and the story which exists as the product of carefully polished thought"—is wrong, that her stories exhibit more "convergence" of aim and method than otherwise. An illuminating discussion of the stories, from the earliest to 1963.

Cullinan, John. "Anthony Burgess's 'The Muse': A Sort of SF Story." *Studies in Short Fiction* 9 (1972):213–20. One of the few critical discussions of one of the few Burgess short stories.

Hughes, Douglas A. "V. S. Pritchett: An Interview." *Studies in Short Fiction* 13 (1976): 423–32. In the course of the interview Pritchett comments on the pleasures and problems of the short story as a form, on the place of the short story in contemporary culture, and on his earlier statement that the short story is a "minor" genre.

"International Symposium on the Short Story, Part I." *Kenyon Review* 30 (1968):443–90. Included are comments from short story writers from many countries on the state of the art and the economic problems of publication. English short story writers are represented by Christina Stead.

"International Symposium on the Short Story, Part II." *Kenyon Review* 31 (1969):58–94. See Part I above. John Wain represents the English short story writers.

"International Symposium on the Short Story, Part III." *Kenyon Review* 31 (1969):450–502. See Part I above. Elizabeth Taylor represents the English short story writers.

"International Symposium on the Short Story, Part IV." *Kenyon Review* 32 (1970):78–108. See Part I above. Edward Hymes and H. E. Bates represent the English short story writers.

Laski, Marghanita. Review of *Such Darling Dodos and Other Stories* by Angus Wilson. *Spectator,* 28 July 1950, p. 128. An unfavorable but interesting review.

Nemerov, Howard. "Sansom's Fiction." Review of *Something Terrible, Something Lovely; The Passionate North;* and *A Bed of Roses* by William Sansom.

Kenyon Review, 17 (1955):130–35. Unfavorable commentary on Sansom's short fiction.

O'Faolain, Sean. "The Secret of the Short Story." *United Nations World* 3 (March 1949):37–38. The "secret" is that the short story tends to prosper more in societies where there is ferment."The more firmly organized a country is [i.e., England] the less room there is for the short story, for the intimate close-up, the odd slant, or the unique comment."

Painter, George D. Review of *A Touch of the Sun* by William Sansom. *New Statesman,* 24 May 1952, p. 625. Interesting assessment of Sansom's development as a short story writer.

Pritchett, V. S., et al. "The Short Story." *London Magazine* 6 (1966):6–12. Contributions also from William Sansom and Francis King. Alan Ross, the editor, maintains that neither the financial nor the artistic situation of the short story is as "depressing as is often alleged."

Raban, Jonathan. "Going Strong." Review of *Collected Stories* by V. S. Pritchett. *New York Review of Books,* 24 June 1982, pp. 8–12. Perceptive review praising Pritchett's talents.

Review of *A Beginning and Other Stories* by Walter de la Mare. *Times Literary Supplement,* 14 October 1955, pp. 597–99. Interesting commentary on the collection under review as well as a helpful survey of de la Mare's career.

Review of *Seven by Five* by H. E. Bates. *Times Literary Supplement,* 13 September 1963, p. 688. A brief but perceptive survey of Bates's career.

Review of *The Stories of William Sansom. Times Literary Supplement,* 10 May 1963, p. 340. An overview of Sansom's fiction to 1963.

Stern, James, et al. "Some Notes on Writing Stories." *London Magazine* 9, no. 12 (1970):6–16. Included are comments from Brian Glanville, Elizabeth Taylor, William Trevor, Michael Field, Jonathan Raban, and Frank Tuohy. Alan Ross points out in the introduction that "good stories continue to be written and they sell at least as well as most novels."

Theroux, Paul. "V. S. Pritchett's Stories." Review of Pritchett's *Collected Stories. Saturday Review,* May 1982, pp. 56–57. High praise for Pritchett from an American reviewer.

Index